Praise for the writing of bestselling author Stevi Mittman

"If any writer is going to sit on the throne so recently vacated by the wonderful LaVyrle Spencer, it just may be Stephanie Mittman. With *A Kiss To Dream On*, she proves that she can spin a story of real people dealing with genuine problems as love—not fantasy love, but true love—grows between them."
—*barnesandnoble.com*

"One of those special books that will make your heart smile.... Sit back, kick off your shoes and enjoy."
—Debbie Macomber on *A Taste of Honey*

"Stephanie Mittman has the gift for touching readers' hearts."
—*Romantic Times BOOKclub*

"A terrific read!"
—Pamela Morsi on *The Marriage Bed*

"Miss Mittman might very well be the standard against which all future Americana romance is judged."
—*Affaire de Coeur*

"Mittman's characters walk right off the page and straight into your heart."
—*Booklist*

"Ms. Mittman's characters are a work of art!"
—*Rendezvous*

Stephanie Mittman

Stephanie Mittman (Stevi, as she's known to her friends) didn't start out to be a writer. In fact, she had a nice career going as a stained-glass artist. She won Best in Show at the Washington Square Outdoor Art Show, and her first three-dimensional stained-glass dollhouse became part of the permanent collection of the Museum of the City of New York followed by private commissions and museum shows.

And then, in the early 1990s she went on vacation without a good book. She went without a computer too, and the first pages of her first novel were written on hotel stationery. Now her office walls boast several awards from *Romantic Times BOOKclub*, *BookRak*, *Affaire de Coeur*, among others, all framed in stained-glass frames.

She is the proud author of eight novels, including *The Marriage Bed*, RITA® Award finalist *A Kiss To Dream On*, and Doubleday Book Club offerings *Head over Heels* and *The Courtship*.

After spending most of her life (and her money!) on Long Island, she currently makes her home in Upstate New York with the husband she's adored since high school and two cats who insist on walking her keyboard several times a day. You can visit Stevi's Web site by going to www.stephaniemittman.com.

Who Up MAKES ^ These RULES,

Anyway?

STEVI MITTMAN

WHO MAKES UP THESE RULES, ANYWAY?

copyright © 2006 Stephanie Mittman

isbn 0373880804

This edition published by arrangement with Harlequin Books S.A.

® and TM are trademarks of the publisher. Trademarks indicated with
® are registered in the United States Patent and Trademark Office, the
Canadian Trade Marks Office and in other countries.

TheNextNovel.com

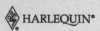 HARLEQUIN®

PRINTED IN U.S.A.

This book is dedicated with gratitude to:

Irene Goodman, agent supreme,
who never lost faith in Teddi or me

Tara Gavin, the editor who could see
in Teddi what others couldn't

Miriam Brody, Cathy Penner and Janet Rose, who
managed to laugh heartily, edit gently, suggest tactfully
and cheer wildly through all thirty-two versions of Teddi

And to my husband, Alan, who lives with
Teddi's alter ego and keeps her sane

CHAPTER 1

My *name is Teddi Bayer.* Not as bad as, say, Candi Kane, but still...

No biggie, you think? Then picture this: a newspaper ad for Bayer Furniture the Sunday after I was born. There I am, naked except for a big bow around my neck, superimposed on a bed of teddy bears. Below me are the words IN CELEBRATION OF THE BIRTH OF OUR LITTLE TEDDI, BUY A COUCH THIS WEEK AND GET A FREE TEDDY BEAR! BETTER STILL, BUY A BED AND MAKE ONE OF YOUR OWN!

Fast forward twelve years and imagine a raucous bunch of adolescent boys trying to cop a feel of my mosquito-bite-breasts to see if I'm "stuffed."

And my parents expected me to turn out normal?

Somehow, despite my name and my genes, for thirty-six years I've managed to defy the odds. That is, until today, when, to show that they are team players and can embrace a common goal, my entire family—and that includes my too-good-look-ing-for-his-own -good husband, Rio—came together to make sure that I go smack, stark-raving, way-over-the-edge mad.

You think I'm exaggerating, right? Well then, let's take them one by one, shall we? First there's my mother, who called me in every aisle of Waldbaum's this morning to tell me what food I should *not* buy for our big family dinner tonight. Every *single* aisle, where she somehow knew exactly what item I was putting into my cart just as I was reaching for it. My best guess is that it's all the shock treatments she's had. They've no doubt given her this incredible psychic power. And is she saving the world with it?

No, she's just driving me nuts.

Witness:

"How much chopped liver are you buying for your father?" she asked the moment I was at the deli counter ordering it. "You always buy too much."

I might have been a tad snippy when I told her, "Only half a pound," and added, "Is that all right with you?"

Of course, she was snippy right back. "Half a pound? That'll never be enough. Not that I would ever tell you what to buy." She said this as if she hadn't told me to get the challah, not the Italian bread in the bread aisle, not to buy the plums because knowing me they were bound to be too soft, and to resist the cheap mints in the bulk-food aisle I always get instead of the exact-same-for-a-higher-price ones in the gourmet section. "You're a grown woman. You have a mind of your own. You should do what you want."

She pauses, maybe to take a drag of her cigarette, and then continues. "Of course, I haven't lived with your father for more years than you've been alive without learning something. I thought I could help, but I see I was wrong. I'll never make another suggestion."

Yeah, if only. "Mom, you've helped," I told her, searching

the glass cases for some arsenic in cream sauce, which, if I'd had it for lunch, might have spared me the dinner party from the dark side I knew was to come. "You're always a help."

"Well," she said, "all I've ever wanted is for you and David to be happy."

I told her we are happy. My older brother, David, is, anyway. Of course, he is a thousand miles south of New York, basking in the Caribbean sun and enjoying life without a phone, or so he tells us. Not that it matters. I know the drill. "David and I are both happy."

"Happy? Of course you're happy. Did you lose a child?"

This is why we cut my mother plenty of slack. Yes, it was almost thirty-five years ago, and yes, the rest of the family thinks that little Markie's death has become a weapon with which she bludgeons us regularly. Still, I don't know that I'd be any better. Gives me the chills just thinking about it.

I told her I was thankful I hadn't, which satisfied her, and she moved on to critiquing my wardrobe until I crinkled a package of rice crackers near the phone and shouted that I was losing her. Before you feel too sorry for her, know that she called me back once I was in the car and asked if I'd gotten her favorite French vanilla creamer—which amazingly I had actually remembered—and told me now she uses the low-fat kind. Zipped my rain slicker back up, grabbed Alyssa out of the safety seat and ran back through the puddles. But, not being a dummy, didn't return the regular so that when she hated the low-fat I'd have the right one on hand.

Of course, that's not nearly enough to drive anyone over the edge, so throw in my three kids. Today Dana, my oldest at eleven, had to stay after school, only she forgot to tell me so I wasn't home for Jesse when he got there. And Jesse, who's nine-going-on-six when he isn't nine-going-on-forty, forgot to tell me he was supposed to bring cupcakes for some bake sale at school and brought home a rather nasty note from his teacher about responsibility—presumably his. And post food-shop-from-hell, Alyssa, our little Princess Cupcake at nearly five, announced she couldn't hold it in until we got home. My car will probably never smell quite the same.

But you're still skeptical. You don't believe it's a plot, do you? Then add my neighbor's husband, who, while not technically related to me, is like a brother-in-law, since Bobbie and I are as close as sisters could be. Tonight he up and left her and their twin girls, Kristin and Kimmie. I am fully aware that this is not my tragedy, but hers. And I swear that I was there for her. I held her, I cried with her. In fact, I think I took it worse than she did because it was more of a surprise to me. But I'm claiming it as part of the plot to speed me over the edge because it opened a box of fears that I have managed to keep locked since the day that Rio and I got married—that someday, somewhere down the line, Rio would realize he didn't love me and climb into the candy-apple-red Corvette I brought to the marriage and drive off into the sunset without me.

Anyway, back to Bobbie, who showed me a drawerful of sex toys which didn't save her marriage, and told me, "Mike's screwing a hypnotherapist. In fact, they've been screwing around for centuries—in other lives, or so he says."

"Other lives?" I am sure my eyes were like saucers, but this stuff was really hard to believe. I mean, yes, Mike's into all sorts of natural supplements and he thinks that ginkgo biloba actually staves off Alzheimer's, but the man's a chiropractor. They all believe in that stuff. But they don't all go off to find alternative universes. "Since when does Mike believe in past lives?" I asked her.

"Since he needs an excuse for screwing around in this one."

She claims she's less upset about his infidelity than the problem of who will adjust her. "I mean," she said as she cried in my arms, "that man knows how to stop my migraines. He knows how to get rid of the pain that runs down my leg. Who's going to get rid of the pain in my ass?"

All I could do was hug my very best friend tightly and tell her the honest truth—that it looked like he was already gone.

I know, I know. You're thinking that I'm taking all this too personally. But then, you don't know about my father, who has been leading my husband to believe that one day he'll be running Bayer Furniture, and who chose tonight to tell him that at seventy, he still has no plans to retire. I think he takes a perverse pleasure in screwing Rio because, in addition to Rio screwing his daughter, he feels that Rio screwed him by not converting to Judaism, as he promised he would.

Which brings us, finally, to my husband, Rio, who actually believed that tonight's dinner was going to change everything and that my father was suddenly going to see the light and bankroll a Bayer Furniture Clearance Center for Rio to run. And now that that boat has sailed, he is standing in the doorway to our bedroom on the fence about whether to blame me or have sex with me. This despite the black negligee I've got on—a nightgown, I might add, which my mother gave me two years ago, telling me it would stop Rio from even *thinking* about cheating.

You'll remember I locked that fear in a box before today. Now I'll worry about it every night for the rest of my life, along with the greatest of my fears—that some day, just like Mom, I'll have a second home at the South Winds Psychiatric Center. And that I'll have a phone set aside exclusively for me there just like the one reserved for her, which is pre-programmed with dial-direct connections to her favorite florist and the local Chinese restaurant, which delivers moo shu pork at the touch of a button. And that I will have sheets stored for me just like the three-hundred-count ones kept in a locked hospital closet for my mother. (Only mine, of course, will be seconds from T.J. Maxx.)

And then, like me, my poor sweet children will be done for—left to manage without consistent and unconditional love, needing always to walk that thin line, showing love without demanding it in return—or risk pushing their fragile mother over the edge.

And as long as I'm being morbid, I may as well go the final step and acknowledge that worse still, they'll have to live out their lives with the Sword of Psychosis hanging over their heads, always wondering when the men in the little white coats will be coming for them.

Boy, your mood sure can change when you think about being institutionalized or abandoned. Now I'm not any surer than Rio that I'm up for making love. Still, there he is, standing in the doorway, framed by the light like some kind of god. His hair is black, full. It still curls down onto his forehead the way it did the first time I saw him. His chest and shoulders still dwarf his waist and hips. He's the kind of man who walks with his shoulders—a lion's gait, always on the prowl. There's a rhythm to it, and it mesmerized me from the start. It is too dark to do more than imagine the small tuft of dark curls that escapes the vee of his shirt, but if I close my eyes I have no trouble seeing it clear as day. Unfortunately when I open them, he is still standing in the same spot, still unable to decide if he's interested in what I'm offering.

Finally he speaks: "I take it Bobbie's still alive?" Translated this means: how could you leave me to deal with your parents on the most important night of my life to gab with your girlfriend?

I remind him that my girlfriend's husband just left her and that she was really upset. We both were. I don't go into the thing about how divorce is one of the three most traumatic things that can happen in your life, because I'm not sure it's three and because he wouldn't care, anyway. "What was I supposed to do?"

In the dark I can barely make out a grimace. The last thing I want to do is fight with him, but he isn't being fair.

"Didn't she come running when my mother tried to commit suicide?" I ask.

He crosses his arms across his chest, unmoved. "Which time?"

Several, I suppose, but while it means the world to me, I realize it would be wise to remind him of something he cares about more. "How about when Alyssa had that fever and you were off hunting little defenseless deer and I had to rush her to the hospital and Bobbie was here for the whole weekend watching Dana and Jess?" I should have left out the dig about the defenseless deer. I'm not sure he even heard the rest. Anyway, I make a stab at another time Bobbie saved the day. "How about when she climbed on the roof to adjust the DirecTV thingy so you wouldn't have to miss the Indy 5000 or whatever it is?" Surely he cared about that.

Only he says she didn't do that. "You did, Teddi. You don't remember that?" *Me?* I hate heights. Maybe I blocked the memory. When I hesitate, he throws up his hands. "You got brain damage or something? You remember anything anymore?"

His words hang in the air as if we've had this conversation a hundred times before. Maybe we did once or twice. Or a couple dozen. Who's counting?

"Sorry," he says after a while, sitting down on the bed and slipping out of his Italian loafers. "I didn't mean anything by that. At least I saw that you picked up my good suit at the cleaners, finally."

"Your suit?" I guess I don't hear exactly what he's saying, because I'm thinking that I've forgotten it yet again, despite how many times he's reminded me. "I—"

"What? They couldn't get the freakin' stain out?" He's halfway off the bed, running to check.

"It's fine," I say, trying to regulate my breathing because the fact is that I have no recollection of stopping at the cleaners, picking up his suit, hanging it in his closet. Does that make twice this week, or three times, that I've lost some moments in time?

He stands beside the bed, ready to head for the closet. "And they fixed that little tear?"

I don't answer because I only vaguely remember a tear. He complains about not being able to buy yet another new suit and asks if I bothered to tell the tailor.

I tell him that I think I hear Alyssa and we both strain at the silence. Finally I ask how it went with my father.

He shrugs. *Same old, same old*, his body says.

He lifts my chin. "You okay?"

I assure him I'm fine, and because I've had so much practice lately, I lie convincingly.

"Hmm," he says, plumping up the pillows. "Hard to believe Mike really got up the balls to leave your little friend, huh?"

"I guess you just never know about people," I whisper, as if saying it out loud will make it worse. I move over to make room for him and the strap to my nightgown rolls down my arm. "Isn't it awful?"

What I want to say is that any man who leaves his wife should rot in hell, but I am saving that for a time when I feel I am on firmer ground.

Rio lets out a breath that's half a laugh and sits on the edge of the bed. "Teddi, I'm not touching that one with a sharp stick."

"You don't think it's awful?" I ask, and at this point I push the nightgown strap back up where it belongs because there are Godiva chocolates sitting on the nightstand. They have begun their siren song and if I reach for them with the strap across my arm it will cut off my circulation. Hey, before you criticize me, may I remind you that it is a well-known fact that a crisis is not the right time to start a diet.

"Okay. I'll play," he says. "Let's say I say, 'Mike would have to be nutzo to leave Bobbie.' What's your first thought, Teddi?" He watches me struggle to answer without outright lying. "You're off thinking that I've got a thing for her, right?"

My answer is a shrug. What man wouldn't have a thing for Bobbie, with that flat stomach and those perky little breasts, which have no stretch marks even though the woman had twins? How do some women get away with that? This morning I would have felt the usual stab of jealousy, but tonight is a whole new ball game.

"But, if I take Mike's side and say your friend is a selfish, spoiled little you-know-what who'd gnaw the hand that fed her if she was hungry enough, you'll decide that next I'm leaving you, right?"

Well, the thought has crossed my mind...only a million times in the last ten minutes. The truth is that the first time I saw Rio, I lost my ability to speak, to breathe. My first thought was that he had a John Travolta sexy smile, but let me tell you, God was only practicing on J. T. When he got it right, he created Rio. Of course, that was twelve years ago, and John Travolta surprised us all by proving to be a fine wine.... Don't get me wrong, Rio hasn't exactly gone to pot, but where John Travolta has somehow managed to evolve from Vinnie Barbarino to expensive champagne, Rio has only made it as far as Corona with lime.

I don't know what made me say that. I don't even like

beer—with lime or without. And Rio is still handsomer than John Travolta—then or now.

"So what's your plan in that sexy little negligee, Ted? You figuring we can screw each other's brains out so you can be sure I'm really here, and really staying? That about sum it up?" He looks smugly at me while I squirm.

I tell him that I probably would not have put it exactly that way. What I want to say is that he is a hundred percent wrong when we both know damn well that he is a hundred percent right. Always two steps ahead of me. That's Rio. He sees through me like a plate-glass window, knows my thoughts before I even have them.

"You can wrap it in any fancy words you want," he tells me as he unbuttons his shirt and pulls it off, throwing it toward the bench at the foot of the bed and stretching out next to me. "You wanna make me glad to be here, don't let me stop you."

Well, I was asking for it, wasn't I, all dolled up in a black negligee? I run my hand down his bare chest, his curls reaching out to capture my fingers, but all I can think about is Bobbie and Mike and how a wife can just not know. "Look, could you just tell me that our marriage is nothing like theirs?" I ask. He leans toward me, nibbling at my neck while he works the strap of my nightgown down my arm. "I mean—"

"No, it's nothing like theirs," he agrees, freeing one breast from behind the black lace trap I've set.

"And we're happy, right? I mean you are, aren't you?" I ask, wanting to hear him say it, hear him promise.

"I'm getting happy," he mumbles against my midriff as he

tries to pull my gown down over my hips. I raise myself, trying to make it easier, but he's already moving on, leaving the nightgown puddled at my waist while his hands play over me as if I'm an instrument he knows well, on which he is merely practicing his scales. "Happier…"

After a few minutes he stops. "What?" I ask, shifting and grinding my bottom into the bed. "Why are you stopping?"

Raising himself up on one elbow, he lazily runs his finger up and down my arm. Finally he speaks. "So your father and I talked. And he thinks buying the building next door for the outlet center is a good idea."

"I thought he was against it," I say, telling myself it's only the cool May night that chills me, and not fear, not foreboding. "And besides, we're doing fine the way we are, aren't we? Don't we have this wonderful house, these great kids and—"

"—a father-in-law who looks at his watch every time I take a crap. I need to get out of there, Teddi. Can't you understand that? Even felons get time off for good behavior. When do I get my time off?"

I understand what he's saying, but at this point it's simply a matter of patience. "My father is seventy years old, Rio. Boca is calling his name louder and louder every day. A year, two, maybe, and Bayer Furniture will be yours. You'll be able to—"

"Right," he says without enthusiasm. "Next year. And what if in the meantime that brother of yours comes home?"

"And what if the earth stops turning? Now you sound like my mother, Rio. David isn't coming home."

Rio runs his fingers through his hair the way he always does when he's frustrated.

"It's a great business opportunity, but your father hasn't got any vision. It's like he's got cataracts of the brain or something."

"If it's such a good investment, maybe you and my father should explain to the bank—"

"What? You think they'll just hand us over half a mil with no collateral? You live in this dream world, Teddi, but just because you got born with one of those silver spoons, it doesn't mean it's so easy for the rest of us, you know. You want to start a business with Bobbie and *poof*, a couple weeks later you two are painting furniture and selling it in Cold Spring Harbor. The rest of us, us normal people, aren't so lucky."

Luck, my father always says, *is the residue of hard work*. So is my business with Bobbie, but Rio doesn't want to hear that. So instead I suggest that we consider taking all the money we are planning to spend on the kids bar and bat mitzvahs and roll it into Rio's shot at being his own boss.

You're thinking that's a pretty gutsy, generous thing for me to do, and I'd love to leave you with that impression, but I know my husband. His favorite game is *I can't because…*

"Oh, that'd be great," he says as if he's reading from my script. "I can just see working with your father every day if I didn't get his kids *mitzvahed*." It's not a word, but since it isn't happening, anyway, I let it go.

"He'd get over it," I say. My mother is another story, but again, it isn't happening and I know it and he knows it.

"He'd take it out on me every day for the rest of my life. And he'd cut us out of his will. And the kids."

"I'm not saying it would be easy."

"If he'd only retire," he says.

I murmur my agreement.

"Or, we could put up the house."

I didn't see that coming. I thought this was a simple whining session and my job was to sympathize and stroke him through it. He takes advantage of my momentary speechlessness to tell me that the building is going for a song. "By the time we have to pay for college we'll be raking it in faster than we can count it. If we—"

College, I remind him, is right around the corner.

"You're right," he says, flipping onto his back and putting his hands behind his head. "Forget it."

And we lie there for a few minutes in the semidarkness, the security lights out back giving the room an unnatural glow. I make a few tentative movements, test the waters by skimming his chest with my hand, but he doesn't respond.

My mind wanders to Bobbie, lying alone in a king-size bed, so I start raining kisses on Rio's chest, working my way down lower and lower. Above me somewhere, he sighs. Is that a contented, *this is the life* kind of sigh I hear, or is it asking *is this going to take all night?*

After a while, during which it seems nothing I do even remotely excites him, Rio comes to life. He flips me onto my back and teases my nipple with his teeth. He runs his hands down my belly and his fingers wind their way inside me until I am slick and ready and arching against his hand.

I am so close to *there*, to home, to safety. I push myself against his hand, offering myself up to him, straining, lifting

myself from the mattress, cooing, my fists gripping the cov-
erlet on the bed, my neck arching, my breathing loud enough
to embarrass me, on the threshold of not caring who hears
me.

Only he doesn't enter me. Instead he props himself up on
an elbow, and when he should be telling me how beautiful I
am, how rich and full I make his life, he folds his pillow in
half and leans against it.

"What?" I ask, reaching out for him, wondering where the
bliss has gone. "What's wrong?"

"Nothing," he says, and his body seems to relax. I fight to
control my breathing, to come down from the cloud I was lost
in, and as soon as my heart begins to beat regularly he seeks
me out once more, only to hesitate yet again as soon as my
breathing betrays me.

And now I'm wise to his game and I have had enough of
it. I sit up, jumping away from his touch and hugging a pillow to my chest, and ask him point-blank, "Are you trying
to drive me crazy? Is that it?"

He runs one finger up my spine until it reaches my hair.
He sits up behind me, trying to win me over by kissing my
shoulders, my neck, reaching over and using his tongue to
play with my ear. But I refuse to be so easily won. "Am I
driving you crazy?" he asks, knowing that despite my pro-
tests I am putty in his hands, always was, probably always
will be.

I nod, stretching my neck back in search of his mouth. He
lifts my hair, licks the back of my neck and blows softly on
my skin.

"Am I?" he demands, his voice low, his manhood pressing against my hip.

"Yes," I admit, slipping down flat on the bed, trying to pull him into position above me. "Stark raving mad."

He says I haven't seen anything yet, and slips down my body until his face is buried between my legs and his tongue is doing things I swear no man has ever done to any woman before. And he keeps at it even after I think I can't bear it anymore, after I've come and come again and am calling out so loudly that he has to put his hands over my mouth so that I don't wake the kids.

When it's over, and we're lying satiated and sticky and our breaths have evened out, he begins to punch the pillows as if there is no place in the bed that he can get comfortable.

"You okay?" I ask him, realizing that I am the only one who has been satisfied, that, as they say, it's all been about me. "Do you want—" I don't know what I'm offering, I am barely awake, barely able to move my mouth, never mind my limbs.

"I'm good," he says. Only he isn't, and I'm not so stupid that I think his misery has anything to do with sex.

"Maybe I could talk to my father," I offer as he massacres our best down pillows.

"I told you to forget it, Teddi." His voice is dreamy, disconnected.

"But—"

"Forget about it," he says, and I can tell his lips are tight and it isn't easy for him to push the words out. He settles himself behind me, spooning. "Oh, yeah. Did you wash my camos for tomorrow?" he asks, referring to the army camouflage fatigues he wears for paintball. "I gotta leave first thing in the morning."

"Angelina did the wash yesterday," I say, not sure if I actually saw the stupid green clothes that signal a weekend away. "They must be in the basket in the laundry room."

"Thank God for Angelina," he says, sleep dulling his voice. It's a sentiment I've uttered a thousand times since I was a little girl and she came to live with us and take care of my mother's house and family. Now, once a week, she does the same for me. It lets me, once a week, leave the house without Alyssa's three favorite Lil Bratz, a backpack full of Beanie Babies and, of course, Alyssa. It lets me shop for bras without Jesse tagging along and trying all the 38DD bras on his head as if they were yarmulkes. And it lets me listen to the oldies station in the car instead of Dana's Limp Bizkit CD.

And sometimes at the end of the day we sit together at my kitchen table, the way we did at my mother's, and I tell her about my fears and hopes and dreams and she tells me about her wishes for me and by the time she leaves we have conquered the worst of my demons.

Rio's arm snakes around my middle. "You got the gift for my mother, right?"

"Mmm," I say, waiting for his breathing to even out. When I am sure he is asleep I let out the sigh I am holding.

It comes out ragged, and when I touch my chest, I can feel my heart beating frantically. *It was the incredible sex*, I tell myself. Not my forgetting one silly gift. *Everyone forgets things*, I tell myself. I am a busy woman with three children to take care of. There are bound to be a few things that slip through the cracks. The fact that I've forgotten Theresa's present is probably that *covert hostility* my mother is always accusing me of. *Indirect sabotage*.

So what if I also forgot the graph paper Jesse asked me for again and the Beanie Baby I promised Alyssa? So what if I don't remember picking up Rio's suit? It's in the closest, isn't it? Isn't that what counts?

So what if I forget a thing or two? I never claimed to have great organizational skills.

So forget the idea that I am becoming my mother because a thing or two slipped my mind.

Just forget it.

CHAPTER 2

Rio left early this morning in a huff, angry that I forgot to buy his mother's birthday gift. Hard as it is to believe, his plan—despite the fact that it was five o'clock in the morning—was to stop at her place on his way to his paintball extravaganza upstate. What kind of mother wants to see her grown son at that hour? The same kind, I suppose, who irons underwear. Enough said?

So anyway, when the phone rings at eight-thirty, I expect it to be Rio, calling to apologize for being a total jerk.

Instead, a hoarse voice tells me, "We need to get footcials."

"Excuse me?" I have no idea what my mother is talking about.

"I saw it on the *Today Show*," she tells me. "It gets your feet ready for Manolo Blahniks."

I remind my mother that she has given up wearing any shoes with heels higher than two-and-a-half inches, and that, as far as I know, Manolo doesn't make heels shorter than four.

My mother says that I am missing the point. The truth is, I often do. Unlike my mother, unlike Bobbie and most of my neighbors, I can't seem to get my hands on a copy of *The Secret Handbook of Long Island Rules*. All of them deny such a thing exists, but I know better. How else can they all know which is the "right" kind of car to drive this year and where, which piece of jewelry is the "right" one to wear this month and when, and which is the "right" store to buy whatevers this week and why? And it's not only the purchases. They all know the required moves to keep advancing on the food chain, or at least not lose ground.

Several of my neighbors have taught me, for example, that it is perfectly acceptable to miss hospital visiting hours after your husband's bypass surgery if going means missing your standing nail appointment. Of course, this doesn't apply when visiting your new grandchild, but no one, with the possible exception of my mother, would do something that awful.

My mother has no need for *The Handbook*, as she was born knowing *The Rules*. And she has told me in no uncertain terms that she hopes that this genetic trait has simply skipped a generation and been passed on to my children. To her, ignorance of the rules is as serious as diabetes or some other fatal ailment. And it's no excuse.

Bobbie doesn't just know *The Rules*, she probably codified them.

"So what's a footcial, anyway?" I ask my mother because Bobbie hasn't filled me in on this one and I'm afraid that I have missed out on yet another important initiation ritual of Suburban Society.

She describes one in detail, including scrubs and masks, as basically a facial for one's feet. I can't figure out why I suddenly need to know all this until she tells me that, according to Katie Couric, the best ones are in the City. (For those of you who live in other parts of the country, Long Islanders believe there is only one city—and it is not called Manhattan, or even New York—but simply, "the City.") My mother doesn't drive into the City, and thinks that the Long Island Railroad is for businessmen, for women who frequent bargain matinees, and for derelicts, none of which she aspires to be. She wants me to drive her, hence the *we* in "*we* need footcials."

"I have Dr. Cohen on Thursday at eleven," my mother tells me, as if she hasn't had a standing appointment with her psychiatrist for the past thirty or so years. Even I, in the advanced stages of forgetfulness that Rio claims I have entered, can remember that. The man had the nerve to leave me a list with things on it like *brush your teeth*, which he claims I've been forgetting lately, along with several other things.

When I agree to take her at some vague date between next week and hell freezing over, she tells me not to forget, like I always do. I'd argue with her, but then she'd bring up the one time I forgot to send her a Mother's Day card when I was busy giving birth to Alyssa two days before. Then I'd remind her that I did call, and she'd assure me that a call and a card are not the same thing. (I know, I know—it's in *The Rules*.)

"You forget all the time," she tells me as she takes a drag off her Newport Light and blows smoke in my face through the telephone lines. "You're, what's that word? With an *A*? You're absentminded."

I get off the phone, telling my mother that it's apparently time for me to go to my laboratory and invent *flubber*, but the reference sails over her head. From there, the day goes down-hill. I botch up two nightstands I'm supposed to be painting with Spider-Man, not Superman. Jesse breaks his glasses. Dana forgets her wallet on a shopping expedition. Alyssa paints her own nightstands—with toothpaste. Mike doesn't come home to Bobbie and the girls.

And now it's Sunday, and things aren't looking a whole lot better. Bobbie has backed out of our plans to go out to the Hamptons for graduation dresses for the girls in favor of stay-ing home to cut Mike's picture out of every photo in the fam-ily album while watching Olivia de Havilland get her revenge on Montgomery Clift for deserting her in *The Heiress* again. The movie may be PG, but Bobbie's performance is defi-nitely NFC, as in Not for Children. Her daughter Kristin has bailed already, and Kimmie has opted to come with us.

The rain is coming down in sheets. I am in the car with a bunch of kids who have raised bickering to an art form and seat selection to a matter of life or death. They are acting as if it's weird to insist they all buckle up, like this is some new form of torture I've dreamed up, and not a state law. After I assure them we are not leaving the driveway until everyone is buckled, I turn on the radio in a vain attempt to tune them out.

Seven youngsters traveling in a van with their parents were hurt, some of them seriously, when their father, the driver of the van, was fatally wounded by a gunshot in what police are calling a bizarre case of mistaken identity on Sunrise Highway early this morning....

"Great," Jesse says sarcastically, not even closing his book as he flips off the radio. "I don't know why you listen to the news." He looks at me accusingly, though I'm not sure what I'm being accused of. Maybe it's that I can hear such horrors and still pull out of the driveway, heading off for posh shopping in the Hamptons. Shouldn't I have to pull over to the side of the road to puke my guts out over such a story? And if not, shouldn't I have to pull over and puke my guts out that I can hear such awful things, hour after hour, and still go off to get my daughter a dress, my baby a Beanie Baby and my son a new game for his Xbox? Oh, and pick up a nail-patch kit because the acrylic nail on my pinkie is coming loose, and maybe something to cheer Bobbie up, and there's something else…

Do I tell Jesse this? No. I say, "Because a person needs to know what's going on in the world." Better to sound like an old fart than to tell him I need to know what unimaginably awful thing I've managed to avoid so that I can count my blessings while I add new worries to my list.

"Like you can do anything about it?"

I ignore him while silently trying to devise ways to protect the children from death if I were to be shot in the head while driving on Sunrise Highway. Maybe there is another way to get out to the Hamptons without taking Sunrise Highway….

I wonder if it's normal to worry so much, and realize that I've got a new worry to add to the list—how much I worry.

While I head down the LIE, the kids do what kids do. Dana calls Jesse a dork, Princess Cupcake whines about the Limp Bizket CD, Jesse moves his seat back and forth—all the usual stuff that so endear children to their parents while traveling in an enclosed space at a speed at which the slightest moment of inattention could kill them all.

It is one of those how-did-I-get-here moments, the kind I share with any mother whose three children individually are the sweetest kids on earth, but who collectively comprise a band of escapees from *Children of the Corn*.

"Are you all buckled up?" I ask as the rain drums on the moon roof and cars heading the other way send up sprays that hit the windshield and make the wipers whoosh. "Alyssa's still buckled?" The least I can do, in the event of a bullet to the brain, is to make sure that the kids'll be safe in their seats.

"That's three times you've asked," Dana tells me. "Everybody's buckled. Daddy is so right about you! You're gonna drive yourself and us crazy with all your worrying."

"Dana! I'll watch Alyssa," Kimmie says, a little too quickly. "Don't you worry about anything, Teddi."

Right. *Don't worry*, I think as I look back and catch the glance between Dana and Kimmie, the one that says, *You see how it is? Didn't I tell you?*

Kimmie's look, *Yes, I see how it is. Poor you!* says that suddenly I've become a major topic of discussion. Great.

Are my frayed edges showing? Have they noticed something I've missed? Am I teetering closer to the edge of late? Or is it just that there are few things as dramatic as being eleven? My memories are certainly vivid enough and I have nothing but sympathy for Dana. Eleven is the age where *weird* is the worst thing you can be, when you realize that your parents are even weirder than your friends' parents, and when you alternate between denying it to yourself and proving it to everyone else. Of course, when I was a kid, my mother won hands down.

"Really, Mom, don't worry," Dana chimes in. It is a rare appearance by the old Dana, the sweet one who existed before she became possessed by the hormone demon that pimpled her face and put tears in her voice on a daily basis.

"That's my job," I tell her. "It's why they made me the Mom."

Sometimes I have this vision of myself as "Lucy in the Chocolate Factory." Only instead of chocolates, worries keep coming out of the machine, faster and faster, and no matter where I stuff them, bury them, swallow them, there are always more worries. And like with Lucy, anyone watching just laughs at me.

"Maybe you should get over now, Mom," Dana says. "We're supposed to get off at exit 70."

No learner's permit in sight, and already Dana is an accomplished backseat driver. "Yes, honey, I'm putting on my signal, checking my rearview mir—"

"Look out!" Jesse yells.

But of course it is too late. The car is traveling too fast. Did it even occur to me to worry about hitting a deer? There you have it—proof positive that if you don't worry about something, it's bound to happen.

Suffice it to say, the poor little wayward deer can't avoid the optional-at-extra-cost grill guards on my Eddie Bauer edition Ford Expedition.

"You're sure you're all right?" Rio asks for the third time. Standing in our den, still dressed in his camos with his blackened face, he looks like someone who's emerged from a coal mine. Except that along with the sooty face he has touches of blue paint on his left shoulder and right thigh, and dirt everywhere else. "Nobody's neck hurts or anything?"

"We're fine," I say again, now worried about whether or not the kids will be fine tomorrow. Doesn't whiplash take a day or two to show up?

"Some other car didn't make you swerve into the deer or anything?" he asks.

"There's no one to sue," I assure him.

"I wasn't thinking of that," he lies.

Of course he was. No one tries harder to beat the system than my husband, and even *I* thought, for a nanosecond, that it would be nice if there were someone else to share the blame.

"So then tell me one more time." He takes a deep breath and I think we're lucky that he can't breathe and curse at the same time because if he wasn't doing the former, he'd be doing the latter, for sure. "Slowly. From the beginning."

I start again, though I've gone over it all on the phone in detail. "We were going to Southampton."

"After that," he says so tightly that I wince involuntarily. Of all the weekends to hit a deer, it had to be this one—the one he waits for all year? His one great escape from Bayer of the Bronx?

"It was my fault," Dana says, and her dark eyes are a little too bright. "I mean, we could have just gone to the mall."

"I should have been watching the road," Jesse says, kicking the deep green glove-leather couch as he swings his leg nervously. "But Voldemort and Harry were having this big magic fight with the wands that have the phoenix feathers at their hearts and…"

"Don't kick the couch," Rio says. It cost sixteen hundred dollars and he's so ridiculously proud of this impractical, sticky-in-the-summer, cold-in-the-winter, dead-animal sofa that the kids aren't supposed to snack on. He actually left the "genuine leather" tags hanging on it for three weeks after it arrived.

"It was no one's fault but my own," I say. "I mean—"

"It was the freakin' deer's fault," Rio interrupts. "He had no business being on the Parkway—"

"It was the Expressway," I correct him, because I can't leave well enough alone.

You see, both the Parkway and the Expressway run the length of Long Island, and when it comes to hitting a deer I really can't blame Rio for missing the distinction. Not when I've done, according to him (now read this in a deep, husky voice, because that's the way he said it) "a good fourteen hundred dollars' worth of damage to the car on top of dragging me home from Neversink."

"Oh, *excuse me*," he says, all but bowing to me. "I stand corrected. Now that I know it was the Expressway it makes all the difference…."

"I just thought you'd want to know where you nearly lost your family," I tell him, adding, "while you were off hurling paint."

"You don't *hurl* paint—you shoot off rounds," he corrects me right back. Well, "shooting off" is something he has a fair amount of practice doing. And it makes a difference what you call the stupidest sport next to Olympic skeleton races?

"It gets worse," I warn him. Believe me, he is not going to like this part. Not that I had a choice. Even now that I'm calmer, sure the children are fine and that the deer will be, I can't see that there was anything else I could have done.

"I don't see how."

He needs a better imagination. I can think of half-a-dozen ways right off the top of my head.

"I leave eight guys in Neversink who are, let me tell you, never gonna let this go, and you've got a smashed-up truck. I can see you and the kids are fine—thank God—which is more than I can say for the deer. But I guess you could say he learned his lesson, even though it only cost him his life. Me it's costing—"

"Oh, he's not dead, Daddy," Alyssa pipes up, preempting me before I can come up with some way to break it to him gently, gradually, set up the scene so he understands that I had no choice—not really. "He's going to be fine after they osperate."

"Operate," Dana corrects her, sliding an inch or two closer to my left side while Jesse closes ranks on my right.

"First off," I say, sinking to a new low (and setting a terrible example for my daughters) by trying to look cute. "I really am sorry I ruined your weekend. I'm sorry you had to leave your buddies high and dry and I'm sorry that the car has to be repaired and the vet is going to cost a fortune."

I slip out from between the kids and stand, hands on hips. Screw looking cute. If he doesn't get it, is that my fault?

"But I just nearly killed a deer with the kids in the car. I'm feeling lucky that we're all physically and—thanks to that vet—emotionally fine, though I am a little shaky, so if you don't mind…" I take a step toward the kitchen, though I have no idea what I want to do when I get there, and really, what can I possibly say that will make up for interrupting his paint-hurling extravaganza?

"Did you say *vet?*" Rio, refusing to take his eyes off my face, is feeling with his foot for the ottoman. When he finds it, he lowers himself down heavily. "There was a vet there?"

I sit back down between the kids, prepared to defend myself. "Well, Alyssa was crying and saying that I killed Bambi," I say at the same time that Dana starts explaining about how the vet wants to put some kind of plates in the deer's hip and Jesse announces that we called him on the cell phone. I squeeze my son's thigh, trying to warn him to shush, but he goes on adding fuel to the fire. "First there was the police, and they said Mom must be crazy to wanna call a vet, but…"

Rio cuts Jesse off. "You're telling me you called a freakin' veterinarian for a damn wild deer?" His voice is rising ominously, but then all his anger seems to suddenly vanish, replaced by a wary smile. "Oh, I get it. This is a joke, right? One of your damn Jewish jokes, like *you think the repairs on the car are bad? Wait'll you hear about the repairs on the deer!* Right?"

"You know, you sounded, for a second, a lot like the policeman," I say, trying to keep the atmosphere light. "He thought I was joking, too. But really, what was I supposed to do, Rio? That little deer was clearly suffering."

Rio shakes his head. "This isn't a joke or something?" he asks, his eyebrows raising in question.

"The dumb cop was gonna shoot it," Jesse says.

"Don't call a cop dumb," Rio tells our son. Now you need to know here that Rio has worse adjectives than *dumb* for cops on Long Island (and he knows his share of them from back before we were married and his crowd included men with nicknames like Snake and the Nose). "So you're telling me that you called a veterinarian to come and take care of a deer that did two thousand dollars' worth of damage to my car?"

The whole thing is now spiraling out of control. "My car," I correct him, because I like to live dangerously, I suppose. After all, he's got my adorable little Corvette and what do I drive? The "family" car so that I can tote around all these children he isn't taking into account. "What did you want me to do? Back up over it and put it out of its misery?"

Alyssa starts to cry. *Good girl*, I think. I give him a look that says, *see?*

He cuts to the chase. "How much?"

"He estimates eleven hundred." I say it as quietly as I can so that it doesn't sound like quite so much. Is it my fault that this fall Rio will be out there trying to kill the poor little fawn—along with all its relatives?

"Three thousand for the car repairs, fifteen hundred for the deer… You get her a dress?" he asks as calmly as he is capable of at the moment, pointing with his chin at Dana.

Dana opens her mouth, but I answer quickly, not wanting Rio to be annoyed with my little girl. "Bobbie wound up taking them to Walt Whitman Mall. She found a dress at Bloom-ingdale's."

He waits, one eyebrow raised, for me to supply the amount. The price is outrageous, but Dana looks gorgeous in the dress, and it's hard to blame Bobbie for wanting to stick it to every husband she knows. "Around two hundred," I say, trying to sound offhand.

He nods, slowly. "And I take it she can't wear this to the bat mitzvah, right? This is for a fifth-grade graduation dance," he says, making it abundantly clear that he is only pretend-ing to find this in any way rational. What is he thinking, any-way? That I'll be able to get away with a store-bought dress for Dana or for me for the bat mitzvah? Is he kidding? The other mothers are already recommending dressmakers and comparing the cost of dyed-to-match suede heels while they wait in the hallway at shul to pick up their kids from Hebrew school. I may not have actually read it in *The Handbook*, but even I know that the possibility of someone else showing up at her bat mitzvah in the same dress she's wearing would land Dana on a shrink's couch for life, and buy me a permanent place in my mother's doghouse.

Rio claps his hands once and leaves them clasped. "Okay. That's forty-seven-hundred dollars for your weekend. Twenty-eight dollars for mine."

"Hey, maybe we should have gone to Disney World in-stead," Jesse pipes up. When did the kid develop a death wish? Clearly he wouldn't last until the first commercial on *Survivor—Children's Edition*.

"It's one of those Kodak moments," Rio says, shaking his

head. He holds up his hands, framing the scene. "The Day Mom Hit the Deer."

"I'll help pay for the deer," Dana says between sniffs.

"Aren't you the one who spent more today for your little dress than I used to earn in a month?" Rio asks her. I guess he's not counting the hot car parts.

"Me, too," Jesse offers, trying to come to my rescue. "You can take a quarter out of my allowance every week."

"Until you're eighty?" Rio asks him, but I can see that his anger is waning.

"Could the deer come live here when it's all better?" Alyssa asks.

Rio looks as if he's actually considering it, but finally says that he has no use for *canned hunts*.

I try not to roll my eyes the way I do when his hunting license shows up in the mail each fall. "Deer need to be free. And you children need to go to bed," I add, pushing Alyssa off my lap and giving her a pat on the rump.

"Do you have to go to work tomorrow, Daddy?" Princess Cupcake asks, patting Rio's leg as if he's some big dog.

"Your grandpa, *Mr. Generosity*, gave me the day off," he says, sending daggers at me with his eyes, as if I planned this whole thing in order to ruin his big Warpigs Weekend. Tempting as that might have been, I never would have used an innocent deer to do it. "And I only had to promise him my right arm. I guess you and me can go watch Jesse play some ball, okay?" He sends me a *happy now?* look through narrowed eyes.

Just ecstatic, I shoot back with a plastic smile.

"Well, I'm glad you're all okay," he says, and the anger is gone from his voice now, and a huskiness tingeing it instead as he pets Alyssa's head. He stares hard at me and I can feel the caress in his gaze. The temperature in the room rises twenty degrees when he flashes that crooked you've-still-got-it-and-I-still-want-it smile at me.

"I really am sorry," I say softly as he lets his gaze drift down my body until I begin to squirm, what with the kids right there and all.

"No," Rio says softly. "You rescue a damn deer, and I think the whole world would agree with me, you're not *sorry*, you're *crazy*." But he is smiling at me as if he kind of likes *crazy*. Like he's given it some thought and decided *crazy* isn't such a bad thing for me to be.

CHAPTER 3

It's Memorial Day, the biggest furniture-sale day of the year. Rio is back in Neversink, and my father should be at Bayer Furniture and not my front door. But here he is, his sad face peering back at me through the sidelights. He is barely balancing several bags from the new Fairway Market in Plainview, and there is a crate of Haifa oranges by his foot.

I take two of the bags from him and jerk my head toward the kitchen, indicating he should follow me. "So Mom's back at South Winds, then?" I ask. Well, it is more like a statement. It doesn't take Sherlock Holmes to figure out what my father is doing at my door, laden with food, on one of the biggest sale days of the year. Ever since the first time my mother was taken to the psychiatric hospital, my father has been buying groceries to mark her admittance. When I was little, my father did it because someone had to and Angelina didn't drive. Or maybe Angelina didn't buy him what he liked. I don't really remember. I just know that the ritual didn't stop with my marriage to Rio. It doesn't matter that I don't live at home anymore, that I've outgrown the cookies. If my mother goes into South Winds, my father shows up with cookies. It may not compare to gathering around the spinet to sing

Christmas carols on Christmas Eve, but for my family, it's a tradition.

So my mother has lost it again. Well, it is hard to blame her. After all, a thirty-seven-year-old woman goes out to the curb to get the mail and comes back to find her two-year-old on the bottom of the swimming pool, trapped there by his tricycle. Who could expect her to ever be all right again? Even if my baby brother had survived, my mother would never have been the same. But the fact that she had been arguing with a neighbor about the man's dog relieving himself on the lawn where her children crawled and played, while her son was drowning—and that when she returned to the yard it had simply been too late—pushed her over the edge.

Sometimes, in my dreams, I still see myself like the Edvard Munch painting *The Scream*, my hands pressed against my cheeks, my mouth opened wide but silent, as my brother's little red bike tips and goes tumbling into the water. I've been silent in so many dreams that I'm not sure what I really did. What does it matter, anyway? Unlike my mother, whose hospital records stand as a testament to her pain, I've gotten over it. And I keep to myself the fact that I firmly (and uncharitably) believe that my mother's breakdowns have evolved into a case of proving that despite the accident she is a good mother because, thirty-two years later, she is still grieving.

Until now, my mother's returns to South Winds have always struck me as just another spin of the revolving door. But with my dreaded thirty-seventh birthday around the corner, with children of my own and my memory beginning to play tricks on me, I am more shaken than usual.

But my father has enough worries with my mother, so I take a peek in the bags on the counter, tell him how sorry I am, and give his shoulder a little consolation squeeze.

"What was it this time?" I ask as I begin to unload the groceries. Panini. Truffle oil. The navel oranges from Haifa.

My father shrugs. "What was it the last time?"

I have to think. Cousin Janet's son turning three? The drowning at that community pool on the East End? There is always some specific spark that shorts my mother's circuits. "I think last time was seeing that David Bayer obituary," I say.

My mother had gone into a total tailspin, though the paper clearly said that that David Bayer was eighty-two and survived by five kids and several grandchildren.

"Well, these things happen," my father says, though when I ask him if yet another David Bayer has died—which is kind of creepy and makes me glad, for the first time ever, that my name is Teddi—he merely shrugs.

I suppose we probably seem cavalier. It's just that my mother's suicide attempts are so much a part of our lives. Believe me, we weren't cavalier the first time. As I remember it, my father and I were having a lovely time in the TV room, where he was explaining to me why the Amazing Mets would never actually win the 1969 World Series. Anyway, for my part, I was feigning an interest in the game, probably hoping to keep my place on Daddy's lap, and, I suppose, in his heart.

I was apparently enjoying some modicum of success, since, at the very moment Angelina screamed from the upstairs hallway, my father was unscrewing Oreos and letting me lick out the cream. Maybe that's where my strong affection for those cookies comes from—that last moment of normalcy in a family that since then, despite all the cosmetic touches Bayer Furniture's profits can buy, still bears all the scars of that day.

We had no idea, when Angelina shouted and my father half lifted, half pushed me off his lap as he headed for the stairs, that tragedies have long barbed tails they drag behind them. And that, in the case of my baby brother, the tail would come to wag the dog.

"Some coffee would be nice," my father says, reaching into one of the bags and pulling out a stiff white box tied with a red-and-white-striped string.

I reach mechanically for the Braun coffeepot and all the while my mind is trying to go back to the house I grew up in, and I'm fighting it. I don't want to follow my father up the marble steps, past Angelina, who is standing on the landing calling the paramedics on the ridiculous old speakeasy phone my mother had had rewired. I used to wonder if my mother bought the refurbished phone with her suicide attempt in mind, so that it would make the perfect picture.

Except, of course, my mother couldn't watch Angelina using it because she was lying on the floor of her dressing room with one end of my *zayda*'s tallis (the very prayer shawl that my brother, David, was supposed to wear at his upcoming bar mitzvah) wrapped around her neck, and the other around the light fixture that was lying on the floor beside the overturned little fawn-colored Louis XIV stool.

"A *tallis?*" my father had asked, kneeling beside my mother, who was blinking at him and rubbing the side of her head. It must be that my memory is playing tricks on me, because I remembered that not a hair on my mother's frosted blond head was out of place, not a fleck of mascara had flaked from her lashes, and not a drop of her lipstick was on the lush beige carpet beneath her. Even then everything in my mother's closet was beige, from the walls and floor to all the clothing that hung there. In fact, everything in her house was beige, a color I still associate with depression.

"You tried to hang yourself with a freaking *tallis?*" I can remember my father asking.

"My father's tallis," my mother had said, giving me a weak smile that I remember clearly. "I wanted it to be something symbolic."

"You're crazy," my father had said. Well, back then he didn't know the half of it.

"Of course I'm crazy," my mother had answered. "Crazy with grief. I'd be crazy not to be, wouldn't I? What kind of mother would I be if I could go on with my life after I allowed my son to die?"

It takes my father nudging me to bring me back to safety, to my peach-and-moss-green kitchen, where the coffeepot is making gurgling noises and smelling good. "You okay, kiddo?" he asks.

"Mmm-hmm," I say with a nod, still feeling a little dazed as I look into the box of rainbow cookies and mini éclairs. "The kids'll sure love these."

There is something wrong with that, almost as if we are celebrating my mother's return to South Winds. "Why should they suffer?" my father asks, reading my mind.

And I feel the swish of that tragedy's tail and know in my heart that the pain, the fear, the legacy will go on. My little brother's death has had as much impact on my family's lives as his life ever could have. Maybe more.

"It was an accident, June," my father had said at the time, leaning over my mother as she lay on the carpet in her dressing room, the sirens wailing down the street. "A terrible, tragic accident."

My mother—God, I remember this so clearly!—had looked over my father's shoulder, staring at me and my brother. "And David and Teddi? You're supposed to trust me to watch over them now?"

I slam the cup into the saucer and bite at my lip. Is it fair that every damn time my mother goes into the hospital I have to see it all over again, in my mind's eye, playing out like some melodrama?

Only the reels are out of synch. Now we're sitting shiva, black cloths draped over the mirrors, old people sitting on little wooden boxes, tables laden with trays of gefilte fish and cold cuts from Ben's Delicatessen, pastries from David's of Great Neck that it seemed no one was supposed to eat. Then the black cloths removed, boxes gone, and the dining room table set for only four.

A door slams and the memory evaporates as Dana comes into the kitchen with Kimmie. "Is that Grandpa's car?" she starts to say, but then stops when she sees him and the groceries on the counter. Gently she kisses him on one of his sagging cheeks. "Oh, Grandpa," she says softly. "I'm so sorry."

"Such a *shaineh maidel*," my father says while he shakes his head sadly. "I look at her, I see you, Teddi."

Great, I think. *And I look at me and see Mom.*

"So you'll go see her?" my father asks.

I want to tell him all I have to do is look in the mirror, but I nod. Of course I will.

CHAPTER 4

I am in my kitchen, talking to myself, telling myself to breathe. I hear myself dictating each step of making dinner as though that will make everything all right. I am so deep in the abyss that Rio's voice scares the heck out of me and I drop the container of bread crumbs onto the floor.

I stare at the mess.

"And then you drop the bread crumbs," I say pleasantly while Rio shouts at me.

"You just forgot to pick him up?" he demands.

"You will need a broom and a dustpan," I say while Dana tells him something or other, Jesse rats on me, and Alyssa tries to climb Rio's leg. Frankly, I don't much care.

"How the hell could you forget? So busy with your little friend next door you forget your own son?"

Like I need this now? After the day I've had? "I didn't forget *my son*," I say, turning my back on all of them and throwing things directly from the stove into the sink. "I forgot *the time*. I was a couple of minutes late."

"Mr. Bonino had to take me home," Jesse tattles. Where is my staunchest defender when I need him? He was my knight in shining armor when that vet bill for the deer came.

"And he had an appointment at the dentist and I made him late. I don't think I should have to go to baseball anymore." Ah, he is throwing me to the wolves for his own sake.

"You're going. And I hope they have to pull all his teeth," I shout, shoving a glass into the sink while Dana yells at Alyssa for touching only-God-knows-what. "The man couldn't wait a few extra minutes?"

"Whoa!" Rio shouts, thinking that his voice alone is going to restore order. Well, no one even notices. So much for Macho Man.

"Look, Jesse, I told you I was sorry. You want blood?" I demand, ripping off my oven mitts and offering my wrists dramatically. The poor kid mumbles some sort of magic spell, which instead of seeming endearing, irritates the heck out of me. I want to shake him and yell "live in the real world," only who am I to tell anyone to do that? Apparently I've spent most of my life in la-la land.

"You gotta stop this, Teddi," Rio says. "You're scaring the shit out of everyone for no reason."

"Hey," I warn him. "I have a reason. You think Dan Bonino is the only one with a life? I have a life, too, and today it tripped me up."

I throw two measuring cups (for good measure?) into the sink before continuing.

"Look," I tell Jesse. "You're home. You're safe. I told you I was sorry. What more can I say, sweetie?"

I thrust my hands back into the oven mitts and open the oven door, releasing a stink bomb of smoke. Two hours ago it was the osso buco I promised Rio. Now it's *drek*. I shove it on the counter and fan at it for a minute in the hopes that it will respond to artificial resuscitation. Meanwhile, Alyssa tugs at my jeans and says something about Grandma June's bubbles.

Great. Exactly what I want Rio to hear, that this whole mess started with my visit to Grandma June. He blames everything that goes wrong in his house on her, anyway, and now, when it is so not her fault, he'll be off on a tear about his "mad mother-in-law."

"Honey, stop pulling on me. And get away from the stove!" I use my hip to push Alyssa away before shoving the hot dish off the counter and smack into the sudsy water in the sink. When the tears I've been fighting all day start, I reach for the faucet and turn the water on full force, my back to my family.

"Come to Daddy, Cupcake," Rio calls to Lys, like if he doesn't rescue her, her bad witch of a mother will pop her into the oven for dinner. "Mommy's gone off the deep end again and she's not gonna take you with her."

Glaring over my shoulder at him, I deliberately push the canister that says *flour* from the counter straight into the sink. I do this spitefully, though how this will in any way hurt Rio, I don't know.

"Don't cry, Mom," Dana says, patting my back while Jesse—aka *the traitor*—tries to hide behind the wallpaper. I can see that I'm scaring the heck out of all of them, but I don't seem to be able to stop myself. It's like there's a *Good Teddi* hanging above the kitchen, watching, knowing she should be comforting her children, telling them she's all right like a mother is supposed to do. But's there's also a *Bad Teddi* blowing the good one off, pushing the half-full flour canister into the sink, and reaching for whatever is next to throw in.

"Mom?" Jesse asks as Dana begins to grab things off the counter before I can toss them into the sink. "It's really okay about Mr. Bonino. He's a jerk, anyway. It's not like you were ever late before…."

"So, who wants Mickey D's?" Rio asks, acting like going to McDonald's will be a grand adventure. I turn and stare at him, my entire body asking what he can be thinking, and see my three precious children looking at their father as if he's suggested they shoot me and start over.

How come they get it and he doesn't? I wonder as the *Bad Teddi* calmly throws the pile of mail from the counter, one envelope at a time, into the now overflowing sink.

"Christ!" Rio says, reaching over my shoulder to turn off the water and pull the rest of the mail out of my hands. "Have you lost your freaking mind? You're scaring the hell out of the kids. And how are we going to pay these?" he asks, lifting a sauce-and-water-soaked bill off the floor. I want to ask him why it is that he can yell "Christ"—and in front of the kids, yet—and if I take what he calls "the Lord's name" in vain, he is mortally offended?

But it doesn't seem like the right time, exactly.

I am, I think, staring rather vacantly at him. Maybe it's the *Good Teddi* who can see this. *Bad Teddi* doesn't give a damn. I know it's *Bad Teddi* who is thinking this because I never use words like *damn*.

Rio is trying to salvage things around me. "Dana, get your

mother a mop. And Jesse, take Lys into the den and put that mermaid DVD on for her, will you?"

"Again?" Jesse asks, but I look at him sternly, as if someone ought to be listening to Rio and I've decided it is going to be *the traitor*.

"So, you gonna tell me what the hell happened today?" Rio asks me. He is using one of my favorite towels to stop the waterfall.

One of us (The *Bad Teddi?* The good one?) doesn't really want to tell him. There are too many people in my brain. I can't fight them all and Rio, too. "Okay," I say, giving in. "It was something my mother told me on Tuesday."

"Tuesday your wacko mother told you something, so today you burned my favorite meal, which I was looking forward to all day?"

"Don't blame my poor mother," I say, and I feel myself straighten up as if I'm ready to do battle. Only I'm not. Boy, am I not. One of the Teddis is egging me on, shouting, *Tell him! Tell him!* So I do. "Because today I found out that maybe she isn't so crazy. Maybe she isn't even a little crazy. About this, of course. I mean, I saw it with my own eyes. Only, thank God I didn't. Ever, I mean."

Rio's head is sticking forward on his neck like a cartoon character's. "Well, that clears up everything," he says sarcastically. "You know you're getting to be as wacked-out as your mom."

"Thanks," I say as sarcastically as he does. *Sauce for the goose*, someone in my head sings out. "That's exactly the kind of support I need."

He does the fingers-through-his-hair-frustration thing and

I wonder how it was that I actually used to find that gesture incredibly sexy. He isn't shouting, yet. And he isn't throwing anything or banging doors or threatening to leave me.

Now, there's a sobering thought. When he points to the chair, I sit in it.

"Listen to me, Teddi," he says in a come-in-from-the-ledge voice. "You're really scaring me now. I mean, the forgetting things, the overreacting. You know, there might be something to this 'like mother, like—'"

"You won't think I'm so crazy when I tell you what I found out. It seems that all these years, my father and Angelina..." I hesitate.

One thing about Rio—you can watch his brain work. I see him figuring out what I'm leading up to and he looks...well, he looks *amused* as I struggle for a way to put such a delicate matter.

"You mean to tell me that you didn't know that Marty was banging Angelina every time the clock struck *loon?*"

No, that isn't the way I'd put it.

"You really didn't know that?" he asks, shaking his head at me in obvious disbelief.

I get up and pick up a sponge to scrub the counter. How embarrassing that he knows what I never even suspected. "Know it?" I ask, scrubbing hard at the sauce dots that cover the counter.

Rio pries the sponge from my hand. "It's in the freaking tile," he tells me, pointing out the dark orange spots all over the ceramic tiles.

"I told you I should have gotten the Corian," I tell him,

as if a different counter would fix everything. And then I grab the sponge back and scrub some more, anyway, refusing to look at him as I try to decide why I feel ashamed. What have I done to be ashamed of?

"This is all about Marty and Angelina?" he asks. "And you really didn't have a clue?"

"Of course I didn't know! The man's my father! The thought of him sleeping with someone—" I shout. *How do you think he got to be a father? By visiting the cabbage patch?*

"Christ, your father can't order a hot dog without making the waitress blush."

"Oh, he's a harmless flirt." I wait until the *Bad Teddi* stops snickering to continue. "At least I thought he was. I mean, the man is too old to…isn't he? A man can't do it forever, right?"

Now it's Rio who's snickering. "Okay—never mind Marty. What about Angelina? Didn't you ever kinda wonder about her? Like, you know, did she ever go out on a date?"

Why didn't I ever wonder that? Am I so self-centered that I only cared about Angelina in relation to myself?

"So then, did you think she was some lesbo?"

"Angelina a lesbian?" I consider the notion quickly and dismissed it. "No," I say decisively. "I thought she was Mary Poppins. With dreadlocks. She was my other mother. I didn't think she had private parts or private needs or a private life. And if I *had* thought about it, I never would have thought she'd satisfy those needs with my father, of all people! I mean, she's always just been Angelina—not *Devilina!* And what about my poor mother?"

Rio laughs. "Best guess? Your mother knew all along and

was happy as a pig in shit that someone else was seeing to old Marty's needs so she didn't have to."

"That is ridiculous," I shout at him. My voice sounds especially loud because he refuses to shout back. I hate it when people do that. It makes me feel as if I am overreacting. Can you overreact to finding out that your father has been sleeping with both your mothers?

"Which is more likely—" he asks me, throwing an eye toward the doorway to make sure the kids aren't listening "—that June would mess that pink hair of hers or that Marty would mess around?"

"What if Angelina got pregnant? I could have a half sister who's younger than my daughter! Did he ever think of that? And Angelina! What was she thinking? All those years of telling me about respecting myself and saving myself—do you know what she used to say about you?" I ask, rooting around in the cabinet.

"That I wanted to jump your bones?" Rio teases, clearly trying to lighten the atmosphere, to make a joke out of the whole thing.

"Oh, my God!" I say, turning to him with a Spode china teapot in my hand. "She said you'd cheat on me. That all men cheat."

"Well, she'd know, huh?" Rio says, apparently hoping to end the thing right here. "What are you looking for, anyway?"

"I don't know. Anything she gave me so that I can give it back." I hold up the Spode teapot. "Did she give me this or did your mother?"

"You're driving yourself crazy," he says.

But that particular car has left the lot.

I see the two Teddis, in yellow sequins with feather boas like the Supremes' backup singers, dancing across the kitchen singing "Stop in the Name of Sanity"!

"Just stop this whole business, Ted. Now."

I slam the teapot on the counter and pull out a cut-glass pitcher. Carefully, I put it in a Ziploc bag and then in a brown grocery bag. I hold it at arm's length, and despite the warnings from the Supremes, their hands stuck up like crossing guards, drop the package onto the tile floor. It thuds rather than tinkles as it shatters.

Dana pokes her head into the kitchen. "Is everything all right, Mom?"

"Peachy keen," Rio says sarcastically. "You remember this, Dana, when your mother says she's feeling better, or when your grandfather says there's nothing wrong with her. You're watching your mother lose her mind."

"Mom?" Dana asks, and the fear rattles her voice.

"Don't bother her now," Rio says, shooing her away from the doorway. "She's busy going off her rocker."

"Haven't I been good to you," I sing, waving my arms like Diana Ross while Dana backs out of the room. *"Haven't I been sweet…* Make sure Jesse isn't killing Alyssa, honey, would you?" I shout after her.

The old oak clock in the kitchen ticks loudly, as if it is counting the seconds before I explode.

"You gotta stop this," Rio says, picking up the paper bag and gingerly putting it in the garbage. "Or I'm warning you, you're gonna wind up sharing a room with your wacko mother at South Winds."

"How? I mean, what do you suggest?" I ask him. "Forget what my mother told me? Forget being so sure she was wrong, racing over to my parents' house and finding Angelina's nightshirt on the back of their bathroom door?"

He shakes his head at me, shrugging as if he's out of suggestions. Maybe, he suggests, I need some kind of help. He mentions tranquilizers, alludes to shock treatments. "Or maybe all you need is a little time away from the kids, like you say, away from being a mommy."

"A vacation?" We haven't taken a vacation alone, without the kids since...well, since ever.

"Well, not a vacation, per se. I can just see you on one of those. You'd spend the whole time worrying about the kids. I mean, it's not like we could leave them with your mom, and now, with this business with Angel— Hey! What would you say to a week or two at South Winds? You know the staff there and you know—" he starts.

I pull away from him and get to my feet. "Stop saying that!" I shout, grabbing the dishcloth from the counter and throwing it at him. "South Winds is not some kind of resort, for Christ's sake. And I am not crazy!"

He fields another towel and a box of Jell-O. "No?" he says.

And then he has the nerve to laugh.

CHAPTER 5

I am so certain that seeing a psychiatrist is a bad idea that I nearly bolt from the waiting room. What does my mother's doctor know about my needs that he's sent me here to open a vein for this stranger? Why am I the one seeing a doctor? Why don't they instead make every man who cheats on his wife go to therapy? I imagine a room crowded with men in leisure suits. I don't want to make adultery seem fashionable, after all. The door opens and in comes my father, Marty Bayer. In comes Mike Lyons. In comes Michael Douglas. Hmm. This appears to be the M adulterers room. For a second I thank God that Rio's name doesn't start with an M.

And then I remember that Rio is short for Mario.

I am doomed.

I begin to gather up my things, intent on leaving, when the door to the inner office opens and I am trapped. A woman who looks my age, my weight—a normal, everyday sort of woman—looks directly at me and speaks in a normal, everyday voice. I don't know what I expected, but she isn't it.

"Mrs. Gallon?" she asks, glancing at the name on the folder before extending her hand. "I'm Dr. Benjamin. Won't you come in?"

I am frozen in my seat. Until I walk through that door, I am not someone who is seeing a psychiatrist.

"Mrs. Gallon?"

I rise and offer her a limp hand before correcting her. "It's *Gallo*, like the wine." I cross the threshold into her office and turn to add, "Not that I do. Whine, that is. As in complain." I want her to know that I'm not one of those women who's come to a psychiatrist because no one else she knows is sympathetic enough. "I never whine. It's very unattractive— according to my mother—and besides, I have nothing to whine about. After all, I'm married, aren't I? My life is perfect. I don't even know why I'm here. I'm probably wasting your time and the insurance company's money. It's covered, I checked."

With that, I perch on the edge of the oversize leather chair on the opposite side of a solid-looking oak desk cluttered with files and photos and a model of a brain. I put my mother's Louis Vuitton bag (Bobbie insisted I use it so that Dr. Benjamin will know I am a woman of substance) on the floor beside me, but I keep a tight grip on the strap so that if the necessity arises I can make my escape in one motion.

"So, anyway, it's not Gallon. It's Gallo. He's Italian. I'm Jewish. You used to be able to tell from my nose, but my mother insisted we fix that. Luckily the kids got Rio's nose, which was a good break, because I would have had to watch my mother like a hawk to make sure she didn't steal my children from their beds at night and have their noses bobbed. So you already think I'm crazy, right?"

To my horror, I can't stop myself from babbling. Of course

she thinks I'm crazy. I'm talking a mile a minute about my mother stealing my children. What else can the poor woman think?

"You know what a Jewish American Princess's favorite wine is?" I ask, stalling for time. She gestures for me to go on. I do, in a nasally, obnoxious way. "But why can't we go to Florida?"

She smiles indulgently.

"You know *Postcards from the Edge?* Well, my story is more like *Missives from Just Over the Edge.* Though I suppose it really doesn't matter, since it's Mrs. Gallon you think is crazy, anyway."

At least let her think I have a sense of humor.

She looks as if she may be about to laugh, but she doesn't. It is merely an acknowledgment that I am trying. *Very trying,* as my mother always says. Well, I can't just let things sort of hang out there, so I ask if we can start over. "So you say 'Mrs. Gallon?' again, okay?"

I guess she's used to dealing with basket cases, because she seems willing enough to indulge me—even mildly amused, if the little laugh lines crying for Botox by her eyes are any indication. She starts to rise, but I wave her back into her seat.

"No, no. That's okay. I'll pretend you got up. And you can pretend there's nothing wrong with me." I find myself nervously licking my lips, and glance at the closed door, which prevents my sort of slipping out if she happens to look away, which she doesn't. I apologize and explain that I am nervous. "So, what do you think?"

She patiently waits for me to finish making a total idiot of myself, which I must say I have accomplished rather deftly, and in record time. Finally I decide my best move is to simply shut up.

"What do I think? That my secretary hit the *n* instead of the comma. But it was a good icebreaker." Her voice is warm, friendly, inclusive, as is her smile. "Usually I can't get people to start talking right away."

"So then you don't think it's a sign I'm crazy?" I ask her. "All this babbling?" Maybe I can just leave then, having been pronounced all right. I begin to get up, but she motions for me to sit.

She leans back, lacing her hands together, and says very quietly, very calmly, "Why don't you tell me what brings you here today."

Where to start? There's my mother. There's the fact that I am turning thirty-seven, and that is exactly how old my mother was when she went blooey. There's Mike leaving Bobbie, and the business with my father that I can't even give a name to without feeling dirty and...

"I almost hit my daughter," I blurt out. It is as good a place to start as any. After all, it was a box of Cap'n Crunch sailing out of my hands toward Alyssa's head the night of the osso buco disaster that made me realize I need help. "With a box."

"An odd weapon," she says, leaning back in her chair as if people tell her every day that they beat their children. How can she be so nonjudgmental about a thing like hitting my baby? I decide I don't like her at all when she asks, "Why did you choose a box?"

"I didn't *choose* a box," I say, my voice ripe with disgust. "I mean, I didn't set out to hit her. I'm not some child abuser, you know. I was throwing the box at my husband and she came into the kitchen at the wrong moment and…" I take a deep breath and let it out slowly. Now I am not merely an admitted child abuser, I am a spouse abuser too. One more admission and they can book me on Jerry Springer—"Carton Hurlers Who Hurt," or something equally awful. "Can I start over?"

She doesn't snidely ask "again?" Instead, she stares at me as if she can see right through my white man-tailored shirt and straight into my soul. Amazingly, there is no shock in her gaze, no condemnation. "By all means."

"I was very angry," I say, trying to clarify things but stymied by the fact that I don't want to tell her what shattered my ability to cope. "I found out something terribly upsetting and I wasn't taking it very well. And so I broke a pitcher, which had been a gift from this person—the one I found out something about. Only it might have been from my mother-in-law, but I think it was from this person, and my husband suggested that I needed help. So, to prove I didn't, I threw the dish towel. And that's really all there was to it."

"I thought it was a box," she says.

I nod. "After the dish towel," I tell her. Which was after the Minute Rice, which followed the box of Jell-O, which followed the towel, which was all in the house that Jack built.

"Why were you so angry?"

"I was upset, not angry," I correct her.

"You said *angry*."

"No," I say. "I wouldn't say I was angry. I was upset—about this...*thing*, but I wasn't angry." I don't know why she is belaboring the point. I know I shouldn't be arguing with her. She'll only decide that I am belligerent and not like me.

"Why don't you think it was okay to be angry?" she asks. She squints slightly, maybe because the sun is shining brightly into her office, or because she can't see without straining every last dark secret I am hiding.

"I didn't say that." Honestly, I don't remember saying it.

She makes a note in my file (probably that I am argumentative, or repressed or have one foot on the bus to the funny farm), but she lets it slide and asks me how often I am *upset* enough to throw things, and she emphasizes the word *upset* as if it is some code word with which she is humoring me.

It is my own fault, her getting me all wrong. After all, she only knows what I'm telling her. "I never throw things," I try to explain. "It was just that I learned this terrible thing—"

"The one that you don't want to talk about?" And then she asks me if there is anything I *do* want to talk to her about. I ask her how you know if you're really going crazy. And I admit that Rio seems to think I am. She is unimpressed with my husband's diagnosis and tells me that one outburst hardly constitutes a diagnosis of any extraordinary problem that would require psychiatric care.

I ask if maybe she can write that down so that I can show it to my husband. "Or tattoo it on the back of my neck like a care label? 'Do not put in the washer or the funny farm.'"

When she is done laughing, which I'm sure is out of kindness, she tells me that I have a good sense of humor. "The ability to laugh at yourself and your predicament is a gift, you know. And a sign of a sound mind."

I tell her that not everyone feels that way—especially my family.

She caps her pen, smiles and says, "So then, if it was only that one episode…"

And what do I say? "If only." I can't believe it when the words pop out of my mouth. She's all but dismissed me with a clean bill of mental health. What am I doing? Getting my money's worth?

"There's something else?" she asks.

And I tell her about how I'm having trouble remembering things.

"So then you'd say you're distracted?" she asks, making notes on her pad.

"I could live with being distracted," I say, and I can feel the itch inside my nose that means tears may be unavoidable. "But I also remember doing things that I apparently haven't done."

She asks if I can give her an example.

"I can give you a hundred. Like I go to pick up the dry cleaning, and they say I've already picked it up. I argue with them, tell them that they've lost my favorite pair of jeans, and then when I get home, there they are, hanging in my closet. There's planning my daughter's bat mitzvah, which is a whole other can of worms, and the fact that I know I never canceled those invitations, and then there's my husband's suit, which I know I didn't pick up…"

Her expression is sympathetic, but she seems noncommittal. I suppose when you're talking with a psychiatrist, that's better than being committal, if you get what I mean.

Anyway, I tell her that all I want is to be in control again. "I want to take care of my children and house and husband. I don't want to do to them what was done to me."

She says we'll take it one step at a time, then gives me prescriptions for medical tests. Sometimes memory problems can be attributed to physical causes rather than emotional or psychological ones.

"Are you going to test for Alzheimer's? I read an article in *Good Housekeeping* and…"

She cuts me off, apparently not wanting to hear how I scored on their self-test, and assures me she will rule that out, along with any other possible physical causes. She adds that down the road she may want to do a PET scan, and possibly send me to a good neurologist. But she says that in her honest opinion there is a psychological component that needs addressing.

And then I untangle my purse and take it on my lap, as if I don't want to die without it, and I ask the sixty-four-thousand-dollar question. "So, do you think I might have a brain tumor or something?"

She tells me no, flatly, though I notice she doesn't laugh at the idea, either, but promises not to ignore or rule out any underlying organic cause for my situation, to which I respond with the ultimate question. Would something like that be fixable, like if it was a tumor, or something?

She refuses to allow me to get on that train and tells me that in her office no hypothetical fears are allowed. She says again that she'll do some routine tests, and then adds that she wants to check my hormone levels and things of that nature. Then, unbelievably, she tells me it could be as simple as early menopause.

I look down at myself. I've had better days. For example, that time when the kids all had the flu and I was going through a super Tampax an hour and I had to run to the drugstore because the Genovese delivery boy was out sick and they couldn't get the baby aspirin to me. I looked better that day. "I know I look, like, totally crappy," I admit. "But I'm not anywhere near old enough for menopause. I'm not even sure I'm done having children."

"Some women—" she starts, as if it's all over from here, all a giant downhill skid.

"Are you saying I can't have anymore children?" I ask, jumping up from my seat and grabbing my purse all in one motion. "Because I am still a very young woman! I have a five-year-old daughter!"

"Mrs. Gallo," the doctor says, and I could swear that she is actually amused by the whole thing. "No one said you were old or that you can't have more children. Many women have children during perimenopause and often during menopause itself. Sit down and let me explain." She waits, and when I don't sit back down, she adds, "Please."

"How old are you?" I ask her snidely. "Past childbearing?"

"Okay," she says. "Perhaps I should have said *premature* perimenopause." I think she is actually smirking at me.

"I could have more children," I make clear as I ease myself tentatively back down into her beige leather chair. "If I wanted to."

She nods, but the look on her face says I need more children about as much as the Old Woman in the Shoe does, and she's right. And I don't want more kids, so why I'm so offended I'm not sure. Except that I don't want her thinking I'm old. *That* old. I remember an Archie Bunker episode where Edith is going through her changes and Archie demands that she change immediately, and as I am recalling it, Archie morphs into Rio. He will not be one of those doting, understanding, let-me-turn-on-the-air-conditioning-for-you-in-February husbands. "You can give me HRT then, right? And that'll fix it?"

She hands me a sheet from her prescription pad with a name on it and tells me that if it turns out to be hormone-related we can try HRT. And that, in fact, she wants me to see this ob-gyn specialist.

I put it in the pocket of my purse. "And if it's not perimenopause?"

"Then I can help you."

And if it's a tumor, or one of the other things she's mentioned?

Unlikely, she tells me, but that we'll face it if that's the case.

"Well, any of those things would be better than going crazy. Maybe even my dying of something would be better for the kids than…"

"Mrs. Gallo, you are going to be fine. Your kids are going to be fine…."

"I am the most important thing in my children's life," I say as I rise to leave. "I want to be the best thing."

"Believe me, Mrs. Gallo," she says. "I understand."

Behind her on the credenza are two smiling teenage faces. I believe her.

CHAPTER 6

"I don't want that man here," I tell Rio as I try to find the holes in my earlobes that have been there for twenty-some-odd years and have chosen the night of my daughter's Awards Assembly to close up.

Rio reminds me that *that man* is (a) my dad, and (b) in my living room. "And three," he adds, switching to numbers and holding up some fingers, "he's your husband's boss."

I ask if he's trying to cheer me up.

"I don't know what I'm trying," Rio says, sitting down on the bed and throwing up his hands. "I just thought it'd be nice to have a normal evening around here for a change—one that's normal for the rest of the world, not normal for you Bayers." Lately it feels like we are all scaling Everest, and the mountain gets higher and colder every day. Like Sisyphus. The mere fact that I can remember the name of the myth heartens me.

"Grandpa's here!" Alyssa shouts from downstairs. Well, so much for feeling heartened.

"We're coming," Rio yells back. "Will you forget the freakin' earrings? We're gonna be late." He starts out of the room.

"Wait!" I press my hands down the front of my skirt. For a week Rio has been looking at whatever I put on, cocking his head and asking if something is new, or why in the world I am so dressed up, or look so grungy, or why I am dressed so…something. "Do I look okay?" I ask. We've long ago passed the stage where I try to look perfect for him, and somewhere along the way he has become, instead, my mirror. *Do I have lipstick on my teeth?* I'll ask him. *Does my panty line show?* Questions that only a few years ago would make me perfect for him now reveal all my flaws to him, so that they won't be seen by the rest of the world. Why does this happen?

Without even looking at me he tells me I look good, and I now know the answer. A wife asks her husband because she doesn't want to know the truth.

And if he can tell me I look good without even looking, what else can he lie about that I'll be perfectly willing to accept, rather than know the truth?

He stands by the door to our bedroom and waits for me to pass him.

"Well, don't you look pretty?" my father says as I come down the stairs. "You don't look old enough to have a daughter going into junior high."

"It's middle school, Grandpa," Dana corrects him. In her little heels she is able to reach his cheek, and she gives him a peck that sours the cream I had in my coffee. I keep my eyes glued to Dana, my head turned away from the adulterer who used to be my father.

"Such a *shayna punim,*" he says, looking, I suppose, at Dana, at what he thinks is her pretty face. "I wish your

Grandma June could be here to see such *shayna punims*," he adds, trying to include me, though I've turned so that he can't see my face at all.

"Where's Angelina?" Dana asks. "Isn't she coming?"

"No," I say, ending the discussion before it can begin. I'll be damned if I'll let Angelina fill in for my kid's grandmother the way she filled in for my mother with me. Before I knew she was filling in for a wife with my father, too. God, it's all so confusing. "There isn't room with Bobbie and the twins joining us. Find your brother and tell him to get his nose out of whatever he's reading and get down here. Alyssa, if you're bringing any babies with you, you'd better get them."

We wait in silence for the room to empty of children. When they are gone, I wish they were back. I can't look at my father. If I look at him, I won't be able to keep myself from imagining him hovering over Angelina, knowing that the lips that have kissed my forehead a thousand times have nibbled at Angelina's breasts.

I actually think I may be sick, standing here in the hallway with the man I have grudgingly admired for most of my life.

Before I can think of how I can get him to leave, he asks Rio how his back is doing.

Carefully angled so that my back is to my father, I address Rio. "What's the matter with your back?" He hasn't said a word to me about anything hurting.

"I musta pulled something moving some furniture or something," he says offhandedly. "It's nothing."

"Is that what the doctor said?" my father asks.

"What doctor?" It's like watching an interview on *Sixty Minutes*. You hear Morley Safer ask the questions, but you only see the man being interviewed.

"He says I need a little therapy," Rio says. "He does this thing, this traction, and it helps."

"When did you go to the doctor?" How can he not have mentioned it to me? Suddenly he isn't telling me things?

"Thursday afternoon," he says. "I told you, it's nothing for you to worry about. I need a few treatments is all."

"You told me?"

He waves the conversation away. "Okay, I'm telling you now. There's nothing you gotta worry about. The doc says a month, tops, and I'll be good as new."

"And you didn't tell me because…?" I ask, trying not to look as put out as I feel. A mother is supposed to be the linchpin of the family, the sun around which everything orbits and by whose force it all stays together. What will keep my family together if I cease holding on so tightly?

He raises an eyebrow at me as if to ask if he has to spell it out. "You got enough doctor worries," he says, glancing at my abdomen as if the fact that the ineffective new estrogen patch I got from Dr. Benjamin's ob-gyn is somehow a reason to keep this from me. "And it's not like you'd remember if I told you, anyway," he says, and adds a laugh to show he's joking. And then he touches the tip of my nose as if I am one of his children instead of his wife.

Just what I want my father to see—that I still haven't grown up.

"And finding out I don't know things is supposed to stop

me from worrying?" I snap at him, though I am really talking to them both. "That ought to work great."

"Sor-ry," he says, as if I'm being unreasonable here. He looks at my dad and adds that he hates to see me all worried and upset and starts talking about how lately I haven't been my old self.

Well, duh! Let me pull the rug out from beneath you and see if *you* can keep all the crystal in the air!

His voice trails off and everyone seems to be waiting for the person next to them to break the silence. I, dying to be anywhere but between my father and Rio, take off for the kitchen. Both men follow me. I wonder if I start cleaning, will they both follow suit? It is too tempting not to try, so I pick up a sponge and start cleaning the ceramic stovetop. Naturally the men just watch.

Finally my father clears his throat. "So, almost the birthday girl, huh?" he asks. I ignore him, throwing the sponge toward the sink and picking a rubber band up off the floor.

"Yup," Rio agrees when I don't answer for myself. "The big three-seven." He has to remind my father what year it is?

"Thirty-seven?" my father asks. Not surprisingly, he looks momentarily stricken, as if he is remembering my mother at thirty-seven, but he just asks about the big birthday plans as if we are flying to Paris for lunch.

"Breakfast in bed," Rio says proudly. *And I'll be cleaning this kitchen for an hour.*

"Then all the gifts," he adds, gesturing toward the kids, only they aren't even standing there. Dana will have bought me whatever Bobbie, who has shepherded the outing to the mall, has deemed essential to my fashion development. Jesse will have insisted on paying for his gift himself, which means as many things as he can buy for under eight dollars in the makeup aisle at Genovese. Alyssa will pretend for the rest of the week that one of her forgotten Beanie Babies is now her most favorite and then present me with it as her greatest sacrifice.

And from Rio there will be something from Victoria's Secret so hot that I won't even be able to open it in front of the kids and which I'll return on Monday.

I am an ungrateful wretch. No one should buy me anything.

But, if they are going to, anyway, maybe they could get me something they think I'd actually like? A good book from Dana? Tickets to a show from Rio? Something handmade from Alyssa? And from Jesse? Twenty minutes of his undivided attention to talk about anything that interests him.

"Then we'll head on over to my mother's place," Rio continues, while I daydream. It's clear that even he isn't thrilled about going to his mother's for my birthday dinner. "My sister Gina's birthday is Sunday, too, so my mother makes a big fuss or something."

"Well, here's a big fuss from me," my father says, pulling out a small robin's-egg-blue Tiffany's box from his pocket. "And your mother." One thing I'll say for my mother, even if she is in South Winds at the moment, she's got my father trained well.

He pushes it toward me, but I can't take it. I raise my hands and twirl away from it, backing out into the foyer. I want nothing from him except a denial that I can believe. And that is something he can't give me, not even wrapped up in a robin's-egg-blue box from Tiffany's.

My father puts the gift on the little shelf of the hall tree. I will have Rio give it back to him on Monday.

"And Angelina sent you this," my father says, picking up a party bag and trying to hand it to me in the foyer. I back away as if the bag contains ricin.

"Great," I say. It is the first word I have uttered to my father since finding Angelina's nightshirt on the back of his bathroom door. "Please return it to her."

"Now, Teddi," my father starts, but the girls have come back into the hallway and are standing around where they can hear everything.

"We won't discuss this," he says firmly, in a tone I remember from my youth. Authoritarian. In control. "You'll keep the gift because what's between your mother and me has nothing to do with you."

I roll my eyes, take the party bag and hand it to Dana, telling her to put it in the trash on our way out. My father accepts the bag back from my confused daughter just as Jesse bounds down the steps, *Harry Potter* in hand. "Hi, Grandpa," he says, his face radiating joy at the one grandparent he actually likes.

"Hey, Jesse! You all set for the big game tomorrow?" my father asks, ruffling my son's hair as he hugs him against his chest.

"It's just a practice," Jesse tells him. "I guess you can't come, huh?"

My father looks confused and shoots a glance at Rio. "She changed her mind?" he asks, but Rio only shrugs.

"Curt Schilling—just a practice?" he asks Jesse. "What? Only the World Series counts with you as a real game?"

Jesse scrunches his nose, and I have the uneasy feeling that if I were married to Robert Klein he'd be doing that spooky "wooo-oooo" sound right about now.

"Didn't your mom tell you about the game tomorrow? Yankees and Red Sox? You and me sitting in the Mickey Mantle Legends Suite? Now, how's that for big news?" There is silence in the hall. "Your mother didn't tell you?"

"His mother didn't know," I say, not confining my annoyance to my father, but directing it at Rio, too, who has clearly agreed to this little grandpa-grandson trip without so much as informing me, never mind consulting me.

Again my father and Rio exchange looks.

"No one told me," I repeat through clenched teeth, and if Rio says he did, he is out and out lying because he wants me to let Jesse go.

"You don't remember the phone call last Saturday?" my father asks. God, he is getting older by the minute. I look away, afraid I might soften toward him if I look too long, too close. "You said as long as I didn't let him eat too much crap he could go? Rio told you to put it on the calendar?" Jess is all but doing backflips, slapping his forehead, exchanging high fives and low fives with his grandfather.

"I spoke to you on Saturday?" I ask. Impossible. How could I have spoken to him if I'm not even speaking to him?

"On me you hung up. You spoke to Rio. You don't remember? It was the day he came home early."

"What day he came home early?" I wish Jesse would calm down for a minute and that the girls would stop arguing over whether or not Alyssa can bring Bratz and Beanie Babies to the assembly.

"Saturday," my father says. "I sent him home early because you were upset. You feeling better?" He looks damn proud of himself, as if he's fixed everything.

"Rio did not come home early on Saturday," I say, feeling my husband come up behind me and watching my father look over my head at him.

"I'm getting her one of those Palm Pilot things tomorrow," Rio tells my father as the kids begin to get restless and Dana starts yelling at Alyssa for touching her.

"It was Saturday," my father says. "Don't you remember? What? Is there something in the water in this house?"

Rio is trying to signal my father to drop it. "I'm getting her a Palm Pilot tomorrow and teaching her how to use it. It'll be fun. She'll love it. It'll fix everything."

"He did not come home early," I say, telling Dana to take Alyssa to the bathroom, make sure she goes and get her hands clean, and telling Jesse to calm down, no one has told him yet that he can go. "And no one has to 'teach me' how to use a PDA."

"Okay, Teddi," Rio says, adjusting the top button on my blouse. "You know how to use everything with buttons." He winks at my father. "How 'bout you tell Jess he can go, and let's get to the assembly."

I nod at Jess, and nod again when he holds up *Harry Potter* and raises his eyebrows. "Can I take this to the assembly?"

"But not to the game," Rio tells him. "Or you'll tune it out like your mom does when she's reading and all."

"I don't tune out," I say. "And you did not come home early any night this week."

"Okay, Teddi," he says agreeably. "And I didn't bring home McDonald's, either."

Unfortunately this does have a familiar ring to it. (We are, singlehandedly, trying to save McDonald's stock by upping their sales.) But it wasn't early, was it? "At dinnertime," I agree, waving away the gift my father is still trying to give me. When it is clear he isn't going to give up, I take the stupid bag, set a good example for the children by telling him he should be sure to thank Angelina, and place it on the floor next to the hall tree—where I will retrieve it on Monday and send it right back to Angelina by certified mail. And that will be that.

"Because I was fixing the grill on the Expedition," Rio says, after asking Jesse if he doesn't know how to tie his own sneakers, and threatening to get him ones that close with Velcro if he can't tie his ninety-eight-dollar Adidas T-MACs.

"The grill's fixed?" I ask, opening the door and looking at the car in the driveway. "When did you do that?"

There is silence behind me. I turn and look at Rio.

"Saturday afternoon. You don't remember *that?*" This time Rio makes no attempt to hide the glance he exchanges with my father.

Everyone is staring at me. Rio's leg is shaking. His eyes avoid mine.

Sheesh! Who can keep track of everyone's schedule? Especially with the week I've had? Dr. Benjamin told me not to let these things throw me, not to make mountains out of molehills, not to look for things that aren't really there. But what about not seeing what is before my eyes?

Rio's right. I need a Palm Pilot. One of the ones that can

communicate with my home computer, my cell phone, my voice mail, my answering machine, the TiVo in the den, the VCR in the bedroom, the alarm system, the sprinkler system and beings from other planets. That'll fix everything. There's nothing like gadgets to simplify life.

Everyone is still staring, waiting.

"Oh, yeah, last Saturday," I say, nodding my head and watching Rio let go of the breath he is holding, as if his life depends on my remembering he came home early. "McDonald's. I remember now. The same day you fixed the grill and told me about the ball game."

CHAPTER 7

"What did you ask me?" I ask Rio as I sign a paper for Jesse saying that I am aware that he has lost his math textbook (which I'm not, or wasn't, but they don't have a box to check for that, and besides, it is almost a relief that someone else has lost something) and that attached is $18.43 so that his last report card isn't held up.

"Milk?" Rio says, as if that is a question and he is waiting for the answer.

"White. Comes from cows. High in cholesterol. Kids drink it," I answer, figuring that ought to cover it.

"Funny," Rio says, lifting Alyssa off his lap and setting her down on the couch. "I don't suppose you got any?"

"In the fridge," I say, looking through my wallet. "Did you borrow any money from me?"

Rio ignores me as he walks to the kitchen, and I pull out my checkbook to write a check instead of giving Jesse cash, since suddenly I am down to seven dollars. I am sure I had about forty when I went off to get milk and a couple of other things after seeing Dr. Benjamin.

"Where in the fridge?" Rio asks, standing at the kitchen doorway.

Men are impossible. It isn't bad enough that they all apparently believed the "lock" function on the dishwasher means they can't open it (which explains why they pile dirty dishes on the counter above it), apparently there is also some sort of boa constrictor that lives under the sink, so they can't, ever, scrape dishes or throw empty boxes and cartons out. You'd think that they could actually look in the refrigerator for themselves. What can live in there? Bigfoot?

I roll my eyes at Jesse, grateful that he is only a man-in-training and not a full-fledged incompetent yet, and head for the kitchen.

"Right here," I say to Rio with the air of superiority that a wife who knows she's right has a patent on. I fling open the refrigerator door and reach in—but the two half gallons of milk I bought hours ago are gone. I don't know why, at this point in my mental deterioration, this comes as a surprise, but it does. I bend at the waist and look harder, move the orange juice, the pineapple-orange juice, the tropical orange juice, swearing about how five people should be able to drink the same juice once a day, shouldn't they? But juice is beside the point.

"Jesse?" I call. "Did you and your friends drink all the milk already?"

Jesse rolls into the kitchen on his new Rollerblades—they have retractable wheels, only he never seems to retract them. He is going to kill himself skating around with his nose in a book. He looks up at me as if he hasn't a clue why he's come into the kitchen.

"Did you somehow make the milk disappear?" I ask him,

trying to be nonaccusatory. After all, I've been jumping down everyone's throats for days and it has to stop.

"Milk? Oh, good. You got some? You got any of those things from the bakery with the whipped cream and—"

"There is no milk. I'm asking if you drank it all," I say, trying to sound more patient than I feel.

He reminds me that he had Sunny D, and, sounding like Captain Queeg asking about the strawberries in *The Caine Mutiny*, I demand to know if there was milk in the fridge when he took the juice. Jesse obviously thinks the answer is of no consequence. He looks at me blankly.

"Well, somebody drank it," I say, opening up the cabinet under the sink and looking in the garbage for the empty cartons. "I mean, there has to be some logical explanation for this. Two half gallons of milk don't simply grow legs and walk away."

"You forgot it," Rio says. His tone is bored. "I guess I gotta—"

I adamantly deny forgetting it. I am rapidly growing tired of him acting as if I am some mental patient with drool on my chin. "I remember quite clearly going to Trader Joe's and CVS rather than making a full-scale supermarket run, and getting two half gallons of milk, soy nuts, shelled pistachios, some of those imitation Cocoa Puffs that probably won't fool Alyssa and a box of Tampax."

"Ah! Well, that explains everything," Rio says after rolling his eyes at the mention of my Tampax. "Maybe you left the milk in the car?"

I didn't, I assure him, but he sends Jesse to look, anyway,

while I continue to deny it. I remember quite distinctly putting it on the counter and then opening the refrigerator door. Okay, maybe not distinctly. It's one of those things you do over and over, a million times during the course of a lifetime—like turning off the faucet or closing the door. But I did get the milk.

Rio leans against the wall, his arms folded across his chest, looking righteous while we wait for Jesse to return.

"What?" I demand, but he just watches with mild curiosity while I rearrange the contents of the refrigerator.

"Hiding in there somewhere?" he asks. "Under the butter? Behind the mustard?"

Jesse comes in through the kitchen door flipping a disk in the air and catching it. "Not in the car. Found Dana's Linkin Park CD, though."

Rio looks at me. "You feel okay?" he asks, coming close enough to all but examine my pupils.

I pull away from him. "I'm fine. Why are you making a federal case out of this? I got milk," I say, speaking as evenly as I can. "I got two half gallons of the red Lactaid, even though I wanted the blue one that's low fat. And the cashier had her nails all done up for the Fourth of July already, red and white stripes with blue tops and little white dots…or maybe it was for Flag Day…" My voice trails off as I consider whether or not it might have actually been yesterday that I went to the store. Without Angelina coming anymore, what is the difference between Tuesday and any other day of the week?

"Was Lys with you?" Rio presses.

Oh, right. Now I'm sure it was today because of her playdate and my therapy session. "No, remember I called you this afternoon and told you that she was at Alexis's and I was going to pick up the pants with the sauce on them from the cleaners?"

"No," Rio answers flatly.

"Now who can't remember?" I ask.

He puts his hands on my shoulders and all but walks me to a chair, pressing on them until I sit. "I wasn't in the office this afternoon. I went to see that back doctor again."

"So then it was earlier," I say cavalierly, as if it isn't the least bit important, while all the while I have the sense that something is terribly wrong here. But I can't put my finger on what it is. "I mean, it must have been earlier, right? When you spoke to me, that is."

"You feel okay?" He pushes my bangs back off my face and feels my forehead. "I don't think that doctor of yours is doing you one damn bit of good. If you ask me, you're worse than before you started seeing her. I'm telling you, Teddi, you seeing a lady doctor is like the blind leading the deaf." He shoots a glance at Jesse, who's standing next to the entrance to the kitchen watching us. With the slightest gesture of his head he makes it clear that Jesse should leave us alone.

Jesse seems to know more than I do and nods, avoiding my eyes as he leaves. There is something familiar about the look that passes between them, and a bitter taste rises in my mouth. I've seen that look. I've *received* it.

But that, of course, is different. Something is wrong here, but it isn't *that*.

"Is it your back? Did the doctor say you hurt something? Is it serious?"

"No, it's not serious," Rio says. "I might have to go back to him a few more times is all. Those therapy treatments are helping some. It ain't me I'm worried about, Ted. It's you."

"Me? I'm fine. I've got a lot on my plate, what with this birthday thing, and my mother being back in South Winds, and my father and Angelina...well, who wouldn't be a little distracted? But I'm really—"

"So I guess you probably planned to get the milk, but you got busy or something and you forgot, right?"

Well, that would be nice, but it isn't so. I remember I even got a Kentucky quarter for change and put it in my jeans pocket.

"No. I got the milk right after we talked," I say, leaning back so that I can feel around in the change pocket of my jeans, but not finding the quarter there.

Rio comes closer, crouching beside my chair and looking into my eyes as if he's going to find some secret there. Softly, almost gently, he tells me that the only time we spoke on the phone today was when he called to say he was coming home. He says there were no discussions about milk or laundry or anything else.

"Maybe all you need is a good night's sleep," Rio says. "How about I run you a bath or something and then get you into bed? And tomorrow you can call Dr. Benjamin and..."

"Rio, I got milk." How many times did my mother swear she bought something and been unable to find it? How many glances did my father and I share that mirrored the one Rio shot Jesse? But this is different. He has to know that, doesn't he? My mother is crazy, yes. But for me there is some other, some better, explanation.

"Don't worry about the freakin' milk," Rio says, putting his hand under my elbow. "I'll go over to Dairy Barn after you're settled." Suddenly he's a saint.

"You know, Rio, I really didn't forget Jesse the other day," I say as I let him lead me toward the stairs. "I lost track of the time…" I don't bring up the ball game, which I have decided not to think about, or the hundred other things I have forgotten lately. Everyone forgets things. That's why there are forty-two different kinds of Palm Pilots. That's why they invented secretaries. And notepads.

"Yeah, I know," he says, guiding me as if I am an invalid. "It's nothing. Too much stress or something. In a few weeks the kids'll be off to camp and you'll get a nice break."

I stop and turn to look him squarely in the face. "This is important, Rio. Listen. I'm not losing my mind. I did get milk."

"Yeah," he says. "Probably Dana drank it, is all. I'll get more."

But if Dana drank it, the empty cartons would be in the garbage. And who could drink a whole gallon? And what about the phone conversation, and the quarter in my jeans?…

"Jesse came in from the car, right?" I ask.

Rio nods.

"And Dana's in her room and Alyssa went to bed, right?" I ask, listening to myself and being ashamed of the pitiful way I sound. "I didn't lose any of them today, did I?"

"The children are good," he says softly. "And there's some good explanation about why the milk's missing. Maybe Dana loaned it to Bobbie and the girls."

It is possible, I suppose. More likely than that they were filming a "Got milk?" commercial down the block and raided my refrigerator.

For more than thirty years I have been telling myself I am fine, convincing myself I am all right, purposefully ignoring every sign that should warn me.

Now the yellow lights are flashing. CAUTION! CAUTION! PROCEED WITH CARE! and closing my eyes doesn't help. I still see them.

"Want me to run you a tub?" Rio says. "Or maybe help you get outta your clothes?"

There is no innuendo in his voice. No sexual connotations. His eyes aren't eating me up the way they usually do.

"I'm fine," I tell him. *I'm fine* I repeat to myself while Rio answers a soft knock on the bedroom door.

"Is Mommy okay?" I hear Dana ask, though Rio has opened the door only a crack.

"I'm taking care of Mommy," Rio says. "She's tired, is all. It's like we talked about, remember?"

"Well, but she was supposed to take me to Saks to look for bathing suits, and Jesse says—" Dana starts.

"Don't go worrying about your mother," Rio says firmly. "That's my job."

"It's nobody's job," I say from a dark corner of the room where I'm thinking I must be crazy if I told my eleven-year-old she could get a bathing suit at Saks Fifth Avenue. "There's nothing to worry about. I must have left the milk on the counter at the store. People do that all the time." And toilet paper rolls jump out of wastebaskets, and daughters-in-law forget to buy gifts, and—

"Of course they do," Rio agrees.

But he is lying.

"Oh! I remember now," I say brightly. "I put the package down on the next car so that I could open the car door."

"See?" Rio tells Dana. "That's all it was."

Well, if he can lie, why can't I?

CHAPTER 8

"It was horrible," I tell Dr. Benjamin as I pace around her office. "I actually accused her of stealing milk from my refrigerator. It seemed so logical at the time. The only logical explanation."

"And what did your neighbor say?" she asks.

"She pointed out that *I* was the one forgetting to get things," I say, when actually Bobbie shouted something like *What the hell do I need to steal your milk for? I'm not the one with the freaking memory problem!* She was having a sleepover for the girls and had, of course, gotten lots of Dunkin' Munchkins and bakery stuff, and bagels and lox for breakfast the next day. According to *The Rules*, you cannot cook for a party. You have to bring in or go out for any food beyond chips. The one exception to this rule is if you've gotten a new piece of equipment, like a Pizzelle Maker, which you can inaugurate at a party but then never use again.

"And she'd gotten Lactaid for Dana, and that was the way I thanked her—accusing her of coming into my house and taking milk out of my refrigerator." I shake my head, a habit that has become so routine that it's a wonder my eyes don't rattle. The two half gallons in Bobbie's fridge were from the

Dairy Barn, and if I hadn't been so totally crazed I would have realized that as soon as I stuck my nose in for the hazelnut creamer.

"Did you really believe that she had done that?" she asks. Unlike the last visit, she is doing an awful lot of writing in my folder.

I admit that I suppose not. It was just that I was inexplicably missing milk and Bobbie had an overabundance.

"Let's forget the milk for a minute," she says, and before she can finish I make some joke about how I've made a habit of doing that already.

She laughs. "I fell right into that one."

She asks me where I'd like to start and I feel like one of those clowns at the circus who keeps pulling scarf after scarf out of his mouth, only instead of scarves, they're worries. There are class trips, disease-bearing mosquitoes, community swimming pools. "You can't even say hello to a baby without the mother looking at you like you plan to kidnap it," I complain. "And if Alyssa isn't glued to my side and I lose sight of her for ten seconds, I stop breathing. Do you know what can happen out there? That someone can swoop down and scoop up my little girl, run into a bathroom with her, change her clothes, cut her hair and walk out of the mall with her before the mall police can even raise one another on their radios?

"Suddenly I'm afraid of everything. Kids with guns, dogs that attack, drunk drivers…if Dana seems depressed, I worry about preteen suicide. If she doesn't want dessert, I worry about anorexia. Jesse hides in books. Alyssa spends too much time looking in the mirror and trying to look cute. You should have known me before…"

"Before what?" she asks, and I shake my head. *Before what,* indeed. The death of my baby brother? My mother's illness? My inching toward the ledge?

"Do you think I'm crazy, worrying about all these things?"

"Are you afraid that Martians will abduct your kids? That the police will mistake them for terrorists? That witches are casting spells over them or that creatures who live deep inside the earth will shovel up and snatch them?"

I have to admit that I am not.

"Then no, I don't think you're abnormal for worrying, and I think that you are acting in a totally responsible manner when you weigh the dangers of any situation and then act accordingly. You aren't inventing dangers that don't exist, Mrs. Gallo. "

"No one else seems paralyzed by these kind of fears." They all seem to go on with their lives as if they live in Metropolis, and while bad things might happen, surely Superman will save them and their children.

"And they are all looking at you and thinking the exact same thing. 'Why, look at that Mrs. Gallo,' they're saying. 'She's got all these balls in the air and somehow she can still get dinner on the table every night.'"

I admit that we go out for dinner more often than I cook.

"Fine," she says. "'Will you look at that Mrs. Gallo? Why, she's out to dinner again, as if she doesn't have a care in the world! How does she do it?'"

"With mirrors," I respond, but I understand what she is saying. Apparently everyone has their own supply of smoke and mirrors.

I tell her that I appreciate her trying to convince me I'm normal, but that I know I'm not. She tells me there is no such thing as "normal"—there are only those who thrive better than others. We are all, to some extent, the walking wounded.

"And in your case, what happened to your younger brother inflicted a wound that can never really heal without leaving a scar. Your mother's breakdowns, your family dynamic— these are all more wounds that you have tried to ignore over the years. Imagine your psyche as your body for a second. You didn't merely sprain a toe, or break a nail. These problems in your life are huge ones. And you have been strong enough to limp around with your leg broken, your arm dangling from the socket all this time.

"Now along comes this betrayal by the two people in your life who saw you through your original traumas, and it's like a—"

"Knife in the back," I say, nodding my head and trying not to cry.

"Exactly. But you've staggered to the hospital, and I prom-ise you that you are in good hands. Hands that respect your strength, your fortitude and your wisdom in seeking help."

"Do you think you can really help me?" I ask, leaning for-ward in my chair. "Once the kids leave for camp I can come more often—as often as you say, if you think that you can give me back my life. I'll do whatever you say. Shock therapy, med-ication—"

"You know, I was surprised when you didn't come in here asking for Zoloft that first day. Since they've started advertising it on television I get several calls a week asking if I can prescribe it over the phone since the caller already knows from the ad that it's exactly what he or she needs."

"I wanted to, but I thought that it would make you think I needed it. *Catch 22*, huh?"

On the way home I call my mother at South Winds.

"I'm playing mah jong," she says. I tell her that I just wanted to check on her and see how she is doing. "I'm in a mental institution and my husband is schtupping the maid while I'm locked up in here. How do you think I am?" she asks.

My cheeks burn as I imagine the women sitting with my mother overhearing our conversation. "Is there anything you need?" I ask. "Anything I can bring you?"

I expect a sarcastic answer, like *a faithful husband, a divorce* or *a gun*, so I am surprised when she says, "I need a manicure." I don't have a chance to respond before she adds that just because she's in a nut house doesn't mean she doesn't care how she looks. "You are how you feel, Teddi. I don't know why you can't grasp the concept. You dress well, you feel well. You wear raggedy old clothes with paint drips on them, you feel raggedy and old. Look at your husband. He dresses like a fancy dandy, and he thinks he is one. Who's to say he's not? Illusions, Teddi. They're all we've got."

Somehow I feel there is a *Rule* in there, but my mother's logic shakes me. I promise to take her for one of those foot facials when she is well.

"Are you happy, Teddi?" she asks me, and the question

seems to come out of nowhere, until I realize she's testing me to see if the lesson has taken.

"Yes, Mom, I'm happy," I tell her. After all, if I say I am, who's to say I'm not?

CHAPTER 9

On my dreaded thirty-seventh birthday I am alone in my queen-size bed. I can hear my family in the kitchen, Jesse still pumped from his trip to Yankee Stadium with his grandfather, the girls shouting about who will cut a flower for Mommy's surprise birthday breakfast tray. *Please let them just make an English muffin and coffee,* I vainly pray, remembering how hard it was to get the dried egg off the stove last year, and how the year before I had to throw out the bacon griddle. It was so far gone that even Angelina couldn't clean it.

"Okay, let's turn the volume down," I hear Rio saying as they head up the stairway like a herd of elephants. Quickly I scoot under the covers and close my eyes, pretending to be asleep so that they can wake me up with shouts of "Happy Birthday!"

"Shh!" Jesse shouts at one or the other of his sisters. "You'll wake her up!"

Of course, he says this so loudly I would need to be in a coma for his shushing not to wake me up. Still, when they open the bedroom door, I am playing my part.

"Happy birthday!" they all yell, and I open my eyes and give them my best surprised look, like I have no idea the day, the breakfast, the rose and all were coming. Rio probably thinks I don't.

"Oh! Aren't you the sweetest family any woman could ask for?" I say, stretching and sitting up in the bed, patting the comforter around me to invite them all to sit down. "Look at this!" I purr as Rio puts the tray across my lap. He's got that *I'm so proud of myself* look I always find so irresistible because he combines it with this raising of his eyebrows that adds *I hope, I hope* to the mix.

Alyssa scrambles up onto the bed. Thankfully Rio knows Alyssa well enough to fill the juice glass only halfway, and put the saucer on top of the coffee cup.

"Happy birthday, Mommy!" our littlest one says, shoving at me the computer-generated card with the Internet-perfect characters and the Comic Sans MS font that Dana has obviously helped her make. Whatever happened to doilies and crayons and each child's card being recognizable? She takes my face in her two chubby little hands and, inches from my nose, says, "We didn't get you a pool for your birthday!"

I grin weakly. Alyssa comes up with the wildest things.

"Of course you didn't," I start to say, until it dawns on me that Dana and Jesse are actually yelling at Alyssa for letting the cat out of the bag. "We said not to tell her!" they shout, while my eyes connect with Rio's for a flash of truth before he looks away.

Impossible. It can't be, I think, unable to breathe, unable to swallow. I wave my hands, trying to tell Rio that I am choking, dying—help me, or get the kids out of the room so they don't witness it.

"It's got all the bells and whistles, Ted," he says, not even realizing that I am going to die, then and there, in my bed with my birthday breakfast on my lap and my children crowded around me. "One of those electric-eye things that can tell if a fly is breathing near it, a special cover that'll hold an elephant or something, six-foot-high fencing around the whole magilla—"

"Are you out of your mind?" I sputter when I can find my voice. I am blinking wildly, pinching my leg hard to see if maybe I'm dreaming and that this is a nightmare from which I can wake up.

"Yeah, yeah, I know," he says, putting his hands up as if I am some customer who doesn't want to go for Scotchgard on the matching ottoman. "I shoulda talked it over with you first, but it'll help my brother-in-law Joey out. Maybe keep his job with the pool guys he works for. And it's not that expensive. Besides, I knew you wouldn't want to treat yourself—"

"Treat myself? Rio! My brother...?"

"David?" He looks puzzled, and then the dim bulb over his head comes to life and he smacks his forehead. "Oh, Jesus H. Christ! Markie! I can't believe I didn't think of that!"

"*You* can't believe it?"

He looks at the kids. He looks at me. He sits down on the bed and stares at the carpeting. I opt for the ceiling.

"Okay, here's what we do," he says. "I'll get some kind of swimming teacher for Alyssa. You know, teach her, and maybe give Jesse and Dana some pointers, too. That way you can stop worrying about anything bad happening to the kids. We shoulda had someone teach her to swim years ago."

He asks Alyssa if she wants to learn to swim. I ask him if he'd like to have bamboo shoots stuck under his fingernails, but he just pats my legs.

"For God's sake, Rio. The kids aren't even home in the summer. They go to camp."

Rio tells me that Dana is nearly too old for camp already, and that Jesse hates it.

"I don't—" Jesse starts, but Rio shoots him a look that shuts him up. I wonder how many times they've rehearsed the whole thing. *We tell Mommy about the pool like it's a wonderful thing, and then Alyssa, honey, you start to cry, and Jesse, you say how you hate camp.*

Rio is still rolling.

I, on the other hand, am drowning. I imagine the Supremes dancing into the bedroom, looking resplendent in turquoise sequined bathing suits with matching Carmen Mirandaesque turbans. They are belting out, for all they are worth, *Baby, where did our love go, and all your promises…*

Rio, of course, doesn't see them. "And there's plenty of time before and after camp, and it'll increase the value of the house by tons more than it costs to put it in…."

I am shaking my head before my eyes are open again. "I don't want a pool," I say, swallowing around the word as if even uttering it can hurt the kids. "We can't afford a pool."

"Hey, everybody knows a pool is to a backyard what a Lexus is to the driveway. It's pure status, honey. Raises our backyard a notch above all the other yards, and ergo all the houses in the neighborhood, making it an investment that can't go down with the market. See? It's like a Mercedes, only instead of losing half its value when you drive it out of the showroom, it increases what the house is worth, and what the owners are worth, too."

These are things that matter tremendously to Rio and about which I couldn't care less. Besides, the danger of a pool so completely outweighs any possible status bump Rio might imagine. "I don't want a pool," I repeat. "And we aren't getting one. We can't afford one and I can't live with one." And that, I think, is that. Why couldn't he get me some nice piece of jewelry like other husbands do? If he is so concerned with status, he could have gone for jewels. Everyone knows a diamond ring appreciates…and so would I.

"Look, Ted, I can cancel the whole deal, but it'd be a mistake. A chance like this doesn't come along every day. The whole thing isn't gonna cost us one penny over cost cause Joey's company is doing it. Who knows if that schmuck he works for will even be in business next year?"

"Who cares?" I ask him back. How can he think that this is about money? *Let's risk the kids' lives and your sanity this year, honey. It's cheaper.*

"Please, Mom?" Jesse begs. I steel myself. If he asked me to let him go bungee jumping with that same pitiful look, would I have any trouble saying no?

"Dad says I can have pool parties," Dana says, "like Melinda Moskowitz."

"You know the damn thing will actually save us a fortune in the long run," Rio says.

Of course, I know better than this. It's another *Rule*. The only way to have home parties is to have someone come in to entertain the children, or to inaugurate some new major purchase. There will be one pool party. The first one. After that, no one will be interested, the parties will return to restaurants, and there will be a very expensive hole in my backyard that I will beg to pave over on a daily basis. Were I to agree in the first place, which I won't.

"Melinda is the most popular girl in the fifth grade," Dana reminds me. I doubt this for two reasons. (1) I've never heard her name mentioned before, and (2) her name doesn't start with a J or an A.

"You can't buy friends," I tell them. It's weak, I know, but it is four against one, and I can't find anything truly awful to say about their wanting a pool. I can't blame them for wishing they had one, even if I am not *ever* going to give in.

"Yeah, yeah. And you can't buy happiness," Rio agrees. Then with a nudge and a wink at Jesse, he tacks on, "but you can sure make one helluva down payment!"

I don't find that as funny as the kids do.

"Look," he says. "You want me to, I'll cancel the whole deal first thing in the morning. Only the way I see it, that means you're gonna live the rest of your life being superstitious, and we're gonna spend this whole year watching you wait for something terrible to happen, instead of saying, 'This is my life, not my mother's, you don't inherit accidents,' and moving on. Come on, Teddi, isn't that what the doctor told you?"

Maybe she did say that a person couldn't inherit accidents. But she didn't say, "so go home and have a pool installed."

"The kids want a pool, I want a pool—"

"And so it's my birthday present?" I ask. "What are you going to give me for Hanukkah? A ski trip for the four of you?"

"We ordered you a float," Jesse pipes up. "It's got armrests that hold your drink and everything. And we ordered water wings for Alyssa and—"

I tell them maybe when the princess is older, but Rio counters that Lys is nearly five.

"By next summer, when we can really use it, she'll be almost six. But hey, if your mother doesn't want a pool…" Rio tells the kids, playing on the fact that there is nothing stronger in this world than Jewish guilt "…I gotta cancel it. Of course, then you guys'll be stuck with the town pool again this year. And you'll have to deal with the crap that goes on there."

Jesse and Dana look appropriately miserable. Lys starts to sniff.

I am not giving in. Not this time, and not on this issue. I haven't caved on Jesse crossing Jericho Turnpike at South Oyster Bay Road, even for Carvel, and I'm not caving for this. It isn't happening. They can read my lips. On this, I will not budge. How he could even put me in this position, I don't know. Is it fair to make me be the party pooper and admit to the kids that I am afraid, when he knows how important it is for me to be a good example?

What kind of example *am* I setting? What kind of message will the children come out of this with? If something is hard, just throw up your hands?

"But Daddy said…" Lys whines at me. Usually Rio doesn't

tolerate her whining, but this time he is letting it go. Heck, he's probably given her a quarter to do it.

"And I was thinking maybe I could talk your father into letting me take off a few Saturdays this summer, what with business being slow then, and we could spend weekends around the pool…us and Bobbie and the girls… Maybe even next Memorial Day weekend…"

Man, he is slick. It's like my father is always saying. Rio Gallo can sell anything. He could probably sell Wonder bread to Hasidim during Pesach.

I feel my shoulders sag ever so slightly.

"And Jesse could use the exercise," Rio adds.

I suppose this is true enough.

"And I wanna learn to do the doggie paddle," Alyssa pipes up. I raise an eyebrow at Rio. Over the top now, no?

"And the hole in my backyard?" I ask, demanding to know how I am supposed to deal with that. "A huge hole anyone can fall into for weeks? Not to mention my flowers…"

"I'll move all the bushes myself," Rio says while the kids whoop and holler. "I swear it. And the hole'll only be there for about three weeks. Being as how I know how you'd worry about Alyssa and the hole and all, I called up Westwood Lake, and they've got kids going as young as Lys, so if you wanna, we could send her along with Jesse and Dana and—"

"Send Alyssa to sleep-away camp?" If the pool is a shock, it is quickly paling in comparison to the idea of sending my baby off for seven weeks. Some lines cannot be crossed. "Absolutely not."

"So then it's settled," he says, as if I said okay, which technically, I haven't. I can still change my mind. They'll be disappointed, but if I can't cut it, the pool is not going to happen. I can try living with the idea for a while. And, if I'm not really on my mother's bus, I'll be able to kiss all my fears goodbye.

It is a huge, enormous, mammoth *if*.

"Happy birthday, honey!" Rio says, reaching beneath the bed and pulling out a box with a bow on the top.

Glaring at him, I move the untouched tray out of the way and lift the lid off the box.

Great. Exactly what every thirty-seven-year-old woman who's borne three kids wants.

A bikini.

CHAPTER 10

Bobbie, her sister Diane, and I have been getting together for a Girls' Night In since Dana and the twins were babies. We've continued the gatherings through my other two pregnancies (watching *Baby Boom*, *Three Men and a Baby*), through the remodeling of Bobbie's house (*The Money Pit*, Mr. *Blandings Builds His Dream House*), through Diane's months at the police academy (you guessed it, *Police Academy 1, 2, 3, 4, 5, 6*), and the fact that Mike has jumped ship isn't going to stop us now.

Bobbie keeps saying that while she may have gotten the husband from hell, she's got friends from heaven. Frankly I feel about as useful to Bobbie as a Hummer on Willis Avenue, but I try to be there for her, at least in body, ready to watch whatever stupid movie she and her sister want. And to pretend that life is normal for her sake.

Not that I couldn't use a large dose of normalcy myself these days. As Bobbie keeps saying, if I stand any closer to the edge, a *boo* from Rio will be enough to send me tumbling into the snake pit. She is not at all pleased about my allowing Rio to put a pool into my backyard. Like I'm happy about it?

No happier than I am about rehashing the birthday fiasco

at my mother-in-law's, the details of which Bobbie has related to Diane.

"I don't know why you always agree to spend your birthday at your mother-in-law's, anyway," Bobbie says, placing the blame on me, as she seems to do about everything lately. She takes another swig of her merlot and offers me some, and I tell myself it is the wine, and not my friend, attacking me.

"What?" I ask playfully, trying to make a joke of the whole thing. "You wouldn't choose to spend your birthday with a woman who thinks you've ruined her son's life? Who purposely forgets every year that you are lactose-intolerant and puts cheese on everything in the hopes of either starving you or confining you to the bathroom throughout the meal because every time she looks at you she sees one of the daughters from *Fiddler on the Roof?*"

They both look at me as if I'm babbling, which, though I've done a bit of it lately, I'm not at the moment. I pick up Igor, Bobbie's cat, and settle him on my lap while I continue.

"Okay, you remember that part in *Annie Hall* when Diane Keaton's grannie looks at Woody Allen—pre-Soon-Yi, when we could still like him—and she sees him like Hasidim with one of those tall hats and long sideburns? Well, that's how Mama Theresa looks at me."

I release Igor, who clearly doesn't want to be held, and reach for a diet Coke, pour some into a glass and clink it against Bobbie's raised one. "Here's to a better meal than my birthday scungilli. I don't know when I'm ever going to learn. You'd think I'd remember from year to year, but lately I can't remember from minute to minute."

Mistake.

Bobbie exchanges a look with her sister. Clearly they have been talking about me. They see what I think I've been hiding. I feel naked. I want to run home, only that isn't where I want to be. Panic swells like a tidal wave, and I want, no, I *need*, to run somewhere. Is Marshall's still open? CVS is twenty-four/seven. So's Home Depot, where I could pick up some new batteries for the Palm Pilot Rio came home with last night.

"You have that estrogen patch on from the doctor?" Bobbie asks, and I imagine myself in my new bikini, complete with a tire patch across my belly, courtesy of the new ob/gyn Old Doc Benjamin has sent me to.

I nod, saying how great it is to now be thirty-seven, patched for possible perimenopause, and on the brink of insanity.

"Did I tell you that the Palm Pilot Rio got me has some kind of beam thing and I can exchange information with other Palms? I studied it for an hour last night. Do you suppose that makes me a palm reader?"

"She's testing herself, you know," Bobbie explains to Diane. "Does it all the time. She's the only woman I know who has to challenge herself at every turn. Can she put up the wallpaper in the bathroom herself? Can she figure out how to uninstall the women-with-boobs game that Jesse put on the hard drive? Can she cut her own hair, even the back?" She mouths the word no at Diane and continues taking me apart. "But does that stop her? No one crams more into a day, expects more of herself and makes fewer excuses than our Teddi. It goddamn drives me up the wall!"

Diane tries to shut Bobbie up, but with almost a whole bottle of her favorite Lindemans merlot, there is no stopping her. She doesn't even notice that I am rather frantically hunting for the Sam and Libby ballet flats I got at DSW, because I am so out of there that my head is already back in my own house, under my pillow, blocking her out. No, she rants on.

"Isn't it enough to survive a marriage and kids? Or, in my case, a divorce and kids? You make me feel goddamn decadent if I give in to one moment of well-earned, totally deserved self-pity."

She stares at me and takes another swig of her merlot as if she is daring me to tell her she has had too much. When I don't, she raises her glass in salute.

"Here's to you, Ted, willing to brave the funny farm for your family's comfort and enjoyment. Bring on the pool, shall we?"

"I don't see what else there is to do," I say. It's a feeble response, but my arsenal is empty.

"You could just say no. It worked for Nancy Reagan, didn't it?" she says.

"I never liked Reagan." I am aware that this is a typical June Bayer non sequitur and yet I can't help myself. "Still, I can't imagine what it was like for Nancy to watch her husband slip away. Or maybe I can imagine. All too well. And now I'm the same age—"

"You're letting this birthday thing get to you," Bobbie warns me, as if that thought hasn't occurred to me, as if I don't now have a psychiatrist (shades of my mother) to point this out to me. "I don't care what age your mother was and what age you are. Accidents are not hereditary, girl. Didn't your new doctor tell you that?"

I shrug an acknowledgment, not anxious to give Bobbie any credit or validity.

"She didn't say you were losing your mind, did she? She didn't say that just because your mother has reality issues, you do, did she?"

Before I can answer, Diane pops her beer and wags a finger at me. "Like I've been telling Bobbie, there's always the undeniable power of self-fulfilling prophesies. Like, I suppose you could drive yourself nuts because you—"

"Shut up, Diane," Bobbie says. "She really doesn't need any help falling over the edge, you know."

"I'm trying to pull her over and ask her to step out of the car," Diane says. Now that she's passed all her tests and is a rookie cop, she feels the need to remind everyone of that fact at every opportunity.

"The way I see it," Diane continues as if I am not there, "she's driving herself to the funny farm. Now, my lights are flashing, my siren's blaring, and I'm saying 'whoa, lady. This is not where you want to go.'"

"So," I ask, pretending to be bright and cheery as I shuffle through the tapes on the table. "What are we seeing tonight?"

"Subtle," Bobbie says sarcastically. "I'd never guess you were trying to change the subject."

They go on joking with each other, but I am finding it hard to pay attention. I hate it when I leave the kids at home alone. Yes, I know that Dana is old enough to babysit, but where she'd be vigilant at someone else's house, will she be vigilant in her own? And where other people's children might be fooled into thinking she was a grown-up with some authority and obey her, is there a chance in the world as we know it that Jesse will? "Earth to Teddi, come in, please," she teases.

"Did I turn off the stove?" I wonder aloud. "And unplug the microwave?"

"You called in pizza for the kids, Ted," Bobbie reminds me. "You didn't even turn *on* the oven or anything."

Maybe I should go home and check. I could slip in the back door and look around without announcing that I'm home, or I could leave the weekly Teddi Roast and—

Diane rolls forward on the couch and puts her weight on her legs. "What is the matter with you?" This from a woman who has no children.

"She's fine," Bobbie says too quickly.

"Yeah," I agree. "I have a possessed house, where laundry goes into the garbage and keys disappear and toilet paper rolls are always empty but—"

"Hey! How many men does it take to change a roll of toilet paper?" Bobbie asks. Suddenly she's Miss Perky-Pants because she senses that I am ready to bolt.

Diane ignores her while I give her a look you might classify as a glare.

"Nobody knows," she says solemnly. "It's never been done!"

"I shouldn't have left the kids alone," I say.

"Speaking of kids…" she says, desperate now for me not to leave "…you know that Mike hasn't called the girls in over a week?"

I can't imagine Rio not talking to our kids for a week. I can't imagine the hurt our kids would feel. "Are you sure he isn't reaching them when you aren't home?"

She gives me a look that says she isn't so stupid that she hasn't asked them. "I suppose he could be trying to contact them telepathically," she says, getting in a jab at the hypnotherapist her husband is seeing. "When I call his office the girl tells me that he's *meditating*."

"Well, it would be nice if he *meditated* on what a shit he is," Diane says.

The phone rings and Bobbie picks up the portable. It's Dana, and she hands the phone to me with a disgusted look that implies it's my fault that Dana has called.

"What's wrong?" I say into the receiver, already on my feet and halfway to the door. It seems like Alyssa's binkie is the latest victim of MIS (*Misplaced Item Syndrome*), a virus that has struck my life with all the force of Epstein-Barr. "I don't know, honey," I tell her. "It was there last night. Did you ask Jesse?"

Dana asks me what Jesse would want with it and I reply, "What would anyone want with that ratty old thing? Do you think some robber broke in and stole it? It's got to be there somewhere. Ask Jesse to help. And call me back if you don't find it.

"And put Alyssa on." I wait, fighting the urge to run across the lawn and look for binkie myself. The truth is that a few months ago, I'd have found it in a flash. Tonight I'd be about as much use as one of Lys's Beanie Babies. I hear Alyssa's sniffle on the line. "Sweetheart? Stop crying. Dana will find binkie. You know, you're getting pretty old for…Lyssie, she'll find it. If she doesn't, I'll come home and I'll find it, okay?"

"Oh no you don't," the childless one says. She takes the phone from me. "Alyssa? This is Aunt Diane. I'll put out an APB on binkie and we'll get to the bottom of this. Can you give me a good description to give to the detectives?"

Bobbie winks at me as we watch Diane in action.

"Eech! And you want this thing back?" Diane says into the phone. "A reward? Sure we could. It's probably the only way you could get anyone to touch it, honey."

Diane holds out the phone to me. "Jesse's yelling that he found it. Guess I'm lucky I didn't set that reward yet."

"Where was it?" I ask, while Bobbie puts two videotapes behind her back and gestures for me to pick one.

The dishwasher? "Hmm," I say, at a loss for the right response. "Well, give it to her and tell Dana to put her to bed, okay? Thanks, sweetie. Yeah, Daddy will be home before me. Okay. Call if you need me."

"Maybe Rio thought it was time to wash it," Bobbie suggests, though we all know that men don't know there's actually water and soap behind the dishwasher door.

"Okay, here's another one," Bobbie announces. "How many men does it take to throw in a load of wash? Seven. Six to go on a search mission to find the washer and one to throw the whites in with the darks!"

I pretend to be amused as I sit down on the couch, determined to get through whatever movie they choose. I will not surrender to panic. My children are fine. My marriage is fine. I love watching movies. They make me forget my troubles.

Bobbie pops in the video and throws the case down on the table.

High Anxiety.

Great. Just great.

CHAPTER 11

I'm sorry I'm late. I couldn't find my car keys. Again. And really, I don't even know why I'm here," I tell Dr. Benjamin. Even I can hear the anger in my voice. I try to erase it, take it back. "I mean," I say softly, "you must have patients that really need your help and I'm taking up your time."

"You don't need my help?" she asks. She has light brown hair and pale skin and wears a pink short-sleeved angora sweater, and all I can think when I look at her is that she is soft. A child would want to crawl into her lap. A husband would want to lay his head there and be comforted.

I am not looking for comfort.

"Well, I'm not angry anymore, so no, I don't think I need any more help."

"All your anger is gone, then?" she asks, looking as skeptical as she sounds. "I must be the best doctor in America. Or maybe you're just the most forgiving woman."

"Or some combination," I say, perching on the edge of the chair since I have no intention of staying. I don't think. Somehow, now that I am in her office I am a lot less sure about leaving than I was while rehearsing on my way over in the car.

"So then you're not having trouble with your memory anymore, either?"

"Okay," I say. "Maybe." There are a million things to choose from. I decide the baseball phone call is the one I want to talk about. "I could swear, I mean, I *would* swear on a stack of Bibles that Rio never called, never asked about my father taking Jesse to a game."

The doctor doesn't say anything.

"Now, of course, it was on a Saturday, so the kids were home, and Rio hadn't gotten me the Palm Pilot yet, and I was running around like a lunatic trying to get stuff taken care of, like getting shoes for Dana's graduation and taking Jesse to Little League and trying to keep Bobbie's spirits up, and I did have the woman from the card shop over to look at invitations for Dana's bat mitzvah, which is a whole other can of worms...."

Dr. Benjamin flips back in her notes. "You mentioned your daughter's bat mitzvah the last time you were here and said about the same thing regarding it."

"I did?" I don't remember. Of course I don't remember—if I can lose a whole phone call with Rio, surely I can lose an offhand comment to Dr. Benjamin.

"Rio and I have been at each other's throats about the whole affair," I admit. "I mean, the children are ours, and we should be in charge of paying for the bat mitzvah and making all the decisions about it, right?"

She seems noncommittal, so I continue. She'll no doubt admire my sense of responsibility when I explain the problem. "If—hypothetically—we let my father pay for it, shouldn't he have the right to make decisions about it? I mean, like if I let him pay for Dana's dress, doesn't that mean that my mother—when she gets out of South Winds—will have the right to come shopping with us, to say what looks good and what doesn't, to tell me I have to have stupid dyed-to-match suede shoes and my dress has to be made by Eleni in Plainview or special-ordered through that little store in Woodmere that she likes?"

I'm wondering what she did about her children's bar and bat mitzvahs, and if I'm offending her.

"Have you told Rio, or your mother, what you are telling me?" she asks.

Like I can tell my mother that. Like I can tell my mother anything. Especially when she's in South Winds playing the poor-me-I'm-in-the-institution card. It's all academic, anyway, since I wouldn't take a dime from my father at this point. It's that Rio doesn't seem to get it. "Listen," I tell her. "If anyone ever lies down on your couch and asks if her husband should go to work for their father, you should tell them that the answer is no."

"How long has your husband worked for your father?" she asks.

"I know," I say. "You're right."

"About?"

I admit that it shouldn't have taken us twelve years to come to this conclusion, and if we'd only been brave all those years ago, by now Rio would be working somewhere where there was at least a chance he'd be happy.

"It's all my fault," I admit. Her lip twitches. "No, really. This one is my fault."

"For having a generous father who took his son-in-law into the business?"

No, for being spoiled rotten and wanting nice things for myself and my family.

"Why is it your fault?" she presses.

"Once I told Rio that my idea of camping in the wild was a motel with chenille bedspreads and one of those wall heaters that clicked on and off all night."

I'm not sure if Dr. Benjamin gets it or not. I think I may see a small smile, but like with a baby, it could be gas.

As Rio's mother always says, *from fig trees you don't get apples*, and I'm not as different from my parents as I'd like to believe. Like any other couple in the Five Towns (that posh area of Long Island where the nouveau riche have *riched* their limit), my parents expected me to marry well and live happily after—in a four-bedroom house with a three-car garage and live-in help. My father had pulled himself up by his bootstraps, or so the story goes, and he didn't want me to have to struggle the way he did. So he bought a big house in Cedarhurst to be sure that the best would be close at hand, and in case it wasn't, he bought my mother a Cadillac, my brother David a BMW, and me that vintage candy-apple-red Corvette. When he gave it to me and called it a *husband-getter*, I don't think he had Rio Gallo—who pulled up in his tow truck when I got stuck on the Northern State Parkway—in mind.

He certainly didn't have in mind a son-in-law who would have the audacity to lie to him about graduating from SUNY Stony Brook, when in fact he'd never even finished Nassau Community College.

If there is a scorecard for potential sons-in-law in that *Handbook*, you can bet that "no college education" is grounds for immediate rejection. Rio probably scored a perfect ten on the disqualification list—or would have if my parents knew about the cobra tattoo on his left shoulder, and the fact that he'd broken the law a couple of times and bent it several more. In the perfect alternate universe my parents choose to inhabit, there are no second chances, no extenuating circumstances. The fact that Rio's father died when Rio was eight years old, that the man had been so underinsured that Rio's mother had to take in wash to feed her children, that Rio and his brother and sisters were prey to a very bad element and that each of them finally overcame the temptation for easy money, count for nothing. The man has a tattoo. Let's all put our heads in the oven, shall we?

I could tell Dr. Benjamin that, but I don't. I think I don't want her to know he has a cobra tattoo.

She watches my mind work, but she doesn't offer a penny for my thoughts. Maybe she's fooled by my T.J. Maxx discount designer clothes and thinks I don't need the money.

"Did you see the gynecologist?" she asks.

I nod, and since the ob/gyn has given me a clean bill of health, I ask, "If I told you that I've seriously considered the possibility that my husband and my father are conspiring behind my back, would you think I was paranoid?"

"Conspiring to do what?" She is leaning back in her chair, studying me while I search for an answer.

"Well, I thought it was to get me to let Jesse go with my father to a ball game—he had these tickets that let them sit in the Mickey Mantle Suite or something."

"A Legends Suite?" she asks, and I can see she knows more about baseball than I do and that this is a big deal. It makes me glad I let Jesse go, even if I didn't know what I was doing.

"I guess," I say, hoping this will make her happy. "Anyway, I'd swear they didn't call, but would my father really stoop so low?"

"You tell me."

"Well, the thing of it is, they'd never have bothered. I mean, Rio would tell me Jesse was going and it would be a done deal. I might have given him a hard time, but he'd have convinced me not to punish Jesse for my father's mistakes. And he knows that." *Just like he knows if he gives me the pool as a gift, and has the kids in on it, that I have to at least consider it.* For a moment I think about telling Dr. Benjamin the pool saga and asking her advice. But what if she tells me to face my fears and get the pool and I find that I can't do it? Or what if she tells me I don't have to confront my fears and I go on, for my whole life, with South Winds hanging over my head, looming ever and ever closer?

"So you're still angry with your father?" Dr. Benjamin asks.

"I guess," I admit, relieved that I've decided it isn't time yet to tell Dr. Benjamin about the pool. Not until I sort through my feelings. Actually, I still might say no, and then I will have told her for nothing. "But I'm not like off the deep end anymore."

The doctor says she is glad to hear it, but I haven't really finished.

"And then they both claimed that Rio came home from work early on Saturday."

"Why would they tell you that?"

"Because it's true, I guess," I say. After all, the car's grill is fixed, isn't it?

"Well, that would explain it," she says, and her lip does that twitchy thing again.

"He *is* trying to drive me crazy, you know." I fiddle with my purse strap, not meeting the doctor's eyes.

"He?"

"Rio. My husband. He bought me a bikini for my birthday."

Is that a smirk? She doesn't only think I am old, she thinks I am fat, too? She's got ten pounds on me, easy.

"What?" I ask her, daring her to say it.

"I was thinking that maybe he was hoping *you'd* drive *him* crazy," she says, and gifts me with a genuine smile. Of course, she's never seen Rio's head swivel around to watch a pretty young girl's firm butt going by before snapping back to me with wistful regret in his eyes.

"I *am* driving him crazy—or my memory is. Or my lack of memory, I should say. I mean the PDA is a help, but there are things you shouldn't have to write down. Like I keep thinking I've changed the toilet paper rolls in the bathrooms and when I come in again, they need changing. And last night? Can you believe that I forgot to turn on the oven? Well, you probably can. Rio had a little trouble, though. I made veal parmigiana for him, but I had to make some Fingers of Death for Alyssa and—"

"Fingers of Death?"

"Fried chicken tenders. Fried food is horrible for you, but

it's all she likes to eat. Rio says it's a miracle she doesn't cluck by now. And I had to make Dana a veggie corn dog because she saw one of those PBS specials on how they get veal, and Jesse was going to eat late because he went over to his friend's house so they could build a guitar, and when it was time to take the veal out of the oven, I realized I never even turned it on!"

"You made four different dinners for five people?" she asks, her soft brown eyes wider than I've ever seen them. Probably she manages to make one meal, like say meat loaf, and it's a take-it-or-leave-it affair. I sit up a little taller.

"Actually, I made five dinners for eight people—Bobbie and the girls came over because Bobbie loves my veal parmigiana, and Kimmie is a vegetarian, so she ate corn dogs with Dana, but Kristin and I don't eat cheese, so we had veal without the parmigiana, though I really did feel guilty about those poor little baby calves."

Dr. Benjamin does an exaggerated slump in her chair, saying she is exhausted just listening to me.

"That's why everyone goes out. But, anyway, my point is that I forgot about the oven," I say sadly, my bubble bursting. "And I could have dealt with all of that, but yesterday I decided to visit my mother at South Winds, where I've been a million times, and three-quarters of the way there I got lost. I got off at exit 62, the way I always do, made a left over the LIE, and suddenly I had no idea where I was, where I was supposed to go."

I feel like I have said magic words. Dr. Benjamin has come forward in her seat and she is staring at me as if I've suddenly grown an extra head—something I could actually use.

"And what happened?" she asks me.

"Well, I got back on the LIE and came home. And I sat in my living room and cried because I couldn't get to South Winds. Ironic, huh?"

CHAPTER 12

Rio and I sit fanning Jesse and Alyssa in the hot auditorium of Thompson Middle School, where Dana will start her march to adulthood in the fall. I have made Rio promise not to remind my father about the moving-up-day ceremonies, though what excuse he's given my dad for taking the day off, I am not sure. Something to do with his back doctor or the physical therapist, I think.

In exchange, Rio has made me promise to consider sending Alyssa to Westwood Lake with Dana and Jesse. He's already sent in the deposit, but he says we can forfeit it if I can't see my way clear to letting her spend the summer in, as Rio puts it, the cool of New Hampshire with a bunch of kids her own age, her sister and brother nearby, and three counselors to her bunk of seven.

"Imagine, Teddi," he keeps telling me. "A whole summer of freedom for us, like before we got married." No matter how many times I tell him it won't be anything like that, that marriage and kids are for life, I don't think he hears me.

Anyhow, he reminds me, I started camp at six myself, the summer following the accident with Markie, and survived. But that was because my mother was so dreading the summer pool season that her psychiatrist actually recommended sending me away.

"You okay?" Rio asks over the kids' heads.

"Of course I am," I snap at him.

"Do you see him?" I ask Bobbie, who is looking around the auditorium for Mike.

There is a sharp intake of breath beside me and Bobbie squeezes the blood out of my hand. "There! With the sunglasses. What's he, incognito?" she demands.

"Is that her?" I cannot hide the surprise in my voice. On Mike's arm is the most ordinary woman, with mousy brown hair hanging out from beneath a floppy hat, and wearing one of those flimsy, flowery dresses that women haven't worn outside their gardens since the sixties. As Bobbie has drummed into me on countless occasions, how you dress on L.I. is the measure of your success. You don't get into a Mercedes S-Class car in ripped jeans unless Ralph Lauren himself has ripped them. And you do not wear out-of-date clothes unless they can be categorized "vintage"—and you can pull off the look. A fatal mistake is thinking that something you've saved from twenty years ago looks exactly like the stuff they've brought back into fashion. It doesn't. The hem is higher. Or lower. The flowers are bigger. Or smaller. The waist is tighter. Or looser.

What Bobbie has been telling me forever finally clicks as I look at Mike's lady friend in her back-of-the-closet faux pas. She is not younger, not prettier, not anything "gooder" than the wife Mike already has. This is who he's left Bobbie for?

"Dr. Phyllis Hepstein," Bobbie all but hisses. "Can you believe he brought her? The girls will be devastated. Do you think I should—"

"I think you should send him that Dr. Joy Brown book," I whisper back. "Everyone knows you're not supposed to bring 'the other whatever' to anything that involves the kids. Sheesh!"

"I think I should—" Bobbie starts, handing me her program and her purse and getting up from her seat as the auditorium fills with the sounds of muffled crashing from the area of the stage. "Is this on?" comes blasting throughout the room, followed by a feedback whistle that must be calling all the dogs within a twenty-mile radius.

"Not now," I say, pulling on Bobbie's perfectly tailored celadon silk mother-of-the-young-graduate jacket. Personally, I can't wait to see Bobbie standing next to Miss Salvation Army circa 1969, but the ceremonies are starting. I glance over at Rio to share a moment of pride, but he is talking to a young woman in a yellow dress sitting behind him, introducing the kids quietly while stragglers hurry into seats. He's got the charm turned up to full power, and I am glad that I never see him selling sofas, as I think it would put the final nail in our marriage's coffin.

I don't know where that thought came from, and because of it I give the girl a friendly little wave that says I am the happiest little homemaker, not bothered in the slightest by some little slut flirting with my husband because I am oh so secure. Rio makes hand gestures of introduction, not talking because the school principal is welcoming the parents, siblings and friends of the graduates. While I am not all that active in the PTA, I do have at least a nodding acquaintance with nearly all the moms. But I've never seen the woman in yellow before. Maybe she is an older sister or an aunt to one of the kids. I feel the slightest twinge of jealousy that I am around the corner from menopause and this girl looks like she could practically take her place among the graduates.

The ceremony proves to be only slightly less boring than listening to Alyssa list her sixty-seven Beanie Babies one by one. At least I am not required to appear interested. They call out every child's name, read their list of activities and accomplishments—what, when asked in kindergarten, they hoped to be when they grew up, and what they now hope to become. This only seems to last for four or five days. It must, because Alyssa has to go to the bathroom three times during the calling of the roll.

Bobbie offers to take her the third time, but I have this vision of *Circa '69* following them, a cat fight breaking out, hair flying, Alyssa crying, the whole nine yards. And so we all go.

"She shouldn't be here," Bobbie says from behind the door of her stall. "She has no right to see my girls do anything."

"Bobbie," I sort of whine, trying to warn her that we aren't exactly alone in the ladies' room. Besides not knowing who is already in the stalls, there is a line of four or five women waiting to use the toilets. "I'm washing Alyssa's hands and then we'll wait for you outside."

"What? I'm supposed to be discreet?" Bobbie asks, raising her voice indignantly.

I look into the mirror and see several women watching me. Among them is the girl in the yellow dress. I offer her, along with everyone else, an apologetic grimace. The girl takes it as an invitation and steps out of line to introduce herself.

"I'm Marian Healy," she says. "I, like, used to go here."

"Well, do you want to go here now?" one of the women in line asks.

The girl titters. I feel two hundred years old. *I haven't tittered in a dozen years.*

"I saw my husband talking to you," I say, trying not to sound suspicious. After all, lately I've been suspicious of everyone but the doorpost.

The girl nods very vigorously, and her dark hair continues moving even after she is done. "I work at the deli he goes to sometimes," she says. "He's always very nice to me, very polite. Some people treat you like the furniture when you work in a deli, but Rio doesn't."

Well, furniture is Rio's bread and butter. He notices furniture. He sizes it up, takes its measure, intuits its worth.

"He's very nice. Polite."

"Yeah," Bobbie says as she dries her hands. "You said that."

As we head back to the auditorium, the girl in yellow calls after us to wait. We turn, but she seems to have forgotten what she wants to say. So I encourage Alyssa to blow her a kiss while Bobbie rolls her eyes, and then leave her in the hall and go back into the too-hot, too-crowded, too-boring ceremonies.

"Where's Dad?" I whisper to Jesse as we take our seats again.

Jesse looks up at me as if I'm not supposed to be there. "Who?" he asks.

I take the book from his hands, shut it and hold it in my lap.

"Suzanne Weinstein, chorus, grades four and five," Dr. Meredith drones on.

"But it's boring," Jesse whines, kicking his leg back and forth. "I listened when they did Dana and the Ks."

"…band, grades three, four, and five. Best speller runner up, second grade…"

"I left Dinky the Doo-Doo Bird in the bathroom!" Alyssa says, loudly enough for several heads to turn.

I clap a hand over Alyssa's mouth. "Dodo," I correct. "And shh!"

"…in kindergarten, Suzanne wanted to be a ballerina," Dr. Meredith says. I glance at the stage. Poor Suzanne Weinstein is a cute little butterball who, at eleven, has probably already been put by her mother on the waiting list for stomach-stapling surgery.

"Dinky Doo-Doo's in the bathroom!" Alyssa says more loudly as she pulls away from me and heads for the aisle.

Rio is swaggering down the aisle toward us, doing the shoulder thing, Dinky in his hand, that girl in yellow a foot or two behind him. He holds the Beanie Baby out to Lys while Dr. Meredith drones on and he nods toward the girl, who obviously found it for her. Rio picks up Alyssa and holds her close enough to Miss Yellow Dress for her to give her a big thank-you hug. It is like a momentary time warp—Marian Healy looks like I did ten years ago, and Alyssa looks pretty much like Dana did. And Rio's gazing at her the same way he used to gaze at me—nether regions, chest, lips, eyes. The flare of jealousy is doused quickly when his gaze shifts to me and he winks as if he's taken stock and I still measure up. How it is he can look at another woman and make me feel good about it is simply amazing. There's an art to it, and he's a master.

"And that concludes our list of graduates," the principal says, and the audience cheers, and the graduates take off their hats and throw them up because they are tired and it is hot and they all want the whole thing to be over.

As we gather our belongings and stand up, I catch a glimpse of Mike, his arm around his flower child.

"It's not fair," Bobbie says when I pat her gently on the arm.

I can say something sympathetic. I can agree. But I give her the standard answer because it says it all and we have said it to each other a million times—when her father died, when my mother goes back to South Winds. When I found out that my father and Angelina had lied to me for my entire life and that I can't turn to Angelina with my hurt.

"Who ever told you life was fair?"

I hear the words, but this time they aren't mine. They are the words of my childhood, and they belong to my mother, her answer whenever I dared to complain about anything being unfair.

Who ever told you life was fair? Was it fair to Markie? Was it fair to me?

And people wonder why I think I have no right to be unhappy.

If life were fair, my dear little girl, I'd have my bouncing baby

boy and all would be right with the world. Don't talk to me about
unfair. I have that market cornered.

My mother's pain has always been the standard by which everyone else's is judged, and if yours falls short, well then, what right do you have to complain? When I think about it, it's true. Compared to June, the rest of the world is lucky indeed.

Not that, at the moment, I think I ought to tell Bobbie that.

CHAPTER 13

The days before camp get progressively crazier. I have agreed to paint camp trunks for several customers and now it appears that my children will wind up like the shoemaker's children, only instead of no shoes, they will have plain trunks. And I buy toothbrushes, toothpaste, plastic toiletry cases, all of which disappear. I hide bags of candy in the kids' trunks for them to find when they unpack. Instead they find them as I'm packing. I put stamped envelopes addressed home in Dana's and Jesse's trunks and postcards that Alyssa can color and mail. They are now precolored. I buy more toothbrushes, toothpaste, plastic cases to replace those Misplaced Item Syndrome victims, and pack them, knowing the kids will have duplicate sets when both turn up. They, in turn, disappear, and my children accuse me of forgetting to get them in the first place. And the second place. And I buy more.

The night before camp I host the Annual Gallo-Lyons Pre-Camp Barbecue. This year, in addition to my parents, because my mother is "unavailable" and my father is "unacceptable," Mike is also palpably missing and Rio comes home from work early to take on the task of single-handedly making perfect hamburgers (and veggie burgers) for eight.

He is in an excellent mood, kissing me on the cheek as he comes in the back door, unbuttoning his work shirt and loosening his tie with a flourish, as if he's practicing for a job at Chippendale's. "Just gonna put on grungies," he says as the kids come into the kitchen. On his way out he pats Alyssa's head and fakes a punch toward Jesse's middle.

"Patties are ready when you are," I call after him as I spot the remnants of the Lyons clan crossing their backyard and heading for our deck. Kimmie and Kristin are wearing cut-offs and immaculate white T-shirts, the short sleeves rolled up evenly to reveal already tanned arms. The Ks have their hair pulled back in high ponytails and I can hear their flip-flops smacking as they climb the steps and join Dana on the deck amid squeals as though they haven't seen one another in a year and a half.

Bobbie follows in a pair of deep orange capris and a crisp white halter blouse, a bottle of wine in hand. She has jeweled slides on her feet and I can see her toenails are perfectly polished, which reminds me of the footcial I never took my mother into the City to get. I look down at myself and notice that my white capris sport Alyssa's handprint and something that may be hamburger juice near the hip. My pink V-neck T-shirt is stretched out and the hem hangs unevenly. My Keds are spattered with paint. My mother is right. Dress like a wreck and you feel like one.

Rio sails back into the kitchen, whistling, and blows on the back of my neck. "You are so hot," he whispers, pushing up against me. "As soon as all these kids are outta here, I'm jumping you on this very counter…and on the kitchen table…."

"Rio!" I squirm away from him and catch Jesse frowning at us, as if he can't believe we still want to touch each other when we are clearly so incredibly old.

Rio grabs up the plate of hamburger patties with one hand, lifts it high like a waiter in a crowded bar and heads for the back door, strutting to the music playing in his head. "Oh, and the dining room," he says over his shoulder. "And from that god-awful chandelier in the hall."

As he goes out the back door Bobbie comes in, tickling his middle as she passes him. "What's that they say in It's a Wonderful Life when Harry's got his hands full of plates? Gotta light?"

Rio's eyes drift down the front of Bobbie's shirt. "You're lucky my hands are full, sweet cakes," Rio tells her. "I'd make you forget all those old movies."

She rolls her eyes at me. "Promises, promises," she says as she puts the wine bottle on the counter and rummages in my utensils drawer for the corkscrew. She comments on Rio's unusually good mood and my cheeks burn. "At least someone's getting something," she says.

"Someone's talking a good game," I answer back as the girls file in. "Are you all abandoning Daddy?" I ask them.

They say something about the smell of lighter fluid being annoying—ever notice how everything annoys eleven-year-olds, except their own behavior?—and swipe the bowl of potato chips off the counter and take it into the den.

Rio comes back in to get the rolls after a while, and Bobbie and I call for the girls to help set the table, bring out the soda, get the show on the road. The Lord of the Grill declares the burgers done to perfection—not an easy chore when Jesse likes his burnt, I like mine rare, Bobbie likes hers medium well—and brings the platter to the table.

"This looks terrific," he says, and he squeezes on mounds of ketchup and adds a slice of lettuce, another of tomato, and prepares to take a bite. Everyone watches him because the honor of the first bite always goes to the griller. Why this doesn't apply indoors where I cook every meal, I can't say. At any rate, he licks his lips, opens wide and digs in.

"Holy shit!" he says, spitting the burger onto the plate and grabbing Alyssa's out of her hands before she can get it to her mouth. "What did you put in these? Kerosene or something?" He takes a swig of soda, rinses his mouth, runs to the railing and spits it out onto the lawn.

"Very funny," I say, picking up my burger. My husband has the sense of humor of a fourteen-year-old, and I take a bite before he can turn this into a half-hour situation comedy. Only he isn't joking. "Don't eat it," I say as I spit the meat into my hand. "Oh my God, don't eat it!"

"What'd I tell you," he says while the kids all push their plates away and Bobbie sniffs the meat to see if it has gone bad.

"Pepper. Too much red pepper," Bobbie pronounces without taking a bite.

"Impossible," I counter. I don't use red pepper in my burgers. I use salt, garlic powder, onion powder and paprika.

"Don't eat that," Rio says to Jesse, who, as always, is spaced out and not paying attention. He starts collecting everyone's plates. "Guess I have to run over to Mickey D's. Make a list."

Bobbie says she's got burgers in the freezer and will defrost them in the microwave. "Take me five minutes," she says, sashaying down the stairs with a wave. If I didn't adore her, I could easily hate her guts.

Rio brings the plates into the house and I follow a minute later to examine what's on the counter. There are my jars of spices: garlic powder, onion powder, red pepper. Rio picks up the red pepper and raises an eyebrow at me. "Well, that was fun," he says sarcastically. "What comes after poisoning the kids? Hiding razors in the candy?"

"It's not like I did it on purpose," I say. I can't believe I'd make such a mistake. Where is my head at, anyway?

"You sure you didn't subconsciously want to make the kids sick so they wouldn't go off to camp tomorrow?" Rio puts the spices back in the rack in the wrong order.

I pull them out of his hands and put them where they belong so that a mistake like this doesn't happen again. "Are you asking me if I purposely planned to make our children sick? That's just...sick."

"So what, then? Another one of those 'lapses?'" he asks, putting quotes around the word. "Isn't that what your fancy doctor calls it when you're having a nutzo moment?"

I really don't like how this conversation is going, and I tell Rio as much. He says he doesn't like how our life is going, but quickly takes the comment back and offers to take the kids out for Carvel after dinner so I can relax. "Maybe you should take a nice bath," he says, and winks. "Get, you know, in the mood." He even offers to run and straighten up the bathroom for me, admitting he just threw his clothes from work in the general direction of the hamper.

After Bobbie's perfect burgers, Rio takes all the kids out for ice cream, leaving Bobbie and me to clean up from dinner.

"You okay?" she asks me when we're alone. "You seem more frazzled than usual."

I ask if not being able to make a simple hamburger wouldn't frazzle her. She admits it would, but we both know this is one of those hypothetical questions that have no basis in reality. Bobbie's husband left and she still has a stocked freezer. She isn't likely to screw up hamburgers.

I sit down at the kitchen table and Bobbie sits next to me, giving me a concerned look that makes me uncomfortable.

"I know I put paprika in," I tell her. She tells me it doesn't matter, but she's never sat through a meal at my mother's table pretending that the food tastes fine because her mother would come apart if it didn't. She's never seen my mother put sugar on eggs or salt in coffee or stand with the cream in her hand wondering what she's supposed to do with it. I have. My father has. Rio has.

A bath seems like a good idea, and I send Bobbie home and go up to take one. As I'm running the water I hear the kids and Rio come home, hear him shushing the kids and telling them to lay out their clothes for the trip up to camp tomorrow. I start to slip my foot into the water just as he opens the bathroom door to check on me. It's freezing cold.

"How can we be out of hot water?" I ask Rio. "There must be something wrong with the water heater."

Rio runs the water in the sink, sticks his hand in and pulls it out quickly. He shakes his head at me.

"Well the bath's cold," I say, indicating he should touch it while I gather a towel around myself. He sticks his hand in gingerly, like I can't tell hot from cold, and then turns on the cold-water tap, feels it and seems satisfied. "Why are you turning on the cold water?" I ask.

Only he tells me he's turning on the hot water. "Jecz. Hot on the left, cold on the right," he says, his shoulders sagging. "I'll run it for you."

"Rio, the faucets are backward," I say. I ought to know. They've been driving me crazy since we moved in more than a decade ago. "Remember, even the house inspector noticed it when we were buying the house?"

"And remember that we switched it about eight years ago because it was driving you crazy? Guess we were too late on that one, huh?" Rio exhales a breath so deep it raises the hair on his forehead.

All I can manage to say is "we did?" as I try the faucets and find that sure enough, we did.

He gives me a hand as I climb into the tub and then stares at me for a good minute before walking out of the room and shutting the door behind him.

"Rio?" I call out, and he tips his head back in. "Dana asked me today if my father and Angelina were…you know, doing it."

"Look, Teddi," he says. "You can't go falling off the deep end, burning things, forgetting things, throwing things, every time you hear something upsetting, you know? You're gonna wind up hurting someone. Why do you think the kids are going away? Because they're safer away, that's why.

"Just remember, Teddi. If you don't get on top of this thing, you're gonna hurt someone you love."

CHAPTER 14

The mall is teeming with mothers who have just put their kids onto the camp buses and dutifully looked forlorn as they waved goodbye to responsibility for two months. Despite Bobbie's reassurance that Lys will be fine, I feel like I should be arrested for child neglect or endangerment or something. I stop in front of Gap Kids, where I occasionally buy Alyssa clothes to wear to my mother's house. Everything in the window is an exact duplicate, in miniature, of what is in the window of the real Gap—sort of Princesses-in-Training…or training *pants*, anyway. I remember Alyssa's little stretchy things. I remember shoes that fit in the palm of my hand. I remember her thinking I could fix anything. "She's a baby. You know how fast they change? She'll come home doing new things and I won't have been the first to see them."

"Ahh," Bobbie says, getting the picture now. "So this is about you, not Lys. Okay, well, you are on vacation, girl. You and me. What do you say? Should we head for Elizabeth Arden's Red Door at Saks? Ask them to match a foundation for us at Sephora? Spend two hours trying on lipsticks at M.A.C? Or should we be boring and settle for being made over at every counter at Bloomingdale's?"

"I'd just as soon go on home," I say. "And let the money I put in my account this morning settle in and feel at home. Maybe it'll get comfortable enough to start multiplying."

"Come on, Teddi, please? We've got the whole mall and no whiny kids who want to spend an hour looking at every CD in the Wall before deciding they don't have enough money to buy one. We can stop at the cash machine again on the way home and see how much interest your money earned while I had fun spending mine."

"Nobody's gonna touch every card in LeMarc's while I hurry to pick out one that doesn't drip schmaltz?" I ask, trying to get into it.

"Hell, girl, you can get a year's worth of birthday cards and no one will have to go to the bathroom before you can pay. Well, maybe I will, but you won't have to take me. Or watch!"

"If we go to the Body Shop, will you behave, so that I don't have to tell you that the testers are meant for people who are actually planning to buy?" I ask. Now I am on a roll.

"You could try on fifteen bras at Victoria's Secret and I promise not to put even one on my head or giggle or anything. I won't even sigh and tell you that I'll wait outside."

A woman with a stroller walks by, stopping at Gymboree and struggling with the door. I run to help her and then stand with the door open, debating whether or not to go in.

"I miss them," I tell Bobbie.

"I'm sure people miss psoriasis, too," she says in answer. "But that doesn't mean that they can't enjoy themselves while it's gone. Wanna get something to eat?" She looks at me and asks if I've lost weight. I've tried Atkins, I've tried

Weight Watchers. I've tried the grapefruit diet, the cabbage soup diet and the Scarsdale diet and I'll tell you this: nothing works like the Fear of Losing Your Mind Diet, where everything tastes like sawdust, and the weight melts right off.

We stroll toward the upscale pizza place, our sandals clacking on the marble floor we agreed was a mistake from day one. In the winter it's slippery from the snow people track in, and if you don't wear shoes with leather or rubber soles…well, as Bobbie says, people who buy plastic shoes only get what they deserve.

As I said, the mall is crowded, full of too-old-to-be-shipped-off-to-camp teenagers who are hanging out, nothing-more-pressing-to-do mothers who are wasting the day with their babies, don't-stick-me-in-a-senior-center-while-I-still-have-money old people who are resting on the benches keeping cool, and actual the-kids-are-gone-and-now-its-my-turn shoppers who can take advantage of the summer sales already in full swing. I generally come to the mall only for gifts, and, I'm embarrassed to say, to buy makeup. According to Bobbie, and hence, *The Rules*, you have to buy your makeup at Saks or Lord & Taylor, where the salesgirls fawn over you and put all those little samples in your bag since it isn't discounted anywhere, anyway. As Bobbie always says when we are at the Chanel counter, anyone who buys makeup at Macy's is begging to be ill-treated.

"So, what does Dr. Benjamin say about your memory lapses?" Bobbie asks me once we're seated and handed menus.

"She says I'm fine." It's sort of the truth, since she has said that all my tests have proved that there is nothing *organically* wrong with me.

"Does she think that sleeping pills would help?" Bobbie asks.

Now, I know that I keep forgetting things, but I never told her that I'm having trouble sleeping. This fact must be written on my face, because she confesses that Rio has told her about our "nocturnal situation," as I have taken to calling it.

"And when did Rio start confiding in you?" I ask, my voice a whisper. "Are you and he talking about me behind my back?"

Bobbie picks up a napkin and calmly and deliberately wipes at the corner of her perfectly-lip-glossed-in-this-summer's-new-shade mouth. Her back is ramrod straight, and if looks could kill, I know the waiter would have to step over my poor dead body to serve Bobbie her grilled chicken Caesar sandwich on focaccia bread. Bobbie doesn't even bother to answer me.

"You had this conversation *when?*" I repeat.

Bobbie points a freshly refilled French-tipped acrylic fingernail at me. She tells me that she is only answering me because she thinks I must really, truly be getting sick. "If you could think that Rio and I—" She shudders. "Last week when he helped me drag out the camp trunks to the truck. Remember? After he managed to get up your three, he came over and moved my two."

Of course I remember. I warned against it, what with his back hurting from moving the furniture at Bayer, but did he listen? No, so the very next day he had to run to the therapist again. I don't dare try to say I'm sorry to Bobbie, because I know that if I stop biting the inside of my lip, I'll start to cry and I'm not sure I'll ever stop.

Bobbie reaches across the table and lays her hand over mine. "How could you think that I would keep anything from you, or that Rio would betray you?"

"You've kept lots of things from me. Important things. You kept Mike's affair from me for nearly a year, didn't you?" I throw this in her face because I didn't learn about it until he actually left, and I guess I'm still mad about it. "I mean, I tell you everything. I told you about how I called out dirty things in my sleep, even. And you couldn't tell me—"

"Well, you told me it happened once, and you didn't tell me what you said, actually." She raises one of her eyebrows, a gesture I have tried to emulate and failed miserably at. She is trying to tease me, I guess, but it's too late for that.

"I told you *Last Tango in Paris*. You know what I must have said."

"Yeah, but did you say, like 'Rio, I want it in the—'"

"Shut up!" I say, glancing around her to see if anyone is still paying attention to our conversation. The women at the table to our left are each on cell phones. On our right, two women who have enough makeup on to attend the Academy Awards are arguing with the waitress about whether or not their IBC root beers are diet. Both are claiming to be diabetics who absolutely can't have sugar. Odd, since they are splitting a slice of *dulce de leche* cheesecake. I suppose eating only half the sugar won't kill them.

"Or was it like—" Bobbie continues, but I override her.

"How do I know what I said? I was asleep. Why don't you ask Rio?"

She ignores my question.

"And why didn't you tell me about Mike?"

"I didn't tell you," Bobbie says, "because if I did, you'd have expected me to kick him out. And because, if it had blown over and he didn't leave me, like I was praying he wouldn't, then every time you looked at him, you'd remember, and every time you looked at me, you'd be disappointed."

Well, she is right. And I would have been more than disappointed. I'd have been appalled.

"I don't understand how you could have known and still wanted him to stay."

"The same reason that would make me take him back in a heartbeat if he showed up at my door," Bobbie tells me. "I love him."

"You love a man who ran around behind your back, then walked out on you and the girls? How could you love that?"

"Well, we can't all be married to *Mr. Perfect*," Bobbie counters sarcastically as the waiter delivers our food and I look down at my vegetarian sandwich on which they've put the mozzarella after I specifically asked them not to. Bobbie notices and goes to call the waiter, but I stop her. "You can't eat that, Teddi. Aren't you going to send it back?"

"And get the right sandwich in time for dinner?" I ask, knowing from previous experience how long that would take. "Watch," I say, peeling the cheese off the grilled peppers and setting it on her bread plate with a flourish. "Something I can fix! All by myself—no help from anyone. Done deal."

"But they got it wrong," Bobbie attempts to explain to me, as if there should be consequences for them. I sense a new

Rule. "People who work here resent people who eat and shop here," she explains to me. "This is total passive-aggressive stuff, this getting orders wrong, and you have to call them on it or they'll put peanuts on an anaphylactic kid's sundae and watch them die."

I'm not sure what the *Rule* actually is, but I am relieved my kids have no major allergies, since clearly everyone is out to get them.

She's taken some of the joy out of my accomplishment, but I tell her that I was able to make the sandwich right myself. It isn't something I can say all that often, and I am actually glad for the chance, though I think that ought to exhaust the subject.

"Where were we?"

I remind her that I was asking how she could love someone who treated her like dirt.

"Because I don't walk around in rose-colored glasses. Because I don't like to eat alone. Because the world is based on couples with two children and I want to fit into it again. And because I'm weak, okay? And my life isn't the magical one yours is, maybe. But Mike's a good father—better than mine ever was. Like he takes the girls to both Burger King and McDonald's because Kimmie likes the fries at one and Kristin likes the chicken nuggets at the other."

"And do you love the way he probably hand feeds those fries to *Circa '69*?" As far as I am concerned, Phyllis doesn't even rate a name.

Again Bobbie says she is weak, and all I can think is that if Bobbie is weak, I must be a bowl of mush.

"Okay, how about how he can make me feel sexy and innocent all at the same time?"

There was a time when Rio could do the same for me. When did that stop, and why hadn't I even noticed before this moment? Must be that old "taking things for granted" thing *Redbook* is always warning against. "Do you love how he can make you feel seduced and abandoned? Bobbie, the man is sleeping with another woman. He's left you and the kids—"

"That's right," Bobbie tells me. "And I still love him, so why do you think that you can decide if I should or shouldn't?"

"Because I know what you're worth. Because that man isn't good enough for you. That's why."

"Maybe he just needs some time."

"A year wasn't enough?" I demand.

"Not for him," Bobbie says.

"Just tell me this one thing," I say. "I'm surely no expert on the *Rules of Long Island*. You're always having to remind me why I have to buy baby gifts at Bloomies and not Macy's, but I do know the *Rules of Marriage*. They're called vows and they involve little things like honesty and fidelity. So explain this to me. Why don't the rules apply to him?"

CHAPTER 15

I am standing at the edge of the abyss. Bobbie is next to me, but in reality, I am alone. I see a mass grave in some Third World country. I see the crater from a dropped bomb.

Funny, because Rio sees a pool.

"It's not too late to fill it in and forget the whole thing," Bobbie tells me. "I'll even have my landscape guys replant the roses for you."

I cannot look down into the hole. I cannot look anywhere else. "Don't be silly," I say, taking the tall drink with the umbrella Bobbie is pushing on me, despite the fact that it is the middle of the day.

"Rio wants a pool," I hear myself say, as if he is the pharaoh, or the king, or Donald Trump, and nobody can tell him no. "And the kids want it. And it's not as if I believe in history repeating itself. Aren't you the one who says that just because my mother has problems doesn't mean that I—"

"Problems? Your mother is in South Winds. Again," she says. "And it started with a pool in her backyard not unlike this one, right?"

One thing about Bobbie. She doesn't dance politely

around subjects. There are days I treasure her for this. Today isn't one of them.

"What does your Dr. Benjamin say about the pool?" she asks. I'm grateful that she has asked very little about my sessions, as if she is aware that, as close as we are, there are still boundaries between us that I need her not to cross.

I tell her that we haven't discussed it, which is, after all, the truth. "I mean, it's my decision, not hers, right? Why would her opinion carry more weight than what my husband and children want?" It would probably be more convincing if I wasn't sniffing at the moment and gasping at my upturned roses, my raped lawn and the hole that looks like Haleakala Crater.

"Because she's a mental-health professional who cares about your sanity?" Bobbie asks. "Or because you know she'll tell you to tell Rio to fuck off and forget the pool, and you're afraid to do that?"

"Do you really think that telling Rio I don't want a pool is harder than living with this deathtrap in my yard? That I'm taking the easy way out by allowing this?"

I see the lightbulb go off for Bobbie as she smacks her forehead. "You ought to ask your shrink what it is about you that keeps making you raise the goddamn bar, Teddi. Why do you always have to be stronger today than you were yesterday?"

I tell her that she wouldn't understand. She's never come up short. With the rum only halfway down her throat, Bobbie chokes. She goes around in a circle, coughing and trying to pat herself on the back. "Rio's right. You are as crazy as a loon. *I* never come up short?"

It's hot out and I know my rose bushes are going to die if

their bare roots aren't soaking in water, but I can't seem to move myself to do anything about it.

Bobbie is still going on about my standards. "You think *I* never fail? Of course I don't. Set the bar low enough and even I can't. Keep raising it, the way you do, and you're bound to reach a limit eventually."

Well, the pool isn't going to be my limit. "A stupid pool is not going to beat me."

"And you don't see how talking to the shrink you're already seeing might help you get over this totally moronic, self-imposed, test-yourself, go-to-the-mat hurdle?"

Unless I manage to take charge of the pool situation, I have decided not to confide in Ronnie Benjamin. If it beats me I won't need her to point it out to me. And if I conquer it, she'll be the first person I brag to about it.

"Well, what do you talk about, then?" Bobbie asks me. "Or would you rather tell me over my rightfully renowned chicken in plum sauce, which after all these years, I certainly ought to do divinely?"

"You know we could have called in Chinese," I tell her while I kick at a dirt ball until it tumbles over the edge and rolls down and down to the bottom of what is to be the pool.

"Yup, with Mike gone and the kids away, that's what I need," Bobbie says. "A time-saver."

She cringes when I look at her sympathetically.

"Well, I appreciate the fuss," I say. "And this," I add, raising the hurricane glass she's brought me complete with fancy laser-cut paper napkin and sipping gingerly.

She ignores my thanks and presses me about what I talk

to Dr. Benjamin about. I hate it when she refers to her as my "shrink."

I tell her about how I report on all the things I keep forgetting and we talk about what I can do about it.

Bobbie suggests I make lists, preferably in my Palm Pilot. Everyone she knows keeps lists, she says. She offers to go shopping with me for a different Palm Pilot or a little notebook or something, anything.

"Rio got me a Palm, remember?" I tell her. "But I'm interested in fixing the problem, not working around it."

"Naturally," Bobbie says, and there is contempt rather than admiration in her voice. I try to explain how I feel about relying on mechanical things that I really don't even understand.

"You know how annoying it is when you go to a register and you find the four pennies that would stop the cashier from giving you ninety-six cents in change, only she's already pressed the buttons and she doesn't know how to add or subtract without them?"

"You might lose your gizmo," Bobbie extrapolates, and I nod.

"I hate it when they can't add. Why do they hire people to make change who can't add?"

Bobbie gives me a look that tells me I'm flirting with untethered status and I change course and tell her about my new memory-strengthening plan that involves hiding things around the house to see if I can find them again the next day.

"Nothing valuable," I say. "Or should I say nothing *else* valuable? I could have sworn I put my good earrings in the freezer, but they weren't there this morning."

Bobbie suggests that I either tell her where I'm hiding things or make an answer key, but I say it wouldn't be a test then.

We stand shoulder to shoulder staring into the hole. "So what movie do you think Diane's bringing tonight?" Bobbie asks, knowing that neither of us actually care. *"The Deep? Twenty-Thousand Leagues Under the Sea?"*

I try to laugh and sip at the same time, and wind up snorting and coughing.

"You have to do better than that. Imitations of people drowning—" She stops herself, mortified by her reference to someone drowning in a pool. "I'm so sorry, Ted," she says soberly. "I didn't mean—"

I wave away the apology. "How about that awful one with Shelley Winters on the boat? Or what about something with David Schwimmer?" I offer gamely.

"Dirty Harry and the Dead Poo— Oh, shit. I did it again." Bobbie smacks herself on the forehead. "If I can't stop thinking about it, kiddo, I don't see how you—"

I pick up my sandals. "I hope Diane's bringing one of those cop movies," I say, making it clear I don't want to talk about the damn pool any more. At least I hope it's clear. "The Eliot Ness ones with Robert what's-his-name—" I stop in my tracks and bite at my lip, a habit my mother abhors. "Why can't I remember his name?"

"Stack," Bobbie supplies. "Don't you think that Robert Stack looks a little like Mike around the eyes?"

"Why can you remember his name and I can't?" I ask, heading toward Bobbie's house with my empty glass in one hand and my sandals now in the other.

"Because he reminds me of Mike? And Mike likes his women 'stacked'?"

"Mike likes his decks stacked," I say, relieved to be talking about anything but the pool-to-be. "How many aces does one man need?"

"Who knows what another person needs?" Bobbie asks, sounding very philosophical. "Look at you and Rio. You've got all this class and he's…" I promise myself that if she dares to make again that crack about how Rio and I are a match made in one of those children's flip books where you can put the fireman's hat on the clown's body and add a mermaid's tail, I will head for my own house and never look back.

"—a good father and a good, patient, loving husband," I finish for her.

"Well sure," Bobbie agrees with a knowing look. "Every husband is."

"Damn!' Rio shouts, jumping up from his lounger in the den. "Did you see that?" I look in the direction he's pointing—the base of the far wall—and see nothing.

"What?"

He says it must be from the pool excavation. Okay, he says it's from the *damn hole*. I still don't know what it is.

"It's dirty?" I ask, getting up to have a closer look.

"It's a friggin' mouse," he says. "Now I've got a goddamn friggin' mouse in my house." He's shaking his head and looking at me as if the pool was my idea. I am standing on the couch. The leather couch that Rio is so proud of and doesn't let the kids eat on.

"There!" he shouts, pointing behind me and running with the newest issue of *Redbook* in his hand.

"Call an exterminator," I tell him, pointing at the phone as if he doesn't know where it is.

"I'm not paying some loser fifty bucks to put down the same poison I can buy at Home Depot for three bucks," he says, grabbing up his wallet and his keys.

"You're leaving me here?" I shout as I watch him head for the garage door.

"Somebody's got to keep their eye on him," he says. "You can do that much, can't you?"

"I'll go get the stuff at the store," I offer, but my shoes are all the way across the room and I'd have to run barefoot on the floor.

And besides, Rio's already gone.

CHAPTER 16

Today I have managed to find South Winds. This time the irony is that I am ashamed of myself for being proud of myself for getting here. Anyhow, I got here and now, shoulders back, grin in place, I breeze into my mother's room.

Sun streams through the windows, which for security reasons have neither drapes nor miniblinds, but the old-fashioned roller shades with cords too short for hanging yourself. Naturally the room is beige, maybe with a hint of pink, as though it has been painted to match her unique shade of hair.

In this wing of the hospital, where patients are in various stages of recovery and considered minimum risks, June is allowed her wall phone (no cord long enough to reach around her neck); her own sheets (three-hundred-count Egyptian cotton, in ecru, of course); and an abundance of flowers (all in plastic vases). It is amazing what the hospital deems dangerous. Do they really believe my mother would break a Baccarat crystal vase in order to slit her wrists? Then why do they bring her morning orange juice in the scratched-up kind of glasses they use in diners?

I find her sitting by the window, studying her nails in a beige chair made out of that fabric you could stick a pen through. "What are you doing in here on such a gorgeous day?" I ask her, handing her the requisite box of Godiva chocolates I have brought with me.

"Waiting for you," my mother says, glancing at the clock with a grimace and tossing the box of chocolates onto the window sill where the sun will melt them in a matter of minutes. She pretends she doesn't want them, but there would be hell to pay if I didn't bring them. "I didn't want to miss it if you called to explain how come you're so late."

"I couldn't find my keys," I say, moving the box to the nightstand.

"Which explains why you didn't have time to get the paint off your hands," she says, poking the box until it is nearly off the edge of the table. "Or change your clothes. I understand perfectly."

There is one lousy speck of Superman Blue paint on my right hand. And the floral overalls are clean and, if my mother were more flexible about fashion, kind of adorable. Bobbie, another arbiter of fashion (as everyone is but me), tells me they fit my image perfectly. Possibly that is a veiled insult. I decide not to move the candy. If my mother wants shards of great chocolate, so be it.

"Have you told Rio that I'm coming home with you when I get out of here?" my mother asks, her Louis Vuitton train case sitting on the foot of her bed.

I give her the Hertz answer: "Not exactly."

"And what does 'not exactly' mean? I'm telling Dr. Cohen to sign my release papers this morning. I'm packed. I already called the florist and told him to deliver my welcome-home bouquet to your house."

THE EDITOR'S "THANK YOU" FREE GIFTS INCLUDE:

▶ Two NEW Harlequin® Next™ Novels

▶ An exciting surprise gift

YES! I have placed my Editor's "thank you" Free Gifts seal in the space provided at right. Please send me 2 FREE books, and my FREE Mystery Gift. I understand that I am under no obligation to purchase anything further, as explained on the back and opposite page.

PLACE FREE GIFTS SEAL HERE

▶ DETACH AND MAIL CARD TODAY!

356 HDL EE3H　　　　　**156 HDL EE3G**

FIRST NAME	LAST NAME

ADDRESS

APT.#	CITY

STATE/PROV.	ZIP/POSTAL CODE

Thank You!

(H-NXT-02/06)

The Reader Service — Here's How It Works:

Accepting your 2 free books and gift places you under no obligation to buy anything. You may keep the books and gift and return the shipping statement marked "cancel." If you do not cancel, about a month later we'll send you 3 additional books and bill you just $3.99 each in the U.S., or $4.74 each in Canada, plus 25¢ shipping & handling per book and applicable taxes if any.* That's the complete price and — compared to cover prices of $5.50 each in the U.S. and $6.50 each in Canada — it's quite a bargain! You may cancel at any time, but if you choose to continue, every month we'll send you 3 more books, which you may either purchase at the discount price or return to us and cancel your subscription.

*Terms and prices subject to change without notice. Sales tax applicable in N.Y. Canadian residents will be charged applicable provincial taxes and GST.

If offer card is missing write to: The Reader Service, 3010 Walden Ave., P.O. Box 1867, Buffalo, NY 14240-1867

BUSINESS REPLY MAIL
FIRST-CLASS MAIL   PERMIT NO. 717-003   BUFFALO, NY

POSTAGE WILL BE PAID BY ADDRESSEE

THE READER SERVICE
3010 WALDEN AVE
PO BOX 1867
BUFFALO NY 14240-9952

NO POSTAGE
NECESSARY
IF MAILED
IN THE
UNITED STATES

I don't look at my mother. "The kids send their love. Dana is learning to dive and Jesse is memorizing the Morse Code—no doubt to send secret messages to other wizards. Even Alyssa sounds all excited about finding salamanders under the rocks after it rains."

"That's nice, dear." My mother rubs at a speck on the window. "The cleaning staff tries to make it over here on their break from McDonald's. Did you have Dana's room cleaned for me? Her rug needs a good steaming, I'm sure." I think about bringing her home to my mouse-infested house and shudder.

"What?" she asks me.

"Dana's got a part in the play," I say, ending the topic. "Can you believe they're doing *Sweet Charity*? I guess if they could bring it back to Broadway, they can bring it back to Westwood Lake."

"Tell me you aren't going to drag me up there to see her in it and expect me to pretend that she can sing," my mother says as she lights up a Newport Light under the No Smoking sign.

"You're not supposed to—" I point at the cigarette.

"*I* am not supposed to?" she demands. "*I?* What about your father and what he is not supposed to do? Is he supposed to keep his wife and his mistress in the same house? Is he supposed to offer to share the same bed with me that he shared with her?"

"Mom, I don't think that Dad—" I start, and am almost grateful when my mother interrupts, since I really don't want to defend my father's behavior, especially to my mother, who, in my weakest moments, I have to admit may have driven him to it.

"I bore you in my body," June says, clutching a stomach that, despite her age, is still remarkably flat. Well, two tummy tucks will do that. "I had Angelina stay up with you when you were sick. I made your brother take you with him to the movies. I gave you that necklace your father bought me for my fiftieth birthday…." The one that she had him replace with something she considered more suitable to the occasion, which means that it had to have fifty diamonds, for one thing, and be set in platinum for the other.

"I was there for you every step of the way. Who do you think hired that man to teach you to ride a bicycle? Do you think your father would have thought to do that? Who do you think he would have engaged to help you with your diet?

"But if you don't want to help me now, when I need you, when you finally have the chance to pay me back for all I've done for you, well…I can certainly find a hotel or a spa that will send a cab and—"

How ironic that my mother is asking for payback! Rio would get a good hoot over that one—if I weren't actually bringing her home. I don't think Rio is going to laugh about anything regarding June until I have her back in Cedarhurst where she belongs.

"Are you going to live in a hotel forever?" I ask. "If coming to my house for a little while is going to help you work things out with Daddy, then Rio and I will pick you up when the doctor says you are ready to come home and we'll take you to our house."

"For a woman whom everyone seems to think is ready to sign herself in here, you sound pretty sure of yourself," she says.

My mother refuses to talk to my father. She refuses to talk to Angelina. How the heck can she have any clue about where my head is? "Excuse me?"

"Was that supposed to be a secret?" She raises her eyebrows until they disappear behind her plastered bangs. "Your brother didn't tell me it was a secret."

"You've been talking to David?" I ask, not sure if it is my mother who is off the deep end again, or me. I remind myself that even if she had talked to David, which is as likely as a sale on beachfront property in the Hamptons, David can't know that Rio is concerned about me.

"I saw him yesterday," June says, fluffing her hair before reaching for another Newport. "Isn't it wonderful that he's come back? I invited him to join us for dinner tonight at your house to celebrate."

"Well, let's wait until you're released for that, shall we?" I say, trying to sound reasonable while inching toward the door, since if my mother is seeing David, Dr. Cohen had better put off her release indefinitely. God, next it'll be Markie, and then watch the accusations fly.

"Teddi!" The voice—manly, deep, and yet with a childish eagerness—comes from behind me.

Slowly I turn around, not believing the image in my mother's unbreakable mirror.

"David?" I ask, but the frog in my throat steals the word. He nods sheepishly. Dear God, I'm sharing my mother's hallucinations! Now we've both got Beautiful Minds, and it's like in the movie when the kid who wasn't really there doesn't get any older, because except for the tan, no one would ever guess David has spent twenty years in the tropics. He is still dressed in khaki pants, a white sport shirt with a collar, and a navy blazer with brass buttons. He has on brand-new cordovan tasseled loafers and his hair looks freshly cut. His alma mater, Harvard, would be proud of him. That is, providing they didn't know any of the details of his life. He spreads his arms. "The prodigal son returns," he says with ease, and I can't help but think that will be the way Rio will see it.

I cannot think of a thing to say.

"Nothing? No 'hello'? No 'long time no see'?" he asks, coming toward me awkwardly, apparently unsure if he should take me around and hug me, or kiss me, or maybe simply shake my hand.

Do apparitions get confused, too? I can hardly ask old Mom if the man we are both seeing is real. He stands in front of me, waiting for me to do something. I offer my cheek to him and he kisses it lightly, leaving a whiff of something that may be English Leather. I touch my cheek and it is slightly damp. David is real. "Welcome home," I say when I can find my voice. "How long have you been back?"

"Since Monday. Rio didn't tell you? Ran into him on Tuesday at the store. He looks real good." While he apparently assesses me, I try to hide the fact that my husband didn't bother to mention my brother is back. It isn't as if the guy has come back more than two or three times in what—twenty years? And Rio didn't say a word. "You do, too. I should have called you when I got in, I—"

"What about me?" our mother asks, preening. "I don't look good?"

"Yeah, Mom, you look great," David says, with more resignation than warmth. "You always do."

"So, David," I say, pretending I'm not reeling, and am not going to call Dr. Benjamin from my car before I even pull out of the lot, even if it is July Fourth. "What are you doing back? Nothing's wrong, is it? I mean, how come you're here? Not here, but… What brings you back?"

I can't believe that no one has told me. My father can call me for the kids' camp address when Rio is there with him every day, but he can't call to say my brother is home? Of course, he probably figures that Rio told me.

"What do you think he's back for?" June asks, blowing her smoke toward the ceiling where the smoke detector winks at her. "He's here to take over Bayer Furniture."

Things fall into place with a thud. That's what took Rio so long to get home on Tuesday night, when he said that he had to stop by his mother's on the way. Married twelve years and he still brings his troubles to her. A man doesn't share that sort of stuff with his wife, according to Rio. A man protects his wife, provides for her. He doesn't burden her with his worries. Not about sex and not about money.

A wholly different set of rules, you see. *The Rules according to Rio Gallo.*

CHAPTER 17

Dr. Benjamin is waiting for me when I get to her office. As I am getting out of the Expedition (every time I say that I feel like I am on safari), I see that she is bending her miniblinds and watching the parking lot. This allows her to see me (a) drop my purse, (b) pick up my purse and drop my book, and (c) drop my handbag as I reach down to pick up my book, which is, it turns out, not my book at all, but Harry *Freaking* Potter!

I can't even look at her as I hurry through the door she is holding open and plop into the unnaturally cold beige leather chair. I blow my bangs off my forehead, or try to, but despite the AC in the car, they are pasted there by the hot weather.

"Hot out," I say, trying to compose myself.

She says nothing, but pours me a tall glass of cold water from the carafe on her desk. She is in waiting mode, anxious to discuss what couldn't wait for our usual Tuesday appointment.

"So you know, I assume, that your husband called me yesterday. He says he is very worried about you."

Yeah. "Munchkin Syndrome by Proxy," I say with a grimace.

"Münchhausen by Proxy?" she asks, apparently thrown

off kilter. She fingers the brain model on her desk, tracing a crevice with her finger.

"Whatever. The one where you make your kid sick."

"Do you mean to say that you think your husband is—"

My diagnosis is off. Only *I* know what I mean. What else is new?

"Maybe what I mean is self-fulfilling prophesy. That's what my friends keep saying. The thing is, Rio is so afraid that I'm going crazy that he's making me crazy."

"How so?"

I don't know. "Forget I said anything. It was a wayward thought, after all."

She suggests that wayward or not, we run with it, insisting that I wouldn't have brought it up unless it was truly bothering me. And anything bothering me is worth discussing. What a concept! Imagine if husbands felt that way? Dr. Phil would be off the air!

Screwing up my courage because I'm not sure I want to know the answer, I ask her if she thinks I could be paranoid.

She is supposed to say 'Do *you?*' We both know the drill. We've run it before. Only this time she simply says, "No," looking at me as if she wants to know if that will put an end to it.

"Why not?" I ask. "I mean, how can you tell?"

She looks at me as if to ask if we really have to play this game. "Okay, do *you?*" she asks with so little interest I'm not sure I'm supposed to answer.

I have valid reasons. Like suspecting that Bobbie and Rio are having an affair behind my back. I suspect everyone of everything. Even the guy at the Dairy Barn. "I drove through there—you know I have this milk problem—and he asks me what the heck I've done with the six gallons of milk he swears I got the day before, which must have been a very busy day." I take a breath and forge ahead. "Okay, same day. I go to the new dry cleaners to pick up Dana's rug. Only the guy says he put it in my car for me the day before, which I'm sure never happened. And he winks at me! I go off the deep end, ranting and raving and making a general idiot of myself telling him how the rug matches all the colors in the pillows in Dana's room, and then I come home and, of course, it's in Dana's room."

Dr. Benjamin nods and waits for me to go on, which I do without taking a breath.

"And so, by now I'm a deranged lunatic, a *paranoid* deranged lunatic, and I decide that Rio is tricking me somehow. So instead of asking him if he picked it up, which would have been a neat trick since he worked late on Tuesday, I call back the cleaners and inquire about the car he put it in, you know, like it doesn't really matter, and I'm thinking they'll say it was a Corvette, and all the while my heart is racing and I'm thinking 'I've got him now.'"

The wind leaves my sails and I hunch my shoulders and wonder why she has to crank the air-conditioning up so high that I need a sweater in July.

"Of course, the fact that Rio wouldn't do that to me doesn't even compute at this point, you know? Because I'm so sure it's not me. Which of course it must have been, because the cleaner says he put the rug into a Ford Expedition."

"Well," Dr. Benjamin starts to say, but I wave her effort away.

"It gets worse," I admit. "He says he put it right next to a zillion gallons of milk and a half dozen of Alyssa's Lil Bratz. Of course, he doesn't call them Alyssa's…

"And then I thought the kids were pulling some stunts, like the plastic stuff for camp?" She nods to show that she remembers the toothbrush holders. "Only these things keep happening even though they're away. Like when I called to change my nail appointment and apparently I already had. And it keeps happening, over and over again, and I keep thinking it's someone else, and it keeps turning out to be me.

"And Rio thinks I—" I start, and then stop myself when she raises a warning finger.

"Do *you* think?"

I admit I don't know what to think, and she shuts my folder, leans back and asks, "Are you ready to talk about the aspirins now?"

"Oh, for God's sake! Rio told you, too? Why didn't he just take out an ad in *Newsday?* Get it on the six o'clock news? It was nothing. I had a headache and I went into the kitchen to take some aspirin. I took out the bottle, a glass—you know. And then the phone rang. It was Rio, saying that he was almost home, did I want him to stop for anything. So I said I was taking some aspirin for a headache and I asked him to stop for milk, which as you know I seem incapable of keeping in my house for some reason that I can't explain."

"And that made you upset, thinking about the problem

with the milk, and you took some aspirins. How many?" she asks.

"No, I wasn't upset. And I'm not done. So, then he asks me to check to see if he left his keys to the shed on the dresser in the bedroom. See, he went to that stupid paintball store and he keeps the stuff in the shed all locked up, and…well, anyway, I went upstairs and then the doorbell rang and there was postage due on a letter from Canada. It seems that Rio has some sort of stupid idea about going hunting in Saskatchewan or something, and then I thought I saw the mouse that Rio saw the other day and—"

"I thought you told me you were having trouble with your memory." She has opened my folder and is scribbling as fast as she can.

"And as long as I had the mailman at the door—" I say, reaching across the desk and tapping the folder indicating she should get down every word "—I thought I could give him the letters for the kids. And then Rio came in, and my head was pounding like crazy and I took three aspirin, but then I looked at the stuff on the counter and the truth is, I couldn't remember if I took some already or not.

"And I thought I might have taken two doses." I fold my arms. "And that's the aspirin saga. And why he got so upset and acted like I was suicidal, I can't tell you."

She stares at me, waiting for me to cough up some other details. Like maybe she wants to know about David, but I don't know that I'm really ready to talk about that.

"And the deer?" she asks.

Violated. It is the only word I can think of to describe how

I feel. I get up and walk over to the window, adjusting the blinds until I can see into the parking lot. I don't really expect to see Rio out there, but I wouldn't be surprised if he was. I don't think I'd even be surprised if when I peered out, I found him peering in. Must be more paranoia because it's as if Rio is storing up damaging evidence against me. I mean the deer thing was a long time ago. Why bring it up now?

Tonelessly, I tell Dr. Benjamin about Bambi, and say I'd do it again, given the chance. Then I amend my statement so she'll understand that I mean I'd save the thing, not hit it, again.

"If I had hit a deer with my kids in the car when they were young, I'd have moved heaven and earth to save it," the doctor says.

I'm grateful for the admission, because Dr. Benjamin's respect matters to me more than I want to admit. It would be different, I think, if she were a man. Then I could think that she doesn't understand, can't know how I feel, would feel differently if she'd borne children. The fact that she's a woman means I can't get off the hook so easily, and it means that if she can do it, I ought to be able to, as well. I wish I knew exactly what *it* is.

"I keep seeing that deer in my dreams, and Alyssa is crying and I wake up with my heart pounding...." I tell her. I don't mention the other things that wake me up in the night because I am too embarrassed.

"That I can help with," she says, pulling out her prescription pad with the kind of smile that says she wants to be on my team. "Mild sleeping pills."

My team has been decimated by players that have either

been put on the disabled list or fouled out. It feels good to have a substitute with all the right moves.

"Any other odd instances since last week?" she asks. "Any high drama?"

"Well, Rio's making sure that nothing too terrible is going wrong," I say.

"He's very solicitous," Dr. Benjamin responds.

"Overbearing." The word pops out of my mouth before I even realize it.

"What makes you say so?"

"Actually, Bobbie, my neighbor, says so. She seems to think that all his coddling is making things worse. Like I told you about how he bought me this Palm Pilot to keep track of things that I want to remember? So he keeps telling me to put this or that in it, calls me from the office to tell me things and asks if I've put them in my Palm, as if it's the easiest thing in the world to do, which it isn't, especially if you have long nails. And I get all crazy about whether I put each stupid thing down in addition to whether I did it. Some things I put in after I've done them and then check them off. And Bobbie keeps saying that if I don't drive myself crazy, Rio'll do it. But Bobbie's going through a hard time and—" I stop myself, almost sucking in the last of my words.

"And?"

"Oh. I thought you'd tell me not to talk about Bobbie because I'm supposed to talk about me."

"You think Bobbie might be a little jealous of the attention that your husband is paying you?" She makes a note on her pad.

"What did you write?" I ask.

She looks at me and considers a minute. Then those little Botox beggars near her eyes crinkle. "Get milk," she says.

I can't help laughing. I lean forward but she shifts so that I can't see the yellow pad.

"Bobbie's jealousy," she reminds me. "Does it bother you?"

"You mean is that yet another thing I feel guilty about? That my husband is there and hers isn't? That I've got money and she's got to be having financial trouble with Mike gone? That my life is perfect and I have no right to be coming apart at the seams?"

"Is that something you need a 'right to do'?"

"I have no problems. I mean, other than that I'm losing my mind. I have a husband. I have children. They're happy kids, healthy kids…."

"So you feel that there is some sort of fairness doctrine operating here? That emotional and mental health is somehow an earned capacity?" She seems amused by the notion.

"More like the other way," I admit. "That if everything is all right—"

"You mean that if, for example, a mother were to accidentally be responsible for the death of her child, she would have a right to a breakdown, and to subsequent breakdowns?"

She is referring to my mother. The facts seem to speak for themselves.

"And that a woman who seemingly has everything going for her has no right to a breakdown. Have I got that right? That you only are allowed to experience difficulties if you—"

"Yes."

"You aren't serious."

"Well," I hedge, not wanting to disappoint her. "I really don't think that I have a right to complain about anything. Which makes me all the more irritated that this is happening to me. I should be fine. My life is fine."

"Is it?" The line between her eyebrows deepens. She really could use some collagen or something.

I don't know what to tell her. I'm still trying to work up to the fact that Rio kept from me David's coming home, but it's such a Pandora's box that if I lift the lid, even a little, who knows what will come flying out?

"What's bothering you the most at this moment?" she asks.

"Well, you know, the pool thing is getting to me a little."

"The pool thing?" she asks.

Of course I've mentioned it to her, haven't I? I'm sure I have. "The in-ground pool we're getting?"

She was leaning back slightly in her chair, and now she comes forward with such force that she looks as if she's part of a catapult act in the circus.

"I didn't tell you?" I ask as innocently as I can, as if it is merely some detail I've left out, not something I've agonized over. "Rio got me a pool for my birthday."

"He did," Dr. Benjamin says, nodding as she tries to take this new information in.

"Well, the kids wanted one, and Rio did, too, and his brother-in-law works for the company and he loses jobs very quickly so it seemed like a good idea, while he had the job, and maybe to help him keep the job, too, if we ordered a pool."

She waits for me to finish while I loft out there in the wind, untethered, pretending that the pool is no big deal.

"So they started digging the other day. Big hole. Huge hole. Looks like the foundation for a new Wal-Mart."

The doctor is unnervingly quiet, which only makes me feel all the more strongly the need to fill up the dead air around us.

"It's going to be organically shaped, black inside instead of blue, so it doesn't look like a pool, but more like a pond, which is good so that it doesn't really remind me of anything. Not that it would bother me. I mean if it looked like another pool."

"By that you mean the one in which your baby brother drowned," she says. "I mean, why mince words if it doesn't bother you, right?"

I am too busy swallowing and trying to sit up straight in my chair to answer her.

She flips open my folder to check on something and then reminds me that my birthday was several weeks ago.

"Well, that was why I thought I'd mentioned it," I say, but her grimace says she isn't buying it.

"Well, I don't see why my husband and kids shouldn't have what they want just because of something that happened years ago to someone they never even knew," I add.

"Someone they never knew? Funny, but I thought when we discussed your brother's death we were very clear on the fact that it happened to you—that the tragedy of losing a baby brother belonged to you as well as losing a son belonged to your mother."

When I say nothing, she continues.

"You remember that discussion? It seems to me that it's a matter of convenience, suddenly, whether the tragedy is yours or not. Is that the case?"

"Convenience?" I shout at her. "That's a terrible thing to say! Like I'm using it as some excuse. Well, this proves I'm not, doesn't it? If I used Markie as an excuse, we wouldn't be having the pool put in, now would we?"

"Why *are* 'we' having the pool put in, Teddi? The real reason?" Damn those eyes of hers, that can peel off layers of my soul and pin them to the wall.

"Rio wants—"

"And what about what Teddi wants?" she says before I can finish. I tell her as much. "Are you telling me you want this pool? Was that what you were about to say?"

"I'm not opposed to it." No one, except those members of my family who want the pool desperately, would even pretend to believe me. "I mean, there are four of them and one of me. It hardly seems fair that I should impose my will on the whole family because of something that happened over thirty years ago."

She is writing furiously in my file. After a moment she looks up. "I want to be sure I have this right. Now our feelings are subject to majority rule? I thought it was a merit-based system last time. Now we vote on how Teddi can feel and what is supposed to bother her after how long. Tell me, would their votes change if it happened last year? Is there some cutoff?"

It is not the way she is making it sound. It isn't like my

family has ever said I shouldn't be bothered by what happened to my brother. "This really has less to do with them than it does to do with me."

"How so?" she asks.

"Well, I want to be over it, to wipe that fear, and all the others, away. To take charge of my life and not let the past, or my mother, or my fear of repeating her life, rule my own."

"Nice speech," she tells me, asking whether or not I buy it.

"I should be over it," I say adamantly.

"If I could remove one word from the English language, or at least forbid the uttering of it in this office, it would be *should*."

"Well, a pool will prove that I am over it." *I hope*, I add silently.

"And the fact that you're trembling means...?"

I don't answer her. What can I say? That I am scared to death and never should have agreed to the pool in the first place? That the challenge is too great? That, as Bobbie says, I've set the bar too high?

"The fact of the matter is that some things are never gotten over. Yours is not some irrational fear based on what might happen. It is a memory rooted very soundly in what *did* happen. And if you want to work on getting over it, we will do that. The pool itself concerns me less than your refusal to see that you have a right to the security that comes with knowing you have prevented a possible calamity by simply not having a pool in your yard."

I shrug a little, as if she might have a point, but I'm not willing to concede it.

"Do you understand what I'm saying? That you have a right to say no to the pool—you don't need excuses, reasons, arguments, though in fact, you have them. What you want, or don't want, is as important as what your husband and children want or don't want."

"Yes, but there are four of them who all have rights, too, don't they? Why should my rights supercede theirs?"

"Well, they can easily live without a pool, can't they? Now, tell me the truth, Teddi, can you as easily live *with* one?"

CHAPTER 18

I am waiting for Rio to get home from work. He is usually in a good mood on Mondays because my father is off, which leaves him the run of the store. Only tonight he comes home in a foul mood. Bobbie and I watch him grimace at the hole in the backyard and the lack of progress that is being made on the pool that Joey's company is putting in. There is a bulldozer and something called a Cat, but the bull appears to be dozing and the Cat isn't digging any holes, either. Neither has shown any signs of life for several days. The surface dirt has dried and blown around in the light breeze, coating and recoating the new deck furniture with a film of dirt despite how many times I wipe it down.

Just inside the back door, Rio slips out of his dusty loafers, grimaces at them, too, and glances at the empty stovetop.

"So as usual, there's no dinner?" he asks, opening the oven door and peering into the oven. How long can a person keep the same expression? "We gotta get some help in here, Teddi. Someone to do the cleaning, some cooking. Angelina'd be happy to—"

"I thought you said this morning that you wanted to go out for dinner tonight," I say, ignoring the comment about Angelina and the dirty oven. "Remember, you said you wanted to try that new Italian place on Cold Spring Road?"

"How about you giving us a little privacy, sweet cakes?" he says to Bobbie, signaling with a jerk of his head that it is time for her to leave.

"I thought that Bobbie could come out with us," I say, but Bobbie is halfway out the door, making excuses about having to call the kids at camp and trying to make it look like Rio isn't throwing her out.

"Well, that wasn't very nice," I tell him after she leaves.

"Yeah, well, my day wasn't what you'd call nice, and now I get home and there's no dinner." He looks at the oven again as if dinner is going to magically appear there.

"You said you wanted to go to that Italian restaurant that serves family-style," I remind him.

"Okay, sure. If that's what you want," he says, pulling out a chair at the table and sitting down in it.

"I was going to make chicken, remember?" I say. "But I had to go visit my mother, and you said—"

He looks at me as if the conversation never took place. As if he never wanted to go out to dinner.

Maybe it never happened. He looks over at the clock on the oven. It reads 3:10. He checks his watch, then looks at the microwave. It reads 7:40. "What the hell time is it, anyway?" he shouts, pressing buttons on one clock and then another. "How do you stand this? It's enough to drive even a normal person crazy!"

"Blew a fuse," I explain. It happens all the time. For the better part of a year, the VCR has been blinking 12:00, along with the clock on the answering machine. At least those two agree and are right twice a day. Actually, it doesn't bother me at all. I find it easier to get used to it than to run around fixing the clocks every day in the summertime, when storms and air-conditioning sabotage the house's electrical system on a regular basis. It's the price you pay for having five televisions, four VCRs, two DVD players, TiVo, Replay and digital Cablevision in a house that was built when a typical family owned only one TV.

"Where'd you go today?" he asks me, taking my hand in his and stroking it idly, as if he is trying to make a connection of some sort. As if we need that.

"Just to visit my mother," I say. "My father was there, and David, and—"

"Ah, the Golden Boy," he says, interrupting me. The subject has been a prickly one since I confronted Rio about not telling me my brother was in town. "Back just the way your father planned it from day one. I'll bet that was one touching scene."

I tell him that the "touching" part involved Angelina's mouth and my father's privates, apparently witnessed by a pubescent David. While my parents and I were horrified by David's revelation, Rio seems to find it pretty amusing. This is because there are three things that Rio thinks he has known about my father from the start: (1) that my father was fooling around with Angelina since forever, (2) that he has been waiting for David to come home and take over the reins of Bayer Furniture, which would effectively cut Rio out of the picture, because (3) my father hates him. The world according to Rio.

So despite the fact that my father hired Rio, that we have lived off Bayer Furniture for all these years, and that there was no way my father could have known that David would resurface, Rio has been waiting for this betrayal to happen for nearly as long as he has worked at Bayer. He doesn't seem to get it that my while my father might betray him, he would never betray me.

Of course, now that I know he's betrayed my mother, I stand on less solid ground on that one.

At any rate, I don't tell Rio how my mother told David and my father that he is anxious to welcome her here, that he's already cleaned out Dana's closet for her and that, unless Angelina is out of the house she shares with my father by the time she is ready to leave South Winds, she is coming home to our house.

We are on tenuous suspension bridges with fraying ropes as it is. There's no point crossing any more of them until it's absolutely necessary. Rio is happy enough to drop the subject of my family after looking upward and muttering *pazzo!* loudly.

"Go anywhere else?" he asks.

South Winds was more than enough for one day. I tell him that I came straight home.

"So then you went to the bank on the way there?" he asks. "Or you don't want to tell me about that little stop?"

It's true. I'm guilty. I deposited a check from Precious Things, where they paid me for the camp trunks and nightstands and an incredible floor lamp with Alice in Wonderland's neck stretching up nearly the length of it. And I did a quick withdrawal at the ATM on the way to the hospital. Get the cuffs. Book me.

"And the bank," I admit readily. "And I also went to the bathroom twice and stopped in Home Depot Expo to look at kitchen curtains for the window that faces the yard. It's all in that gizmo you got me, if you want to check. Or maybe we could get me one of those cute Martha Stewart House Arrest bracelets to wear."

"Don't start with me, Teddi. Not when you're the one in the wrong. You gonna tell me what you're spending all this money on?" he asks, pulling a folded piece of paper from his pocket and smoothing it out on the table. "Is all this for that damn bat mitzvah, or what?"

"All what money?" I look at what appears to be a fax from Roslyn Savings Bank. *Insufficient Funds.*

"You know, you want to spend it all on this little party, Teddi, you go right ahead. My future, our future, what does it matter, anyway, right? But you gotta shell out the money two years in advance? I guess you think it's fair since your father's only keeping me on because of you, and he wants this thing to be the party of the century. So even if I'm the one working my ass off down there in the heat because the air-conditioners are too old to do squat…

"Anyway, you can spend it on whatever you want, but there is a limit to it, you know. And I can't replace it if I don't know it's not there or nothing."

"What are you talking about?" I have taken out exactly sixty dollars since the kids left for camp. And I put in several hundred, which more than covered that.

"Twenty-one hundred and sixty dollars, Teddi," he says, laying his hands palms up on the table. "That's what I'm talking about. And it don't grow on trees, you know. Ask your father. And how come it's gotta be cash, two years in advance? They need two years for the damn check to clear?"

"Are you accusing me of taking out twenty-one hundred dollars?" Okay, I may have made two withdrawals and not just the one I remember. It's been more than a week since the kids left, and Bobbie and I have eaten a few lunches out and picked up a lipstick or two.

"No, I'm saying you took out twenty-one hundred and *sixty* dollars, but the sixty was from your own account, so I got nothing to say about that. But the three seven-hundred withdrawals were from our joint account—an account without twenty-one hundred dollars in it," he says. He points again at a fax on the table. "See here? June 28, seven hundred dollars. July 2, seven hundred dollars. July 6, seven hundred dollars again. How long you think you could keep taking money out before I noticed?"

"Oh my God," I say, panic rising as if I've got three kids in the car and the LIE has just turned to a sheet of black ice. "It must be one of those bank frauds. Someone must be looting our account."

"Right," he says, clearly not buying my explanation. "Look, I'm sorry if I acted, you know, mad. I know I've been dumping on you about this whole bat mitzvah thing, but what does a goy know about chopped liver swans, anyway?"

"Rio, I haven't put down that kind of money on the bat mitzvah. I haven't put money down beyond the deposit, and that was done a long time ago. Which is all beside the point, because I did not take out that money," I say.

"Oh," he says knowingly. "I get it. You don't *remember* taking the money out." He says it amiably, almost with a wink.

"No," I repeat. "I am not demented, and I'm not careless about money. At least not about that much money. Someone is looting our account, Rio, and it isn't me." It happens all the time—isn't that why I gave in and changed my PIN? As bad as it is, I like that explanation better than the one Rio seems ready to accept.

"You didn't maybe give it to Bobbie?" he asks, tilting his head as if he'd understand if I did. "And not tell me 'cause you thought I'd be mad?"

After I assure him, swear up and down that I haven't taken out a dime from our joint account, never mind twenty-one hundred dollars, he agrees to call the bank as soon as it opens in the morning.

"Didn't you tell me you changed that PIN thing?" he asks. When I nod, he asks if I told anyone and I tell him not even him, and before I can tell him the new PIN he says, rather dubiously, that someone must have taken a 'damn lucky guess.' He puts his hand up to stop me when I try to tell him what it is, saying he never uses the machine. Then he stands up, ready to go out to dinner as if it's settled.

"This place you wanna go to take credit cards?" he asks, fingering the Insufficient Funds slip on the table.

"I still have some cash," I say. "At least I think I do."

"You ready to go then?"

I nod, grabbing up my handbag.

"Fine," Rio bites out as he puts his arm around my shoulder and leads me to the door. "This oughta be great."

CHAPTER 19

"And so I open my wallet in the restaurant," I tell Dr. Benjamin between sniffs. "And there it is. Twenty-one hundred dollars. Hundred dollar bill after hundred dollar bill."

She pushes the box of tissues closer to me and I take out a couple more.

"How could a person not know that she took out all that money? How could I not remember that? And then, of course, I went into my whole 'somebody else did it' mode. I told Rio I thought my father had come into my house and put the money in my purse. Only I know he didn't do it because when I brought up money, he offered to send home five hundred dollars with Rio as if it were a king's ransom."

"What about Rio?" the doctor asks.

"Don't you think I thought of that? I thought of Bobbie, of my mother—whose locked in South Winds, for Pete's sake, and naturally Rio. I'd have accused the milkman if we had one. I even thought of David."

She asks me who David is and that leads us down the Oh-Didn't-I-Mention-He's-Back Alley, which the good doctor refers to as Omission Street. When I admit it's unlikely that David took the money out of my bank and put it in my handbag, she seems willing to let the David story occupy a back burner for a while.

"You know how to tell if a paranoid woman has esteem problems?" I ask her.

She gestures for me to tell her.

"She thinks nobody important is after her."

She ignores my joke. "You ruled out your neighbor and your husband, then?"

"This is great. You'll love this. You know my crazy mother. Well, her friend was the victim of computer theft and my mother was so sure that I would be next that I had to promise her I'd change my PIN number, which I did, last week. She says that you're supposed to change it every month or so. She saw it on *Prime Time* or *Dateline*."

"And?" she asks. I can see that she is at her wit's end. I passed mine a long time ago.

"And so no one knows the new PIN. I can hardly remember it myself without looking it up. And I had the money, after all. And I was at the bank those days. I checked it in my Palm Pilot, but I swear I was only making deposits. I mean, I could swear, but then I'd be wrong, wouldn't I?"

She makes some sympathetic noises while she jots some things in my file. She shakes her head as if it doesn't make any more sense to her than it does to me. At least, she tells me, I remember going to the bank. It's a relatively small thing, she says, to forget a second transaction. Well, actually it isn't, but she apparently is willing to make excuses for me.

"Are the sleeping pills helping you?" she asks, grasping at straws. "Are you sleeping well?"

"Like the dead," I say.

She nods, like we're making progress.

Maybe she has time for these games, but I don't. "Okay, look," I say, leaning forward in my chair. "I've come to you for one of two reasons. Well, really one reason, but there are two ways to get there. Either you can simply tell me I'm not losing my mind, which is what I want to hear, or you can fix it so that I don't lose my mind. Either way works for me, as long as I can have my life back."

"Okay. You're not losing your mind," she says, and flips my file closed. "I'll have my service send you a bill."

"What about what's happening in my life? What about how I can't remember—"

She sits back in her chair, as if she has all the time in the world and whether I stay or go doesn't make a bit of difference to her.

I hate it when she does this.

"I know what you're doing," I say, copying her posture, settling in.

"And what is that?"

"Manipulating me. You're hardly the first person to do that."

"Be nice if I was the last, though, wouldn't it?" she asks, giving me that little Team Teddi smile.

I take a long time to answer and surprise both of us by saying that maybe it would, and then again, maybe it wouldn't.

Her jaw drops slightly and she asks, incredulously, "You like being manipulated?"

"It saves making mistakes," I say, defending myself reflexively. "I mean, if I'm doing what is expected of me, then everyone around me will be happy, won't they? And if they're happy, then I'll be happy. So, in essence, doing what they want me to do is the surest way to find happiness, isn't it?"

She says nothing. Okay, so maybe I'm not happy at the moment, but maybe it's because I don't know what everyone wants of me. My God, is that the person I have become?

"It's not like I have no will of my own," I continue in the wake of her silence, unsure where I am going with this. "It's that what I want never seems as important as making everyone else happy."

When she still says nothing, I charge on. "Okay, like I'm going to see my mother. She hates when I wear overalls. If I wear them, anyway, she'll complain and criticize and I'll be miserable, so I'm actually making myself happy by pleasing her, right?"

"And your pool? You're telling me now, honestly, that you're making yourself happy putting that in? Which one of us, exactly, are you trying to convince?"

"How come the only time you talk is to say something mean?"

"Because you're up to it, Teddi. The more we talk, the more I see you getting in your own way, setting limits, relinquishing authority to anyone around you. And here you are, at it again, coming to me to tell you that you are normal, when you already know that for yourself, don't you?"

"Maybe you're right. I do relinquish authority. At least I did. I went from my father's house to my husband's. But it seems like everybody I've trusted to take care of me has let me down. Look at my father, my mother, Angelina. And now Rio thinks I'm losing it and he can't stop it.

"Do I know I'm normal? I don't know."

"I'll help you Teddi, in every way I can, but you're a grown-up now. You don't need someone to 'take care of you.' You're the one with the keys. You're the one in the driver's seat." She is nearly pleading with me. "Drive, dammit, Teddi. Drive."

"I'm trying to," I tell her. "That's why I'm bringing my mother home to my house."

"Despite my reservations?"

I tell her that I feel I have to, for my sake as well as hers. "If she's there, I can't very well fall apart, can I? I have to be strong for her, and have a normal life going on, and show her that I am…"

"…nothing like her?" Dr. Benjamin asks. "Teddi, people aren't meant to live with their mothers once they're adults. Even under the best of circumstances. If, for example, my mother moved in with me, an hour would be too long for both of us."

"I can do it," I say, and she looks at me as if she's seeing that poor wounded psyche, the one with the broken leg and the limp arm and the knife in her back that she told me I was, only now she sees that there's a ball and chain attached to my good leg. "It'll be good to have the company."

She asks me about my husband's job. Another potential source of embarrassment.

"He works, usually, six days a week. That's retail. Sometimes he takes off a Saturday, if my father doesn't mind too much. But if he's off, he usually likes to…"

I really don't want to tell her this, but she leans forward. *Yes?* she asks with her body language.

"He likes to go upstate and play war games," I say with a deep sigh. "It's with paint. Let's say it's not my favorite thing about him. Of course, it's not as bad as hunting."

"Not as bad as if he hunted, you mean?"

"Not as bad as *when* he hunts," I correct her, and I can't believe that after a dozen years of marriage Rio still hasn't given it up, and I still haven't gotten used to it. They always say that you shouldn't marry a man with the idea of changing him, and I wouldn't really change him—not completely—but hunting? Civilized men, as I've told Rio more than once, do not go kill animals. They become veterinarians, they work for animal rights, they stop their cars to bring wounded deer to animal hospitals....

"He really wasn't cut out to be a furniture salesman six days a week," I say by way of explanation. "I mean, my father could do it eight days a week and think that visiting furniture factories in Italy qualifies as a vacation.

"But Rio..." I say, and I've heard him say the same thing often enough "...was supposed to do something more exciting, something hotter, faster, sexier. And I suppose he would have, if he hadn't married me."

"What do you think he'd be doing today?" Dr. Benjamin asks me.

"Oh, maybe be a race driver in the Indy 500?"

The doctor says that sounds pretty dangerous. She's obviously never been on the Seaford-Oyster Bay Expressway with Rio after midnight. The Indy would be a piece of cake.

"He likes danger. He likes to gamble. Maybe he'd be a professional con man. I don't know. Or a spy. He loves all those

James Bond sort of gadgets. He reads the *Sharper Image* catalog the way some men read *Playboy*."

She asks me if I think that Rio resents me for the choices he's made.

"Maybe not *resents*, but it's there."

"And you?" she asks me. "What might you have become? Where might you be?"

At my office in the D & D Building in New York City, decorating the apartments of the rich and famous? In my own design studio, planning color schemes and choosing fabrics with other people's money?

When I don't answer she says, "Becoming a wife and mother can be ambition enough," but neither of us believe it. It's a dead-end job, and we both know it. At some point the kids grow up, the marriage grows stale....

"Yes it is," I say a little too adamantly. The fact is, I don't want to talk to Ronnie Benjamin about my marriage. I want to talk about my mother and how she didn't raise me. I want to talk about my father and how he betrayed me. I want to talk about my kids and how I can save them. I want to talk about the damn two thousand dollars in my wallet, but I do not want to talk about Rio.

So naturally her next question is: "Tell me about your relationship with your husband."

I hate this leather chair. The air-conditioning turns it into an iceberg. "What do you want to know?"

She suggests I tell her what I think she ought to know. Whatever I'm comfortable with.

I tell her that I don't know what's important, and I reread

the diplomas behind her as if I am making sure she is worthy of my secrets.

"Of course you do," she says. "It's *your* life, *your* marriage. No one knows better than you. You are the expert here."

Oy. If I'm the expert, we're in big trouble. "It's a good marriage, I suppose. Rio is good to me. We have three terrific children, a nice house."

It sounds lame. Was this all I wanted from life? Is it all I want now? "Okay, go with this," she says. "My favorite thing about Rio is...?"

...his looks. I mean, the man is killer gorgeous. But how shallow would that sound? I try to come up with something else. *Loyal* makes him sound like a dog. *Adventurous* makes him sound like a bounder. *Dangerous* makes him sound like one of the Sopranos.

"Well," I say. "He's a good father. He works very hard at a job he hates just to support us."

"He says that he hates his job? He's told you this?" Dr. Benjamin asks.

I nod. "Pretty much. But he likes the money."

"And Rio's favorite thing about me...?" she prompts.

"The money," I say with a *do-I-have-to-answer?* look.

"Really?" she presses.

Of course *really*. Am I hot? Am I cool? Am I a good sport about anything the man does? I get up and go to the window. "I hope not. But I can't think of anything else."

"Well, how about this, then," she offers. "Rio *should* love me for..."

That's a lot easier. "Well, first off, because I am a wonderful mother. I care about my kids more than anything, and I try to think about the long-term effects of everything I do with regard to them.

"Also, it would be nice if he appreciated my artistic abilities. He acts as if what I do, my decorating and the furniture painting I do with Bobbie, is some little hobby anyone could do if they wanted to. Which isn't true. I'm good at it. Really good. But Rio acts as if it's something to keep me busy and make dinner late. As if anything I do can't really be worthwhile. Especially lately."

"He's changed?"

"I guess I've changed. No, I *know* I have. I'm so preoccupied and nervous, but he isn't helping it any when he treats me like I'm some mental case. I mean, I am here, so maybe I am, but I think he's making it all worse."

I try to compose myself, but the more I say to Dr. Benjamin, the more things occur to me that I feel I ought to say aloud.

"And this is probably a terrible thing to say, but I think he likes me better this way than self-sufficient. I think it makes him feel more 'the man' to have me needing him to hold me together so I don't come apart at the seams. And the more helpless I am the more Rio seems to love me." I pause for a moment and realize that the more helpless I am, the more I can't even stand, never mind *like*, myself. I ask if she can explain that.

Fortunately, she can. She tells me that I am the kind of woman who values self-reliance and that my *perceived*—and she is careful to stress that word—lack of control over the situation at hand is causing me to condemn myself. She explains that everyone holds certain character traits in especially high esteem, and that learning which traits those are and striving to possess them in abundance is a good way to build self-esteem and contentment.

"And maybe—" Dr. Benjamin says, tapping my folder "—that's a good place for us to start next time."

"Isn't there anything I can do in the meantime?" I beg her. "On my own, beyond therapy?"

"In large measure, you're doing it," she reassures me, pulling out some handouts she thinks may help me to feel in control of my situation. She tells me that there is no magic pill, no secret formula.

"Damn," I say. "I was really counting on a pair of ruby slippers."

CHAPTER 20

Rio is, once again, in a bad mood from the moment he comes through the door. Maybe he misses the kids. I know I do. At any rate, he grumbles at me, muttering something about the *goddamn bulldozers* turning the backyard into some community litter box, as if this is my fault. Let's remember whose idea this pool was, shall we?

Then he goes straight to our bathroom, where he showers, changes and comes down fresh and clean, asking me where I'd like to go out to dinner. As if I really care. Casually he mentions he's out of shaving cream, which is simply impossible, and points out, tactfully, that I am wearing two different shoes. I explain how I tried on one of each to see which looked better and then had to answer the phone, and then got busy with I have no idea what else. By then he's lost all interest in why I have on one sandal and one wedge.

He suggests we call in for pizza and I agree, despite the fact that I hate pizza. I'm not hungry, anyway. After he calls, he turns a MacGyver rerun on the TV and starts going over a stack of bills, mumbling and cursing under his breath, oblivious to me. I would feel slighted, but it is actually a joy to be free of his watchful eyes for a few minutes. It seems like a good time to practice the "neurobic exercises" from Dr. Benjamin's handouts. First I study the den, trying to memorize every detail like the article suggests. Then, with my eyes closed, I get up and walk to the kitchen without stumbling into anything.

Keeping my eyes shut, I go to the pantry, pull out my casual Pottery Barn celadon-green dishes (they're square so I know I've got the right ones) and the oversize glasses with the dragonflies on them and carry them to the table. Then back to the side-by-side refrigerator, which I open, feeling around inside for a liter of soda. I pull one out, realize it might be water, and for a moment stand there, stymied.

Taste, I think, fumbling to open it and sticking my finger in. Can I really set up for dinner without looking?

"Is it Stevie Wonder Night or something?" I hear Rio ask, and I open my eyes before he's finished getting the words out. He's standing with his eyes closed, groping in front of him and wagging his head back and forth.

"I was just practicing." I am embarrassed at being caught in the act of looking foolish.

"For what?" he asks, his head cocked awkwardly and his tongue hanging out of his mouth like an idiot. "A brain tumor?"

"It's an exercise," I say defensively. "I thought you were busy and wouldn't mind."

"An exercise in what?" He leans up against the doorjamb, his arms crossed easily across his chest, looking mildly amused. "That whaddyacallit? Futility?"

"I'm trying to strengthen my memory." It makes sense on

paper. Taking away one of the senses makes you concentrate harder, and that makes the brain work.

"You think you're gonna forget how to set the table? Things get that bad, Ted, I'm checking you into your mother's hotel. I don't think I can take two loonies at the same time."

That's true enough, but after my session with Dr. Benjamin I came up with a plan. "I was thinking it would be a good weekend for you to go up to that cabin your friend has and do some paintballing or something."

He looks at me as if my marbles are coming out my ears. "Go away and leave you alone here with Looney Tunes? What are you, brain damaged? You must think I'm as crazy as the two of you!" His voice actually squeaks with horror as he says it. "Outta the question. No way I'm gonna leave you two here. Not now, with you like this."

There is no nice way to tell him that his hovering is making matters worse. That my self-esteem, along with my mental health, is now in jeopardy. I tell him it will be better if he isn't home, if he is out paintballing in upstate New York. "Oh, we'll be fine," I say lightly. "I'll take her shopping and—"

"Oh, sure. This is a flash—you're not fine. What if you have another accident or something? Hit an elephant this time? Or what if you get lost again? No way am I gonna leave you and your mother to go driving all around and spending more money."

"Is this about money?"

"No, it's not about money," he says, holding one hand to his chest as if I've mortally wounded him with the accusation. "Even though you gotta admit you've been going a little overboard in the spending department lately. I mean, I didn't want to say nothing, but three hundred dollars in the lingerie department at Bloomingdale's? How could a few lousy nightshirts cost so much?"

"I didn't buy—" I start to say, but Rio's eyebrow rises skeptically. I was in Bloomingdale's and I did pick up a couple of things for my mother. And a bra. Three hundred dollars? I really don't think so. But then I didn't think I made those withdrawals, either, so what good is my recollection?

Rio is staring hard at me. His gaze shifts down from my face to my body, making me feel self-conscious. "So you at least bought something lacy, maybe?" he asks as if he is hoping I have.

"I don't think so," I say honestly, not wanting to go down that road. "I think I bought a bra and some stuff for my mother."

"For three hundred dollars?" He is leaning against the wall, looking lanky, looking interested in me for the first time in a long time. For some reason I can't explain, it makes me uncomfortable. I busy myself with putting out the cups and saucers for some coffee.

"Are you sure you're not forgetting something else you bought?" he asks, sidling up behind me, his warm breath tickling the back of my neck. Usually that drives me crazy, gets me "hot to trot," as Rio puts it. Tonight it's so much hot air.

When I tell him I don't think I've forgotten any purchases, he twirls me around and unbuttons the top button of my blouse, taking a peek inside.

"New?"

"No."

He backs me up against the counter and his leg presses against me, inserting itself between my own. I'm not fighting him, but I'm sure not encouraging him, either. He has to struggle, but he finally pulls my shirt free of my jeans and plays with the waistband until he finds the edge of my panties.

"New?" he asks again.

Actually, they are. In an attempt to make myself irresistible I have broken down and bought a pair of those thongs that make me feel as if I'm being violated by a crazed periodontist with a floss fetish.

His fingers splay across my lower back, working their way inside my jeans until they are snug against my naked behind. "Oh, yeah," he says, his breath now hot against my ear. "These are new. And definitely worth their weight in sex toys!"

He is playful, not pushy, and I don't know if he expects me to melt in his arms or swat away his hands. "If you want to, I guess tonight we could…"

Could I sound less enthusiastic? Sure, if I were dead.

"Gee, thanks," he says sarcastically, backing away from me, leaving cold air to rush against the skin above my jeans. "I guess it was a lousy idea, what with how you're not feeling so great." Every day he has a new euphemism for his assessment of my mental health.

"I'm perfectly fine." Slowly, seductively, to prove it, I run my hand down his chest and then halfheartedly struggle to get his shirt out of his pants. When he pulls away, I'm not sorry.

"So you really want me to go?" he asks. "You're not scared to be here on your own?"

I assure him I really, really want him to go. Far.

"What about those mice?" he asks, one eyebrow raised.

"I thought you said they'd eat the bait you put out and take it back to their nest or whatever it's called that mice live in."

He shrugs, as if maybe they will and maybe they won't. I figure they'll see the poison and yell "Raid" or "Brand X," and pack their itsy-bitsy suitcases and leave my home, and I tell him that mice or no mice, I'll be fine.

"I should really go?" he asks, framing my face with his hands and looking into my eyes as if he can find a truth to hold on to there.

"My mother and I will be fine. We'll bond!"

"Yeah, like Krazy Glue," he says, obviously amused at the pun.

"We'll be great, Rio," I assure him again. *We will be*, I repeat to myself.

Just what I needed, a new mantra that includes my mother. *We'll be great. Mom and I will be just great.*

CHAPTER 21

Rio is packing his own bag and heading for the hills. Frankly, it is a relief to see him go. Having him and my mother pick at me at the same time would be more than I could take.

So fine. Let him go. My mother will no doubt be happy to step right into his shoes and tell me I am heading to hell in a handcart, or to the sanitarium in a Subaru.

"I called a service," Rio says when he comes back into the bedroom with the duffel bag he always takes away with him. "Write it down in your Palm thingy. They'll pick you up at eleven and take you to South Winds, wait for you, and take you and the *fruitcake* back here. "

"I could have called," I say. "In fact, I'm capable of driving—"

He harrumphs and warns me, "Don't even say it, Teddi. Don't make me take the keys, or the distributor cap or something. I get *agita* just thinking about it. "

"It was a tiny dent," I tell him, referring to hitting the stop sign at the end of our block on my way home from the doctor's office. "It's not like I wrecked the car. People must hit stop signs all the time—"

"Yeah, well, screw other people," he says. "This is about you. Didn't you tell me that you were on some other planet?"

I'd said I was distracted. What else could I have said? It wasn't like I was driving down the street and thought *I think I'll ram that stop sign*.

"You got lost going to the funny farm last week, you hit a stop sign this week. What's next, Ted? A kid on Rollerblades? It's summer, the kids are all over the place. It's safer for you to take a limo. Think of yourself as so spoiled you don't even gotta drive yourself around. How's that?"

"I feel like a prisoner," I say.

"Great," Rio says sarcastically, shoving clean underwear into the duffel as if he wants to kill it. "Well, you know what, Teddi? I don't give two shits what it feels like, so long as you're safe. If I had my way, you'd spend the weekend at South Winds, where somebody'd be watching you all the time to make sure you're safe."

"Don't say that," I warn him. "What do you think is going to happen to me here? Think I'll burn down the house or drive the car through the den?"

Rio raises an eyebrow. "Maybe you'll leave the kettle on the stove?" he says, knowing that I nearly burned the bottom off the kettle only a few nights ago when I was on the phone with the kids.

"I got an electric kettle," I say, while he continues to throw things into his bag. "People must do it all the time, Rio. That's why they make electric kettles with automatic shutoffs." Not that I believe it myself for a minute, but if I stop finding explanations for my behavior—and excuses—I'll be lost.

"Or maybe you'll pull the plug on the refrigerator?"

I have no explanation for that. Nothing I can even make up. It was like I caught it from that patient of Dr. Benjamin's who I told Rio about.

"Or maybe you'll run out of gas and have to call me from Plainview again to get AAA to bring you some—"

"People—" I start, but he interrupts me, calling over his shoulder as he goes into the bathroom.

"Maybe Bobbie'll tell you that you gotta paint another bunny and you'll start throwing step stools through windows...."

I did not throw anything, so don't listen to him. There is a very simple explanation. I was upset about a misunderstanding with Bobbie and I turned too quickly with a lamp I was painting and somehow broke a window in the garage. And if I'd been smart, I would have had the window fixed and not even mentioned it to Rio. But I've been so upset with myself, and Rio always arranges for those sorts of things—repairs, appointments, whatever. If it's going to cost us money without the joy of shopping, he usually takes care of it.

Just as my father always does. Of course, my mother is incapable, incapacitated. But I can do it. I can do it all. Didn't I start this furniture-painting business myself and then take Bobbie in as a partner when it became too big for one person? Don't I make money at it? And have satisfied customers and even a reputation? I *can* do all the calling and arranging. I just don't, or at least I haven't.

"What's my mother going to think—" I ask as Rio puts his toiletries into the bag "—if I come for her in a hired car?"

"When a limo comes to get her? That it's about time she got what she deserves, I'd guess." He rolls his camouflage pants and jacket into a ball and thrusts them into his bag.

"And when she wants to go shopping tomorrow?" I ask.

"Tell her there's something wrong with the Corvette and take a cab." He is taking the Expedition up to the cabin and leaving the Corvette safely ensconced in the garage.

"She doesn't like the Corvette, anyway," I agree.

"Yeah. It ruffles her helmet," he says. It's possible that if my father had invested in Aqua Net fifty years ago he'd be retired now in a mansion in Boca on my mother's support alone. Everything in his bag, Rio tugs at the zipper, fighting with it as if it is purposely being difficult. It seems to me that Rio thinks everything is always being difficult simply to annoy him. "And don't go crazy with the charging, okay? I left you some cash and right now…well, don't spend more than we got, okay?"

"If we go at all," I say, "I'll pick up a few things to send the kids—some candy and stuff like that, okay?"

Rio stops fighting with the zipper and looks at me. "You know you don't hafta ask me if you can get the kids stuff. You don't gotta ask my permission for anything. We're a little short of cash right now is all. I explained it all to you, remember?"

I know it isn't in my best interest to say no, and so I nod.

"You sure you don't mind that I'm going?" he asks.

There is a piece of me that is terrified that he is going. But another piece can't wait for him to close the door behind him when he leaves. Like so much lately, I don't know what I want. And Rio plays on it, like he always does.

"I'll stay. I mean, you're right about your mother and me being oil and fire—"

I almost correct him, but he hates it when I do, so I admit that the timing could be better, though I don't know how.

He stops what he is doing and takes my face in his hands. "I can stay, Teddi. I don't have to go, if you're feeling shaky or anything. Or if you don't think that you can take care of yourself and June the Loon."

I say I am quite capable of taking care of myself, my mother, Rio and anyone who happens to wander in off the street.

Rio looks absolutely stricken and I have to promise that I will not let anyone wander in off the street—that it's just an expression—but he isn't easily placated.

Finally he gets up, spreads the handles on his duffel and slides the zipper open. He pulls out his camouflage stuff. "I can't go," he says, placing the clothing on the bed beside the bag. "You're gonna need me here."

"To do what?" I ask, wishing he would get going already and let me get my day started. "Hold my hand? Go. You need a break from work, and from all this *mishegass*. You deserve a break. Probably be good for your back. Hey, if I could leave me, I would."

"I'm not 'leaving you,'" he says, bracketing the words with his fingers before shoving some of his clothing back into his bag. "Don't forget that this whole thing was your idea. Jesus, I hate it when you say things like I'm leaving you. Why do you have to be a drama queen about everything?"

"I only meant that if I could take a break from me, I'd go. I was trying to empathize with you, that's all."

"Maybe if you went to South Winds for a couple of weeks, while the kids are away, and—"

I push my hands into the pockets of my shorts. That way I can't strangle Rio. "There's nothing wrong with me…" I say between clenched teeth "…beyond being distracted. Dr. Benjamin says so. And there is no way I'm going to a place like South Winds. Now, if you offered me a couple of weeks in Bermuda…"

"I did offer you a week in Aruba, remember?" he asks. I don't, but there is no chance in hell I'll admit that. "But you said you didn't want to be so far from the kids, with them away and all. I bet you don't remember that, do you?"

"Of course I do," I shout at him, remembering vaguely discussing an island at some point in time, but wondering how I could have passed up Aruba. Not that I could go with the kids away, which is exactly what he claims I said. "Would you go already? There's no reason to worry about me. I mean it, I'll have my mother here to keep me busy. And I can start getting the kids' rooms cleaned out so that when they come home they'll be ready to start school with a fresh, clean slate."

"That's my girl," he says, patting my head and then letting his hand trace the side of my face and cradle my chin. "And if anything goes wrong, you know what to do, right? You call me and I'll call that doctor of yours, or you can call the lady yourself and she'll—"

"Look," I say. "I know you're worried about me, but there is no reason to be. I'm fine, I've been running a house for more than twelve years and I think I can manage a couple of days more without burning it down or defacing it or killing anyone and hiding the body in the basement." *Present company excepted.*

Rio looks contrite. "Okay, okay. I didn't mean to get you all upset," he says softly. "I just love you so much that I—" He coughs, his eyes filling up so that I can't lace into him and tell him if he doesn't stop treating me like a nutcase I might really become one.

"I'll be fine," I say. "You need any help packing?"

"All done," Rio says. "Gotta get my stuff from the shed and then I'm set. I'll meet you in the kitchen and we can have some breakfast or something before I go, okay?"

Rio never has breakfast at home. I've always had this fantasy in my head—probably a leftover scene from some movie—where Rio reads the *New York Times* (that's how I know it's a fantasy) and sips coffee across the table from me. He reaches around the newspaper for a slice of toast (in one of those silver toast holders) and reads aloud something important to me. Of course in my imagination he is wearing a suit with one of those old cravats like in *Life With Father* or *Cheaper by the Dozen*, and not a set of camos and dog tags.

And he is reading the financial page and not the ATV listings in *Buylines*.

"You sure I'm capable of making you breakfast without burning my pans?"

"Don't start," he says. "'Cause I'm not sure of anything. Except that your sarcasm isn't helping anything."

Just go, I think to myself while I smile innocently at him.

"I'll just have a cup of coffee," he says, hefting the duffel bag. "I'll go get my rifles."

"A cup o' Joe," I shout after him, imagining that's what they say when he stops in the diners upstate. Just knowing he is going feels so freeing that I decide to run out to the yard and cut a couple of flowers for our "last meal" before he leaves.

I laugh to myself as I head down the steps behind Rio. Guns and Roses. That's Rio and me, all right.

CHAPTER 22

I'm not so far gone that I don't know a mistake when I see one. But with my mother already here, it is too late to do anything about it.

"You have everything you need?" I ask her after I've spent the entire afternoon getting her settled into Dana's room. Before I even went to collect her, I took down Dana's Ricky Martin posters, removed the collection of Powerpuff girls that my mother refers to as "dust collectors" from the windowsills, and took away all the pillows I made for Dana out of Britney Spears Concert Tour T-shirts. I found a carafe for the bedside table that I painted for Dana, a clock that glows in the dark (though not too brightly) and wooden hangers for all of my mother's clothes. I even found fresh drawer lining (scented—I hope she'll forgive me) for the drawers I have emptied for her use.

"Do you need anything else?" Not that there is anything left to need, as far as I can see.

"I don't know how you can live like this," she says, picking at something stuck to Dana's bedspread. "You need a good maid in here, Teddi."

"I'm kind of between housekeepers at the moment, Mom," I say, not mentioning that my mother's household is, as far as I know, still being maintained by Angelina, and that Angelina is the very reason she is here with me. No use stating the obvious.

"One thing has nothing to do with the other," she tells me as she runs her fingers across the top of the headboard as if she's in some commercial for Pledge. "Your house needs cleaning. You don't have to be here when Angelina cleans it. You can trust her with that sort of thing, you know. I'll leave a message for your father to tell her—"

"I'll get a cleaning service in," I say, my shoulders sagging from the weight of an hour and forty-two minutes with my mother. "I should have done it before this."

"We'll tell your father to arrange it for Monday," June says. She opens Dana's window and lights a cigarette, glares at me and blows the smoke out the window. She is waiting for me to tell her she can't smoke in the house. I am taking her window maneuver as recognition of the rule.

"I'll take care of it," I say, but I know I won't.

"Did you have some idea about dinner?" she asks, looking at her watch. "You know how bitchy I get when I'm protein-deprived."

"Really?" I ask, trying to keep the sarcasm out of my voice and resisting the urge to ask how one tells the difference between her general attitude and her protein-deprived state. "I hadn't noticed."

"Well, you'd have to be paying attention to something outside yourself, dear," my mother says, leaning out to crush the cigarette on the outside of my house before stooping to primp in Dana's mirror.

"Why would you say something like that?" I ask, thinking about what Dr. Benjamin would make of this conversation. *And the reason you let your mother, while you were extending your home to her, speak to you in that manner is?* she would ask. "Why would you say something purposely hurtful to me, when I've taken you in, taken your side, done everything, all along the way, all my life…"

"What did I say?" my mother asks, looking innocent and confused. "I didn't say anything about what you're wearing, as I promised your father I wouldn't. As if he deserves any kindnesses from me!"

"'What I'm wearing?'" I repeat, looking down at my black capris and my man-tailored shirt on which I've fashionably raised the collar and tied the tails around my waist. "What's wrong with what I'm wearing?"

"This is 1997, not 1957, Teddi," my mother says. "And Elvis has left the building."

"Don't you know what year it is, Mom?" I ask. Sometimes I forget that my mother is really sick, and not merely terminally annoying. "It's 2005, Mother. And capris are back."

My mother rolls her eyes. "Well, they shouldn't be. I know! Let's have Dana's room painted for her as a surprise," she says, running her hand down the wall and tugging at a seam in the wallpaper that has 'Dana' printed all over it. "She's too old for this name stuff. She knows who she is, doesn't she? And all this lavender!"

She stands back from the bed, putting up her hands to frame the scene. "I see taupes and beiges and browns. Very sophisticated. Maybe with a leopard throw for the bed."

I put up my hands the same way and squint through them. "And I see Dana screaming her head off and never speaking to me again."

"Your children are too willful," June says. "My children never would have questioned my judgment in matters of taste."

"Your children never had the nerve to have their own taste," I say. "It wasn't until I was twenty that I even knew I had an opinion on what color a wall ought to be. I thought every room was supposed to be taupe and beige and brown."

"Exactly right," she says, fingering the lace curtains through which I wove lavender ribbons to match the ones on the heart wreath Dana and I made together. "Anything else is tacky."

My house is mostly hunter green, accented with bright white and varying intensities of salmon. Dana's lavender bedroom doesn't exactly blend, but self-expression for a teenager is a lot more important than blending in with her mother's color scheme. At least I think so. "Thank you, Mother, for your decorating opinion."

"Not that your house isn't lovely, Teddi. For Syosset. Of course, if this was Cedarhurst, people might assume you were brought up on the wrong side of Peninsula Boulevard. But, since none of my friends will ever see it, what difference does it make? You needn't worry about embarrassing me."

"Thank you again," I say. "It was the primary worry of my life until now. But it's been replaced with dinner. What did you have in mind?"

"Well, if my advice isn't important to you…" she says, her

voice trailing off as she sits down on Dana's bed, looking peeved. She is no more peeved than I am, no more dejected.

My God, did I actually think, *hope*, that one day she and I would bond, have what other mothers and daughters have? Sometimes it feels as if we are actresses, saying the same lines, playing the same roles, time after time, and still not getting anything right.

What role do I play with my mother? The long-suffering victim? The wronged one? The martyr? Isn't that what Dr. Benjamin asked me? Isn't it what she meant when she asked me why I was taking June home to my house? Because I need to be the martyr?

And what role does my mother play? The Wicked Witch of the West? Faye Dunaway in *Mommy Dearest?* Joan Crawford in *Mildred Pierce?*

"Of course your advice is important," I say, kicking myself for being so easily manipulated, telling myself it doesn't count if I am a willing accomplice. "But Dana's at a sensitive stage right now."

"And I'm not?" my mother asks, one eyebrow raised. "I'm not fresh out of the hospital? You're worried about her feelings and not mine?"

"I worry about everybody's feelings," I say. "And right now I'm feeling hungry. How about we walk up to the Plainview Shopping Center and have dinner at Kebobs?"

"Walk?" she asks.

"Well, I thought we could stop at Carvel on the way back and use up the calories."

If my mother knows what is going on, she doesn't say, and

I am grateful. It's not going all that badly until I take her into the kitchen in the daylight.

She clutches at her heart dramatically when she sees the piles of dirt out the window. Actually it is amazing she can see *through* the windows with all the dirt and dust clinging to them. I have had Mr. Windows come four times to clean them, but it is hopeless. Of all the zillions of things I've forgotten lately, how could I ever have forgotten to prepare my mother for the idea of a pool in the backyard? Dr. Benjamin will no doubt have a field day with that little slip.

"Oh, right. I didn't tell you about the pool, did I?" I say as brightly as I can.

"Remember your slippers," my mother says simply. "The floors are cold there."

I ask her where, but she just looks at me like I ought to know. Oh. There.

"Are you okay?" I ask her when I see that she is shaking. "I could close the blinds in here."

"I bet they have some good name for that," she says, fingering the newly upholstered kitchen chairs.

I am about to tell her *self-delusion* when she apparently finds the word she is looking for herself.

"Chenille."

"Actually, it's cordless corduroy," I correct her, tucking one of the chairs under the table. "I've got to turn off the hose on the rosebush," I add as I slip out of my loafers and into the rubber garden clogs I wear in the backyard, noticing as I do that Rio has accidentally left a couple of things by the back door. "Oh, shoot." I hold up Rio's hat and rifle.

"No, don't shoot," my mother says in response.

"Guess *he* won't be shooting," I say. "Guess I'm not really too sorry about that."

"It's a very low-class hobby, Teddi," my mother says as she fiddles with a cigarette but doesn't light it. "It's something you'd expect from trailer trash. And it's time the man gave it up."

I don't answer her because not only do I agree, but what is really going through my head is that a man going hunting wouldn't forget his rifle. I am thinking about how Rio has hardly made love to me for months. And how that's been— like his going away for the weekend—a relief. Holding his rod, I admit to myself that something has been missing between us for a long time.

"I'm an idiot," I tell my mother as I pick up the phone and dial. "I couldn't see what was smack in front of my face."

Bobbie answers on the first ring. "Hello?"

I take a deep breath. When Mike left her she made a big deal about telling me that until I was in her shoes, I couldn't tell her what I'd really do if Rio left. I tell her that now I'm allowed to tell her.

"What are you talking about?"

I tell Bobbie that Rio is obviously having an affair. Rather than poo-poo it, Bobbie says sympathetically, "Oh, baby! You know I didn't wish this on you, don't you?"

"Of course I know that," I say. "I'm lucky that I have you to turn to. Can you come over?"

There is a moment's hesitation on Bobbie's part. "Uh, sure. I can come over for a little while," she says, adding something vague about having something to do.

There must be a new subway line beneath my kitchen, or some fault in the earth disturbed by the pool excavation. What else explains the fact that I feel the ground shifting beneath me? Rio is gone. And now Bobbie has something to do.

"Teddi? Don't be mad. I tried to tell you, but you didn't want to hear it. And I didn't want you to hate me."

I don't say anything. My mother is studying me, her eyes narrowing to slits as if that will help her hear better.

"I knew you wouldn't like this," Bobbie says.

This is ridiculous, I tell myself. Just because Rio is off hunting without a rifle and Bobbie can't come over doesn't mean...ridiculous!

"And I know that you wouldn't do it, if you were in my shoes."

Well, Bobbie's shoes won't be on for long, will they?

"But I've never been as strong as you are."

Oh, puh-lease! I turn away so that my mother can't read my face.

Bobbie waits and then says, "You're not saying anything."

"You haven't actually told me anything yet," I answer, wanting to hear Bobbie choke on the words.

"Well, let's face it. You know what's going on. You could have called it. You know me better than I know myself. You know that I'm weak and I need a man in my life, and I need creature comforts and I'm not getting any younger."

"None of us are," I say, like it is a song to which I often sing the refrain.

"Yes, but you don't have to worry. Rio won't ever leave

you. After all, where can he go? Your father would fire him in a heartbeat."

My mother is crowding up behind me, trying to get close enough to hear Bobbie's words. I can almost hear her whispering *I told you so*.

"And there are the kids. They need a father."

"Don't they all?" I want to sound smart, but it comes out a whine.

"So when Mike asked—no, *begged*—me to let him come home, what was I supposed to do? Kick him to the curb? Stand on my principles? You can't eat principles, Teddi. You can't trade them at the store for the newest Diesel jeans."

"Mike?" I say, only the name comes out garbled by the tears that are filling my eyes.

My mother takes a step back and studies me while I squirm.

"You think I'm horrible," Bobbie says.

I meet my mother's gaze, vindicated. I am thinking that maybe, by some chance, my mother hasn't guessed where my mind ran to, and I vainly hope that I have fooled her. "No, I don't. Believe me, there are far worse things you could do than take Mike back. Far worse!"

"You think I'm doing it for the money."

Of course she's doing it for the money. And the status and the way of life she set her sights on twenty years ago. Isn't it all part of the package she was primed for from birth—grow up, get married, buy a house and fill its closets? And am I any better, any stronger? If I were in her Stuart Weitzman slides, would I teeter on my principles?

Have I ever?

"Of course I don't," I say, knowing it is what Bobbie wants to hear, and wondering, like Tina Turner, what love has to do with it. "But don't be so sure about Rio never leaving me. He could get a job somewhere else in a minute. He could get a woman somewhere else in half that."

There is silence on the other end of the line. "Bobbie?" My mother cocks her head like some spaniel.

"I think she hung up on me," I start to say, but my voice trails off when I hear footsteps on my back deck.

"So what's wrong?" Bobbie demands as she steps through the French doors.

"Nothing," I say, so used to giving that answer I'm not sure if I have ever given a different response to that question. I suddenly laugh out loud, and my mother and friend stare at me as if my marbles are rolling off the kitchen counter and bouncing on my terra-cotta floor.

"I was thinking about when I was having Dana, and my contractions started and Rio asked what was wrong, and I told him 'nothing.' My water had broken and I was in agony, not to mention scared, but what did I say? 'Nothing.' Talk about denial!"

"Honey, you've been in denial so long you could get elected president of Egypt," Bobbie says.

"Well, she might as well get on the ballot now," my mother says. "Seems to me she thought for a moment there that you and Rio were having an affair."

"Mom!"

My mother waves away my horror. "And now that you aren't, it doesn't occur to her that he could be hiding his salami in someone else's icebox."

"You really thought I would sleep with Rio?" Bobbie looks more horrified at the prospect than hurt by my suspicions.

Never good at lying, I nod, sniffing wildly.

"Teddi, your husband is good-looking, but he and I—" She shivers. "No way!"

I blow my nose while she continues to dig her own grave.

"It's not that he isn't… It's that I could never… I mean, there's you and I. I love you. I would never steal your husband. Maybe your Judith Leber handbag—the one with the stones? Or maybe the Gucci sweater your mother gave you. Your necklace with the diamonds… Something material, maybe. But not—" She shudders again, exchanges a look with my mother and then throws up her hands. "Not Rio."

I feel my neck. Is that where my missing necklace has gone? I want to shoot myself for even thinking it. "I guess I figured that I'd leave me if I was Rio. And I'd go running into your arms if I was stuck with me…."

"And I'd let him? You do not need your head examined— you need a fucking lobotomy! What did you think? That since I'm not getting any, anyway, what with Mike gone, I needed it so bad that I'd screw you along with him?"

"This isn't about you," my mother says, lighting up and of-fering Bobbie a cigarette. "It's about Teddi—"

"—who doesn't allow smoking in her house," I say, pull-ing the cigarette from my mother's hand and throwing it into the sink. I turn the water on and watch it soak through the thin paper over the tobacco. Without turning to face them, I admit quietly to Bobbie that Rio left on a hunting trip with-out his rifle.

"And he doesn't strike me as the bow-and-arrow type," my mother adds.

"He put at least two rifles in the Expedition this morning," Bobbie says, her hands folded across her chest. "Of course, I was passionately kissing him goodbye when I noticed this, and not merely getting the paper before the sprinklers beat me to it."

I know he has more than one rifle. We've fought enough about how many he could possibly need. The one with the long-range sight, the one with the night scope, the one with this, the one with that.

"I guess he's not so wrong about me being paranoid," I say, slumping against the counter and shaking my head.

"What's the difference between being smart and being paranoid?" my mother asks.

Bobbie and I both give up.

"A paranoid woman is just looking over her shoulder, while a smart woman is watching her back."

"I ate too much," my mother says when we get back to the house. It is a welcome change from "I can't believe she's taking that sonofabitch back," as though she cares what Bobbie does. Is the message really that she won't take her own sonofabitch back?

With her ensconced in Dana's room, I don't like the prospect. I play my phone messages, which, of course, she listens to intently.

"Hi Teddi. And hi there, June. I'm up at the cabin and I thought I'd just check how my girls are doing. This might sound funny, and I don't want to scare you, but there was a ratty-looking old truck at the end of the street when I left this morning, and now that I'm too far away to do anything about it, I'm starting to worry about it. I'm sure it's nothing, but don't forget to lock the doors before you go to bed. Where are you two, anyway? Give me a call when you get in. I'll leave my cell on. Love you."

Beep.

Beep.

"Teddi, where the hell are you? You should be back by now. I'm not getting any answer on our cell phone, and when I tried to check the messages to make sure nothing was wrong, I couldn't get the damn thing to work right. By the way, Teddi, I apologize for saying you didn't buy those melons I asked for last week. Why the hell you put them under the seat in the car, I don't know, but I'm sure they'll get the smell out at the car wash. Hope your mother isn't listening to this and thinking that, well, you know. Anyway, call me as soon as you get home."

"I don't like that man," my mother says when his messages are finished. She is standing by the kitchen sink. "If I throw up, do I not get the calories from that sundae? Is that how bulimia works?"

How should I know how bulimia works? Does she think that because it's so prevalent on L.I. they're giving courses in it at the local junior college? Maybe she thinks that Dana and I have taken a class together. Maybe we should, what with Dana worrying so much about her weight.

"Did you see a truck?" I ask her, ignoring my mother's less-than-enthusiastic attempts to stick her finger down her throat. I dial Rio's cell phone number and walk to the front window to look out. As I pull the curtains aside, a car seems to speed away from the house across the street.

The Cingular customer you are trying to reach is either on the phone or has traveled out of the area. Please try your call again later and…

"Well, of course he's out of the area," I say to the phone as I press the off button on the portable.

In the kitchen I can hear my mother retching.

"Mother, you get the calories," I shout. If the woman asks,

she has to want to hear that answer, right? "Stop trying to throw up in my sink!"

The phone in my hand rings as I am on my way to hang it up. "Hello?"

There is a slight crackling on the line.

"Rio? Is that you?"

A dial tone replaces the crackling.

"He must be in a bad cell area," I tell my mother, feeling bereft that I can't reach him.

"He's in a jail cell?" she asks, lifting her head from the sink. "What'd he get arrested for?"

"*Bad* cell," I repeat, helping her straighten up.

"Bad dude," she replies, pushing her hair off her face.

"You tired? Ready for bed?"

"You think all men are bad? Or only the ones we know?"

"I think," I say, "that there are good ones and bad ones. Like women, they're human."

"Well, we deserve better," she says. "Look at that friend of yours, taking back the man that walked out on her and the kids. I would never—"

"No, Mom, you wouldn't. That's why you're here, with me, and Bobbie's next door in Mike's arms. And I think you're right and she's right, because we all do what we need—it's as if we send out these vibes and the universe sends back what we're asking for, which isn't always what we want."

"What in the world are you talking about?" June asks.

"Well, maybe what Bobbie needed was to see what life was like without Mike, and when she did, it humbled her. And maybe you need to see what life is like without Dad."

"It won't humble me," June says.

"Then it will strengthen you," I agree.

"And what about you, Teddi? What if Rio is having an affair?"

Does she honestly think this has never occurred to me? That I've never wondered? Can she not know that this is someplace I simply cannot go? Not now? That if I worry about it, I have to allow for the possibility, and if I allow for the possibility, right now in my life, I might as well sign my own commitment papers?

"Mother," I say with all the conviction I can muster, "you heard his message. Did it sound like a man who is away with some woman? 'Call me? I'm worried about you?' Does that sound like a man who is off getting laid?"

My mother looks noncommittal. "It sounds like your father."

"What happened between you and Dad is different."

"How?" June asks.

When the phone rings, I can't resist announcing I've been saved by the bell.

"Where were you?" Rio shouts at me. "I'm going *oobatz* here with worry. I almost turned around and came on home."

"We went up to the shopping center to eat," I say. "Why were you so worried?"

"Christ, Teddi. I got two loonies home alone with matches. You keeping an eye on your mother? Whatever you do, don't let her fall asleep with a cigarette lit or anything, okay?"

"I'll make sure," I say. Even though my mother knows the rules about smoking in the house, I have no doubt that once she's closed Dana's door, she will not hesitate to light up and puff away.

"And keep an eye on her. Jeez, I never should have let you bring her home with you. What if she tries to off herself in our house? In Dana's room? How would the kid ever get over that?"

"Are you trying to scare the hell out of me, Rio? Because you're doing a good job," I tell him, stretching the kitchen phone cord as far as it will reach in order to keep an eye on my mother, who has gone down to the den.

"Two defenseless women," Rio says, almost to himself. "I don't know what I was thinking. I swear I'll never be able to live with myself if something happens to you."

"What could happen?" I ask.

"Oh, a break-in, some rapist on the loose looking for a gorgeous woman...."

"You think I'm gorgeous?" I ask, sucking in my stomach and regretting the Carvel I joined my mother in having.

"I'm telling you you're in danger, and you want to know if I think you look good? Yeah, you'll make one helluva corpse."

"Why did you say that?" I ask. Rio sounds almost certain that something not only can happen, but that it will.

"I don't know," he says, and I can see him scowling a couple of hundred miles away. "It's not like I'm late with a payment or anything...."

"You mean the men you used to know? You borrowed from them again, Rio? For Christ's sake!" I nearly bite my tongue. Rio has funny standards about using his Lord's name in vain. Not that Christ is his Lord anymore, but he always cringes when I say it, while all the *jeezes* that pass his lips don't seem to bother him at all.

"I didn't 'go to them,'" Rio says, and I don't miss the implication.

I don't ask him to explain. My plan was to grow up and be Elyse Keaton or Maggie Seaver, and instead I've become Carmella Soprano. Through the window I see a car with its headlights off cruising down the street.

"I happened to run into the Nose when I was getting the new grill for your car."

"You bought a hot grill for my car?" I can hardly breathe. Is there a bomb in the car like in *The Godfather*? Is Rio safe?

"I looked into it. I mean, I wasn't paying over a grand on top of that vet bill, Teddi," he says.

"Oh, Rio."

"Look, there's nothing to worry about. Bridge loans are nothing to these guys."

"Except that if you don't pay their bridge loan, they throw you off some bridge in a pair of cement shoes," I tell him.

"Nose was like a father to me," Rio says. "He'd never hurt you. You girls have some ice cream and watch a movie or something and I'll see you tomorrow night. I'll take care of everything when I get back."

"Take care of what?"

"The damn battery's beeping, Teddi. I'm gonna lose you."

"Go find a pay phone!"

"I'll recharge it and you can call me later, okay? I'm sure everything'll be okay."

"Rio!"

"Don't forget to lock the doors before you go to bed."

"Go find a pay phone!"

"You're breaking up."

"Rio?"

Breaking up? Try *cracking* up.

My mother finally heads off for bed around midnight, though how anyone can sleep after an entire pot of coffee, I don't know. I've only had two cups myself, and I am wired to the chandelier and jumping at every noise. Must be the three or four Valiums my mother ate as if they were M&M's.

By 1:00 a.m., I've started and put down three new books. I'm pacing between the living room and the kitchen, going from window to window watching for wayward cars and any motion in the bushes. The mounds of dirt in the yard are casting shadows that mock the 'mountains out of molehills' I am making with my ridiculous worries. I have the outside lights on as if I am expecting a 747 to land in the driveway, but I've turned off the inside lights so that any loan shark with the middle name of an animal or a body part won't be able to see inside and get a clear shot at me when he decides to make me an example.

Man, I can be morbid, I think as I feel my way around the kitchen and open the refrigerator for some light. Okay, for some light and some Mallomars. If I am pegged to die, anyway, why not go fat? Will Rio and David and my father groan at the weight of my casket? How embarrassing, I think, but it doesn't stop me from first taking one Mallomar, then two, and then bringing the whole box out along with a carton of milk.

Well, it must take a few hours for the weight to make its way to your thighs, right? I think this while sitting at the counter bar stool fiddling with the box of cookies and peering out into the backyard. I hear a cat screech in the darkness, and one of the backyard lights goes out. When is the last time I changed the bulbs?

Oh, right. Never.

When was the last time Rio changed them? A couple went out during a party for one of the kids. Must have been Jesse, whose birthday is in April.

My fingers search the Mallomar box in the dark, counting the remaining cookies. Four. I've already eaten three. Seven Mallomars will mean a good-size ring around my middle—one of those hang-over-the-top-of-the-jeans rolls of flesh that make it impossible ever to wear a crop top again. Of course, I am too old for crop tops, anyway. Four will mean I'll have to lie down on the bed to zip my jeans up, but they'll still close. If I live, I'll join LA Weight Loss tomorrow. In the meantime, I eat the fourth cookie and fumble in the cupboard for a glass.

"Mom?" I call out when I hear what may be a footfall on the steps. "You up?"

I hear a second step.

Oh, shit.

This is either the price of an overactive imagination or …

"Mom?" I call more loudly. Dark mountains of dirt loom outside, just feet from the deck. I stand in the unlit kitchen, my eyes seeing nothing outside, realizing now that the other backyard light is off, too.

Coincidence? I reach in the dark for the phone and hold it to my chest. Call 911? And say what? That my backyard lights have blown?

I punch in Rio's cell phone number, whispering prayers that he'll be there, that he'll answer.

"Hello?" He sounds as if I'm waking him up.

"Come home." It is all I can get out.

"Now? It's… What the hell time is it?"

I look at the clock on the microwave. It reads 11:02. I look at the one on the stove. It reads 2:18. The one on the kitchen TV/VCR flashes 12:00. "I'm not sure," I whisper into the phone. "It's really late. And the lights in the yard went out and I heard footsteps."

"Jesus Christ, Teddi. The cabin is a good three hours away from home and it's the fucking middle of the night. What lights went out?"

"In the yard. One minute there were two lights on, and then there was one, and now there aren't any."

"They both went out? Shit."

"*Shit?* That's not what you're supposed to say. You're supposed to say that you put them in within minutes of each other, and that these things are probably standard. That they're made to last a certain amount of time. That the lights are always on together, so sure they'd blow at the same time."

That makes more sense than someone winding their way around the hole in my backyard at 3:00 a.m. unscrewing my light bulbs. Unless they want to use the hole to dump dead bodies in.

That's it.

No more *Sopranos* for me.

"Actually, I changed only the one that went out at Jesse's party. I meant to change the other this weekend, but... Anyway, you didn't hear anything, right?" he asks.

I admit hearing a footstep.

"Outside?"

I suppose it could have been, but I don't think so.

"It's probably your mother, right?" Rio asks.

"She's asleep—" I start to say when I hear the flushing of an upstairs toilet and feel like an idiot. "I didn't think she was up."

"Okay, this is what I want you to do. Make sure all the lights inside the house are off. That way no one can see in."

"Who *no one?*"

"No, turn on the light in the den, but do it from the top of the steps. Don't go down there, Teddi. You hear me?"

"Come home, damn it!"

"I'm coming," he tells me, and adds, "What a night for there to be no moon." I can almost see him shaking his head.

"Are you in the car yet?"

"Almost. Teddi, go to bed. It's late. I'll get dressed, have some coffee and be home before you wake up in the morning."

"Go to bed? Are you crazy? What if there's someone out there who wants to kill us? Remember that woman who got killed in her bed while her kids were getting ready for school? It happens, Rio, right here on Long Island."

"I remember," he says. No words of reassurance, no saying that was different.

"And there was that man in the restaurant on Jericho Turnpike," I remind him. "And I can see a car going up and down the street with its lights off," I say as I stand against the wall and peek out the front window.

"Look, I'm on my way, okay? You want me to call the cops and ask them to cruise by?"

"Would they do that?" That would make me feel better. Just knowing they are outside there.

"I'll call them. You make sure the doors are locked. Oh, sweet Jesus!"

"What *sweet Jesus?* Do you think the Nose is out there, Rio? Is that it?"

"No. Nothing like that. I just remembered something." It sounds as if he is fumbling with the phone, maybe getting dressed while we speak.

"What? What did you remember?"

"I told you, it's nothing. I'll tell the police this isn't like the last time. Just 'cause you called them about your father moving your car that time doesn't mean they won't come now."

Look, it was an innocent mistake. Anyone would have called the police if their car was moved out of the driveway. How was I supposed to know that Jesse had given my dad the keys so that he could pull his car into the driveway to unload?

"I told them when they came that it was all a mistake, Rio. They were very nice about it."

"See? Then there's no reason to get yourself all worked up."

"Rio?"

"You have to calm down, Teddi. It's not good for you in your state. "

"Rio, you're scaring me to death."

"Listen. Maybe I should call your doctor—"

I remind Rio that she said something about not being available.

"I'm coming home. Okay? Maybe you should get one of my guns out of the shed, in case…"

"There is one in the kitchen. Come home, Rio," I say. There is no flashlight beam in the yard, no movement that I can see. "Now."

"I'm coming. Make sure all the doors are locked. You want me to stay on the phone with you while you check them? Teddi? Teddi? Shit. Can you hear me?"

"Rio?"

"What are you doing down here in the dark?" My mother's voice drifts down into the kitchen, and then, before I can stop her, she flips on the light, nearly blinding me with its brightness.

"Turn it off!" I shout at her, and then call Rio's name into the phone.

There is no answer.

"What's going on?" my mother demands. "I didn't hear the phone ring. It must be all that Valium. I could sleep through Armageddon."

I think about Rio's friend, the Nose. Is he going to leave some message on my back porch? Is Igor, Bobbie's cat, doomed?

"Why are we standing here in the dark?" my mother whispers.

"So that if there is someone in the yard, he can't see us," I answer.

"Someone's in the yard? In the hole?"

"There's no one there," I try to reassure my mother. "I thought I heard footsteps, but they must have been you."

She makes her way across the room and from the shadows I can tell that she is crouching by the window. "I can't see a bloody thing," she says.

Why my mother chooses that expression, I don't know. It's like her, though, to make a bad situation worse without even trying. "I'm sure there's no one out there," I say. I was right about bringing my mother back to the house. With her here, I can't fall to pieces. "Let's go up to bed."

I turn on the light, mumbling something about just being silly, and lead my mother toward the stairs.

And then I hear it. A scraping sound, like someone dragging a ladder against the vinyl siding.

"Oh, my God!" my mother says, digging her nails into my arm. "Someone is out there."

"Go up to my bedroom and call the police," I say. My mother takes two steps and then turns back.

"What are you going to do?"

"I'm turning off the lights," I say, flipping the switch and then crawling on all fours to make sure that the back door is not only locked, but that the bolt is thrown. Didn't I check it before? Not once, not twice?

Obsessive-compulsive disorder. What a time to develop that. The truth is that after all the years of being terrified that something awful is going to happen to me, it simply doesn't seem possible that it will. The lights, the noises, the car across the street—they're all easily explained away.

For a moment I am calmer, feeling my way along the door frame, rising to the dead bolt and checking that it is straight across. But as I begin to let my hand drop—no, before it actually drops—the bolt turns itself, as if someone is moving it from outside.

Shit. If someone really is breaking into my kitchen, the first thing they are going to find is me. I imagine Rio getting home at daybreak to find my raped and mutilated body splayed across the terra-cotta tiles, my mother on the phone telling my father that Angelina will have to come clean up the mess.

I reach up and turn the lock again, letting them know there is someone awake in the house, in the kitchen. "I called the police," I shout through the door, starting to scramble back and knocking something over on the way.

My hand traces the barrel of Rio's rifle.

"Don't come in here!" I shout. "I've got a gun!"

And then the door bursts open, and instead of everything happening in slow motion, the way it does on TV, everything happens too fast for me to understand. There is a man in the doorway, a light beam that crosses the kitchen and shines in my eyes. There is a grunt and a thud and sirens and lights, all at once.

And there is blood, everywhere.

And in the distance, through some fog in which I feel lost, I keep hearing my mother's voice.

"Oh, my God!" the voice keeps saying. "It's Rio!"

CHAPTER 24

There are three police cars parked in the circular driveway outside my house. I know this because I can see the lights dancing around in the glass doors on my kitchen cabinets, reflecting in the window over the sink, shimmering on the shiny red stains that splattered the walls. And then again, it isn't the first time police lights have ever swirled around a home I've lived in.

Or even the second time, when a month after they came to take Markie away in a body bag, they came back to escort my mother—first to North Shore Hospital, and then eventually to South Winds. But never, in all the intervening years, did I think that the police would come for me.

Uh, not. Haven't I actually always thought they would? A shrill laugh escapes me, and I cover my mouth with my hands, but the policemen have heard. Rio has heard.

"Just let me talk to her," Rio keeps saying, pulling away from the cops, who are still leaning over him, still assessing the damage I've done. "I'm all right. I'm just damn lucky it was the paint gun. I don't get why she…"

The shrill laugh comes again, unbidden, unstoppable. I love his paint gun. Adore it! Imagine that! All these years of complaining about his war games, and now I am thanking God and Mother Nature and anyone who might listen for inventing guns that don't kill husbands who aren't expected home.

"He was in the Catskills," I say to no one in particular, though one officer, a woman who seems a little younger and a lot firmer than I, is crouching beside me and patting me gently every now and then. "And I heard a noise. I thought I was crazy, hearing noises, you know?"

"She's seeing a shrink," Rio explains to the cops, as if the noises I heard were all in my head.

I direct my words to Rio. "No. There was a noise. You were the noise. I'm not crazy, Rio. You were in the yard. Only I don't understand how you got home so quickly."

"I called her from the cabin—my friend's got a cabin up in Wunderlaken—and she sounded scared, so I told her I'd come home. I had no idea she was so—"

"What time is it?" I ask. There is a ringing in my ears, and everyone is still talking and moving too fast for me. No one answers me, but it doesn't really matter. "How could you possibly get home so fast?" I ask. "We hung up five minutes ago."

Rio is sitting on the floor, rubbing at the area on his chest where the latex paint ball hit him. Several times the policemen have tried to help him get to his feet, and each time he starts to get up, he puts his hand up to signal them to let him be.

"I'm a little woozy," he tells them. "Close range, no vest…"

"You want us to call an ambulance?" one of the officers asks.

"No, God no!" Rio tells them. "Not for me, anyway. Teddi? You want…"

"I want to know how you got home so fast," I say. Well, I want that and for everyone to stop taking Rio's version as the truth. "What time is it?" I ask again, trying to remember what time any of the clocks read before. "I was on the phone with you. Mom? Didn't you hear me on the phone with Rio right before he came in?"

"My daughter would never hurt a soul," she tells the cops. Isn't that the sort of thing the neighbors always say when the police arrest some mass murderer? *He always seemed so nice, like he wouldn't harm a soul.*

"Mom," I say, trying not to sound as though I am coaching her. "Just tell them about how I was on the phone right before Rio came in."

She looks apologetically at me. "Well, she *was* holding the phone," she admits. "And then we heard a noise. I went up to call you. I heard the shots."

"Shots?" one of the cops asks.

"Three, maybe four," June says. "Will you look at all that dirt on the floor? We'll need to call a service, Teddi."

"I fired four times?" I ask. That, I suppose, explains the paint on the ceiling and on the cabinets.

"Teddi, honey," Rio says. "You fired half a dozen times. I'd be dead if it'd been one of my other guns."

"And if she had better aim," June says. "If she played more video games with Jesse, you'd have probably gotten it between the eyes. And if you'd come home a few hours ago, when she was sure you were having an affair with Bobbie, you'd have probably gotten it in the—" My mother has the decency to blush.

"Ma'am?" one of the officers addresses me. "Were you angry with your husband?"

"Wait a minute," Rio says, finally coming to his feet and moving toward me. "Where is this going?"

The officer's notepad is out, and he looks at Rio and then at me. "Ma'am? Did you intend to shoot your husband?"

Rio looks shocked. He takes a step back and stares at me. "You thought I was having an affair?" he asks, incredulously. "With 'sweet cakes' next door?"

"When I saw the rifle by the back door," I say.

"So you knew the rifle was there," the officer says.

"Don't you say another word," Rio instructs me before turning toward the cops. "This looks bad, but it's not the way it looks. My wife is...well, she's been...okay, basically, she's been having a nervous breakdown. I never should have left her this weekend. This is really all my fault. I knew she was on the edge..."

"Then you don't want to press charges?" the lady cop asks. "This was—"

"A weapon was discharged here," the other cop says. "We can't just refer it to family court for counseling, Betsy—"

"It was a paint gun," the lady cop, Betsy, says. "I suppose, if he won't press, we could list it as a domestic dispute."

"I was not trying to hurt my own husband," I insist. "I thought he was a hit man."

Rio groans. "A hit man? Jeez, Teddi."

"Because of the loan," I say, a small piece of me worried that maybe borrowing money from the wrong people is a crime and that I am implicating Rio.

"The loan? You mean the bank loan? The papers are in the drawer. Remember I showed you?" he asks.

I guess it is a crime, and I nod. "The bank. Right."

"What I don't get," Rio says, "is that after you called me and I told you I was a couple of blocks from the house, why you—"

"You said you were up in the cabin," I say. "You said you were three hours away."

"Earlier," he agrees, and then turns to the police. "I called her around midnight, and she asked me to come home."

"No, not then. I asked you later. A few minutes ago," I say. The police look at Rio.

"She gets confused. Thinks things have happened, thinks she's done things—bought things, made calls. And she did call me a few minutes ago," he admits. Aha! "But I told her I was nearly home, not to worry. She's been a basket case lately. I should have known something like this would happen. I told the doctor that she was getting paranoid, but her shrink thought—"

"I am not paranoid! I was scared to death, a man coming into my house in the dead of night. I thought he was going to rape and murder me. I was glad the kids weren't here—"

"Oh, my God. The kids. What if the kids had been here, Teddi? What if they'd witnessed this? Or what if one of them startled you and—"

"Stop it!" I put my hands over my ears and begin to hum. "I can't hear this. I can't take this."

"Take it easy, ma'am," the lady cop says, and her hand clamps tightly on my shoulder. What I haven't realized until now is that this woman is not on my side.

"Look," Rio says in a voice that announces how reasonable he is trying to be, despite the circumstances. "What if I promise she'll get help? What if she agrees to go over to South Winds and—"

"We could take her to North Shore Hospital's psychiatric ward for evaluation," the lady cop suggests, crouching and putting her hand on my knee. "Would you like to do that? See a doctor? He might be able to help you calm down a little, you know?"

"I've got Valium," my mother offers. "That's all she needs."

The lady cop shoots my mother a dirty look. "Ma'am? It's against the law to dispense medicine without a prescription, which is what you're doing, in effect, when you give someone else a pill prescribed for you."

"Sure. *That's* against the law," my mother says. "A man can take the distributor cap out of the car he stole from his wife, steal her keys, and that's okay. But when I offer her something that will make her feel better, will calm her down and—"

My mother is making a lot of sense. It is always a bad sign when my mother makes any sense at all. When she makes more sense than four cops and my husband, it is a bad, bad sign.

"I never—" Rio starts, but my mother interrupts him.

"Marty doesn't even know what a distributor cap is. If he says you took it off, then you must have told him you did. And I know that she couldn't drive us to dinner," she tells Rio. Then she turns to me. "The Prince of Pizza here has been whining and moaning about you to Marty and David."

"Who are Marty and David?" one of the cops asks.

"Her father and brother," Rio answers dismissively, turning his attention to me. "Listen, honey. Dr. Benjamin said if you ran into trouble while she was gone, I should call Max Cohen and he'd take care of everything."

"Dr. Benjamin thought I was going to run into trouble?" I ask. I can hear my own voice sounding dazed, confused.

"Teddi, you nearly fucking killed me. I'd call that more than 'running into trouble,' wouldn't you?"

"But she thought?" I ask, a vague memory of some psychiatrist thinking his patient was crazy playing at the edges of my mind.

"What if the kids had been here?" he repeats.

We mustn't disappoint the children. That's what it was. *Miracle on 34th Street,* when Doris doesn't believe in Kris, and he is so crestfallen at her doubting his sanity that he purposely fails his tests at the mental hospital. I am in the same boat as Edmund Gwenn. And it's like Doris Walker predicted for Kris—"Clang, clang, Bellevue."

"Mrs. Gallo?" Two officers kneel beside my chair, one on either side. Rio stands by the kitchen sink, his back to me, but I can see it shaking. "Do you want to go to Bellevue? Is that what you said?"

In the movie it takes a judicial hearing to get Santa out of Bellevue, so I shake my head. "South Winds. I'm willing to go to South Winds."

When Rio turns to look at me, his face is streaked with tears.

"You can use my room," my mother offers. "And my phone. But the sheets are taupe, Teddi, so you might want to bring your own."

The cops exchange glances with Rio. "Her mother," he says, as if that explains everything.

I suppose that maybe it does.

South Winds is nothing like *The Snake Pit*, I keep telling myself on the way over in the police car. I am not Olivia de Havilland. I have been here a million times before. Of course, each of those times I've been in the superior position of considerate guest, dutiful daughter. Now I am one of the wackos. What did my mother say the doctors call South Winds? Oh yeah. *The Bates Motel*. I am stuck in movie mode. Everything reminds me of some movie I've seen a hundred years ago.

But that is ridiculous. There weren't movies a hundred years ago.

I'm losing it, I admit to myself, silently, so that the policemen who sit in the front seat of the car—with a grill between me and them so that if I go crazy (like if I have another paint gun hidden in my brassiere), they'll be safe—won't hear me.

No, I've lost it. Gone down the drain. I wonder why they don't have bulletproof glass like the cabbies in New York. Can't I shoot them through the grill? Does that mean that society thinks cabbies are worth more than cops? They probably have a stronger union.

"How you doing, Mrs. Gallo?" one of the cops asks. I didn't recognize his Brooklyn/Italian accent before. I wonder if he hates Rio for marrying out of the faith.

"I like your new pope," I say. "I mean, he's no Pope John Paul II, but he seems like a nice-enough man."

The cop who is driving takes his eyes off the road to ex-change a glance with his partner. I don't have to see it to read it perfectly. *Loopy*. Well, I am definitely loopy.

"He's a nice man," the officer agrees.

"My mother-in-law thought John Paul was the next best thing to—" I am only digging a deeper hole for myself and unfortunately I'm not so crazy I don't realize it. So I sit here, uncomfortable, wishing the journey will end but praying we never get to South Winds.

Dr. Cohen, who is like some distant uncle to me after all these years of caring for my mother, comes down the hospi-tal steps as soon as the cruiser comes to a stop. On his heels is my father. Each of them takes one of my arms as a police-man helps me out of the car, protecting my head like they do on the cop shows on TV.

Why am I so lost in movies and TV? Because everything feels like a dream, or a show in which I have been horribly miscast?

"Teddi," Dr. Cohen says warmly. I have always liked his voice—low, even, understanding. But I don't like it tonight. Tonight it sounds patronizing. "I haven't seen you in a long time."

"Not professionally," I agree. He only saw me a couple of times when I was in junior high and wearing black so often that my father insisted I was clinically depressed. Dr. Cohen pronounced my ailment at the time as *thirteen-itis*. He'd patted me in a way that would probably be misinterpreted in these days as abuse, but which seemed rather fatherly at the time.

"You okay, honey?" my father asks when we get up to the top step and the bright overhead lights make us all look ghoulish. My father's chin stubble is white in the harsh glare, and he looks older than the Grim Reaper. And about as jolly.

"I'm fine, Dad," I say. "I tried to kill my husband with a paint gun, ruining both my life and my kitchen. I've abandoned my mother, don't know what I'll tell the kids, and feel like I really failed Dr. Benjamin. Other than that, I'm great."

"Don't worry about your mother," he says. "I'm going to go pick her up on my way home. I've let her get away with this crap long enough."

"Not wanting to stay in the same house with your husband and his mistress is not exactly crap, Dad," I say as Dr. Cohen talks quietly with the police officers a few steps down from us.

"Yeah, well, she didn't mind for thirty years," my father says, shoving his hands in his pockets as if it isn't a good eighty degrees outside despite the hour.

"She didn't know for thirty years," I correct him.

But I am wrong. I can see it in his eyes, in the clear-conscienced way he stares back at me, not saying the truth, but not needing to.

"Maybe I shouldn't have told you," he says. "Not now when you're not feeling so good."

Dr. Cohen takes the steps between us two at a time, an impressive feat for a man his age. "Let's get you settled, shall we?" he says, as if he is the lord of the manor and I am an honored guest. "I'm glad your husband decided to call me. I had no idea that you'd decided not to see Dr. Benjamin anymore. There are several other excellent doctors I can recommend—"

I suppose that Rio has decided that if she hasn't cured me it's time to try someone else. Patience has never been one of his virtues. But luckily, the decision isn't Rio's. "I don't want anyone else," I tell Cohen. "I want Dr. Benjamin. Rio must have misunderstood me or something," I add, not wanting Cohen to think that Rio would do something behind my back.

"Well, I'm perfectly capable of getting you settled in and comfortable in the meantime," Dr. Cohen says. He is disgustingly cheerful for 4:00 a.m. "You must be exhausted after the night you've had. Why don't we get you tucked in and get some breakfast set up for the morning?"

"Don't you want to ring for a bellman?" I ask sarcastically, but Dr. Cohen doesn't seem attuned to my sense of humor. I try again. "What's the difference between a psychiatrist and God?"

Cohen looks at me as if my brains are oozing out my ears.

"God doesn't think he's a psychiatrist."

I don't even get a smile.

"A brain surgeon and God?" I ask.

Nothing. I sigh and allow him to hold the door open for me. The brightly lit lobby of the hospital looks very different from all the times I've come to see my mother. Then I've always found the hospital quiet, serene. I know, of course, that there are emotions being held in check, but I've always felt that after all the visitors leave, after all the company is gone, the inmates get to take over the asylum, much the way I used to imagine that after I was asleep at night my dolls and toys got up and went off on adventures.

Sometimes I really get carried away with my own impor-
tance. If dolls can play, why would they care if I saw them?
And if the people here at South Winds are lunatics, why
would they care if I saw them, either?

At any rate, there are no loonies milling about the hospital lobby. There's only a tired-looking nurse, who comes out
from behind her desk to take me to my room.

"I've ordered a sleeping pill for you," Dr. Cohen says. "Your
first night here is bound to be a little strange and I don't want
you losing any sleep."

"Do I have to take it?" I ask.

"What would it hurt?" my father asks.

"Dr. Cohen," I say, letting him take my hand and massage
the back of it softly, soothingly as we stand there waiting for
the nurse to gather a bag of toiletries and a fresh towel for
me. "Could I ask you one small favor?"

"You can ask me for the moon," Dr. Cohen says. "I can't
promise you I'll deliver, but I'll do my best."

"You are going to call Dr. Benjamin for me, right?" Even
if I do get committed, I would have some say in what doctor
treated me, wouldn't I?

He nods. "Of course I will, if that's what you want."

"Well, wait until Monday morning, so we don't ruin her
weekend, okay? And when you speak to her, tell her that I'm
really all right, that it was a misunderstanding, and that I can
explain everything."

"You're not disappointing anyone," Dr. Cohen says, letting
go of my hand as the nurse takes my arm. It's as if no one feels
safe letting go of me unless someone else is holding on to me,

as if I am free-falling and by passing me hand to hand they can somehow break my fall.

I merely nod. Did I really think I was the only liar living on Long Island? Now, that would be grounds for commitment, wouldn't it?

CHAPTER 25

When I wake up, there is cotton in my mouth. I can barely swallow around it, can barely breathe. Gagging, I sit up in bed and put my fingers into my mouth, only to find nothing there at all.

I'd hoped for blissful oblivion—to think, when I first woke up, that I was back in my house, that all was right with the world.

Instead, before my eyes are fully open, I am well aware of where I am, of the fact that the sleeping pill has only half worked. Well, how long can a person sleep anyway? They'd put me to bed when I arrived, woke me several times for what they referred to as vitals, and now I'm not even sure what day it is. I am, however, acutely aware of where I am and why I am here.

There is no clock in my room, and for a second I feel a rising panic at not knowing the time—as if I will be adrift with no anchor in reality. I touch my wrist, feel my watch, and let go of the breath I am holding. It is barely seven o'clock.

Before I am out of bed, there is a soft knock at the door and a head pokes in.

"Oh, you're awake!" a nurse in a Pepto Bismol-pink uniform says. "Good. Doctor's on his way and you don't want to be in your jammies, now do you?"

"Which doctor?" I ask, wondering if it sounds to the nurse like *witch doctor*, and wondering if there is any difference.

"Your doctor, of course," the nurse says, opening my closet. "Oh, what lovely things your husband brought by yesterday. You'll be a regular glamour puss to see the doctor!" Great. It matters what I'm wearing to greet the doctor? Frankly, my mother has always seemed ridiculously overdressed with her bouffant hairdo and her perfectly polished nails at South Winds. Aren't crazy people supposed to wander around dazed, their hair stringy, wearing thin terry robes and scruffy slippers?

"Come on now, honey," the nurse continues. "We need to get washed up and see about getting you a breakfast tray. We don't want to keep doctor waiting."

Well, I'm not crazy enough to find the nursing *we* any less irritating than the royal one.

"I'm not very hungry," I say. "I can wait."

"And have doctor yell at me for not feeding you? I don't think so, honey lamb. I think we'll have some nice oatmeal and maybe a cup of decaf or tea?"

"Whatever," I agree, not willing to fight about breakfast. I can't think of anything worth fighting over.

"Which doctor did you say?" I ask again, praying it will be Dr. Benjamin, then praying it isn't, so that she won't see me like this.

The nurse looks patronizingly at me, obviously thinking that I can't follow a conversation.

"I have two. Well, I have one, but it could be one or the other. Of two." I decide to drop it and put on the clothes that the nurse lays out for me.

"What day is it?" I ask, and am told that I arrived on Sunday very early in the morning and it is now not quite that early on Monday. I've lost a whole day. She compliments me on my flowers and the looks of the husband who brought them and who is now waiting outside to see me.

With a warning to Rio that "doctor" is on his way, and that "nurse" will be back in a moment with my breakfast, she leaves us alone.

He steps into my room gingerly, reminding me of when I gave birth to his children. Like then, he comes toward my bed looking shy and worried with a handful of flowers preceding him. Unlike then, this isn't exactly cause for celebration.

"How you feeling?" he asks, his voice cracking in the quiet of the room. "You okay? I came half a dozen times yesterday, but you were always asleep. I brought flowers," he says, gesturing toward two arrangements on my bureau.

"Thanks," I say, figuring that it is the flowers that have given me the sinus headache that makes it hard to open my eyes all the way. "They gave me some pills and I got a good rest and now I'd like to go home."

"I know, honey, but you can't." He stares at his hands.

"What do you mean I *can't?*"

"Come on, Teddi. You know what I mean. You could have killed me the other night. As it is, you probably took a couple years off my life, scaring me like that, standing there pointing that gun at me, telling me you were going to kill me."

"I never said I was going to kill you," I say. I don't remem-

ber that. I only remember being scared to death that someone was going to kill me. "If you'd only said it was you. If you'd
only come in the front door like—"

"My boots were dirty. For that I deserve to be shot?"

"Of course you didn't deserve to be shot. But I don't deserve to be here. It's not like I meant to shoot you. I thought
you were a burglar."

"A burglar? I talked to you on the phone a couple minutes
before I got there," he says. "I told you I was on the way."

"Yes, but you were three hours away. There was no way it
could be you—"

"No? Well, it was. I got bruises on my chest and paint in
my hair to prove it. And you should see the goddamn kitch-
en."

"I was defending myself and my home. A person has a right
to do that."

"Sure they do, under the right circumstances. But I told
you to go to bed and I'd be right there."

"No, you said—"

Rio sits down on the edge of my bed and puts his head in
his hands. "You went over the edge, Teddi. Round the freakin' bend. A different gun, a different time, and you'd have
killed me, and maybe one of the kids."

The thought is more than I can take. I want to scream, but
it would only make me look as crazy as Rio thinks I am. I want
to hide under the bed, lock myself in the bathroom, climb
through the little window, which I think is too small for me
to escape through. Of course it would be. I am, in effect, in
prison, aren't I?

"I want to go home. I only shot at you because you said you were—"

"Listen to me, Teddi. You haven't been right for months. You can't remember shit, you imagine things that aren't there, and you're a danger now. Do you understand that? That you could hurt someone? That you could hurt yourself?"

"You tricked me," I say. "You told me that you were coming home—"

"And I came home. What the hell kind of trick is that? The same kind that puts money in your wallet?" He is off the bed now, pacing the room like a caged animal. "Maybe they can help you here. Maybe after a few weeks…"

"A few weeks!" My voice comes out a squeak. "Please take me home, Rio. I'll concentrate harder. I'll—"

There is a knock on the door, and Rio opens it. Dr. Benjamin, dressed in yet another of her silk sweater sets, stands in the doorway.

I slip off the bed and come to stand behind Rio in the doorway. "Dr. Benjamin? Thank God you're here!"

Rio is clearly less happy than I am to see her. "What are you doing here? I didn't ask for you to come."

"I did." I say it quietly but with finality.

"And that's why I'm here," she says directly to me, cutting Rio out of the conversation.

"She lost it," Rio tells her, as if it's all her fault and if she'd listened to him… "She went over the edge, like I told you she would. You know, you're damn lucky it was the Tippman Pro Carbine I left in the kitchen, or I'd sue the freakin' shirt off your back."

The doctor looks more amused than frightened. "You want to calm down, Mr. Gallo? You aren't doing your wife any good by carrying on like this."

"You're just lucky I didn't die or I'd be suing you for all you're worth—" Rio shouts again, but she cuts him off.

"Then I guess we're both lucky you're alive," she tells Rio, mirroring his hands-on-hips stance. She shoots me a look as if to ask if I get the irony, but I don't want to go there. My entire marriage has been ironic. At the moment, it feels as if my entire life has been ironic.

"I thought he was breaking into the house," I say, only my voice seems slightly slurred, almost as if I am drunk.

"You all right? Did you sleep?" she asks me. "You think you're up for a session?" She waits for me to nod and then holds the door, motioning for Rio to leave us alone. Before he leaves, Rio signals for her to come out into the hall with him. She tells me she'll be right in and closes the door behind her so that I can't hear what my husband is no doubt telling her.

What? I can't guess? *Teddi's out of control. She tried to kill me. She's a danger to my kids. She's losing her mind. She's blah, blah, blah.*

"Can I tell you my side?" I ask her when she finally extricates herself from Rio and comes into the room. She pulls out the chair from the little desk by the window and perches on it facing my bed.

"There aren't any sides here, Teddi," she says, gesturing for me to hop up on the bed rather than just stand there with my arms folded over my chest.

I sit reluctantly, refusing to lie down.

"You didn't mean to shoot him, did you?"

"Of course not," I say. But there must be something about the way I say it that surprises her, because I can see her filing my answer in the back of her mind. "Did I ruin your weekend? I told Dr. Cohen not to—"

She dismisses my concern with a wave and starts recapping the story as though she's been there and I haven't. When she gets to the part about how Rio told me that he was on his way home, I stop her. I tell her that I am hurt that she is taking Rio's version of the events for the truth.

"Rio was shot," she says. "Only you and your mother were there. Are you saying it was your mother who shot him?"

"Would you believe me if I said it was?"

I can see her struggling with the answer, wanting to say she'd believe me, but she can't. And she tells me as much.

"I see," I say, turning away and pretending to busy myself with the items in my nightstand drawer. There is only so much a person can do with a mustard-colored plastic bowl, a tube of toothpaste, a cheap comb and a sample tube of Neutrogena moisturizer. I put the moisturizer on my hands and then climb up onto the bed.

"Do you want to rest?" she asks me.

"I want to quiet the chaos," I say. For a few minutes neither of us says anything more. Then I tell her about Rio leaving without his gun, about suspecting that he was having an affair with Bobbie, about the Mafia, and being terrified and shooting at Rio when he came through the door.

She tries to appear unfazed by all the revelations—especially about the Nose.

"Had you taken any medication? Valium? A sleeping pill?" she asks, probably hoping that my imagination or my recollection could have been altered by drugs.

"No. I was in perfect control of my faculties. I mean, I was scared to death, but it was normal. I mean considering."

"Considering?"

"The lights in the yard were out. There was a car that kept going up and down the block with its lights off. There was a scratching…."

"I follow all of this," she says. "What I don't understand is why after speaking to him moments before, you didn't know it was your husband coming in the door."

"Because he was three hours away when he called. I spoke to him, he said he'd come home, and then he was there. It seemed like it was only moments, minutes."

"But it was hours after the first call. And the second one was blocks from the house. Your husband says that there will be phone records to corroborate his story."

"I'm already here. What does he need corroboration for? Does he think I'll sue him for getting in the way of my paint ball?"

CHAPTER 26

When I hear the footsteps in the hallway, I turn my back to the door and pretend I am asleep. People nap all the time in this place, from all the drugs, I suppose. Or maybe they are all pretending to, avoiding their husbands or wives or whoevers. I pull the blanket over my jeans and T-shirt and scrunch down as the doorknob turns.

"Honey?" I hear my father whisper. "You asleep?"

I roll over lazily and let my eyelids flutter open. "Dad," I say softly, so relieved that it isn't Rio that I forget I'm angry with him. "Shouldn't you be at the office?"

"What? I can't take off a little time? There's got to be some advantage to being the boss, besides the privilege of worrying twenty-four hours a day."

I ask if Rio is covering for him. Instead of answering, he asks if Rio's been to see me.

I say I think so, but that the doctor has given me very strong tranquilizers and I've been sleeping on and off, so I haven't really spoken to him.

"You hiding from Rio now, Teddi?" he asks. "Like you did from me? What're you gonna do when the kids come home at the end of the summer? You gonna be in here when they get back?"

"The kids," I say, shaking my head sadly. "Whatever am I going to tell those sweet, innocent kids?"

My father gets up and looks out the window. My room has a nice view of the grounds. People are sitting under trees, patients with their visitors, two nurses taking a smoking break.

"Whatever you tell them, it'll be smart. You've got so much more *seyckel* than me, Teddi. You're smarter than I ever was. You'll do a hell of a lot better than I did." This he says offhandedly. Then, sadly, softly, he adds, "I know I failed you, somehow."

"Dad," I start, but it's clear he has something to say.

"You do know I tried, don't you? I really did, but they don't give out instruction manuals when they hand you your kids. I didn't know what I was supposed to do with a little girl…and your mother…well, she wasn't much help.

"When Angelina came along, she tried to show me. Remember those times I took you to that ice cream parlor in New York City? And to the circus? Those were Angelina's ideas. I didn't know what a girl liked."

"Dad, I—" I start again, but he's rehearsed and he waves me quiet.

"I'm not saying that you should forgive me and her. I want you to understand…see that I'm not such a *mamzer* and Angelina's no slut. It sounds bad, honey, but it wasn't the sordid thing I know you're thinking. It came so naturally, after a while, her and me mothering you like we were, that we began to feel like your parents, like a couple.

"And then we were."

I am sniffing, rubbing at the corner of my eye, and he should be happy for the sympathy, but he doesn't look it.

"If any of this is my fault…if I wasn't the kind of father you needed, if what happened with Angelina, and you finding out, made this happen…"

He sits down in the chair by the desk and loosens his tie.

"It's all right, Dad," I say softly. "I've been growing up a little in the past few weeks, and I don't think things are as black and white as I did this spring."

"I always tried to protect you without smothering you. Whatever I did, your mother said I was wrong. When I objected to your boyfriends, she said I was jealous. I wanted you to have a happier life than we had.

"When you brought Rio home…" He stops to open the top button on his shirt. It looks like he is suffocating. "I tried to scare him off. He ever tell you that? He didn't scare. Not even when I presented him with that little agreement that everything you brought to the marriage, everything I gave you both, was really a gift to you. Signed away his right to anything you ever had, any inheritance, the house, any money I ever gave you. And he's been a good worker, Teddi. And a good father…"

"He signed some sort of prenup?" I am staring at him as if he's grown an extra head.

"He didn't tell you?"

I cock my head. This is all news to me.

"Well, I didn't trust him from the first, but you had your heart set on him. I thought about a prenup, but the lawyer told me you'd have had to sign it, so we did it instead as a contract between him and me. We called it an *outside-nup*, which made the lawyer laugh. He said it was a *separate-property agreement* or something like that. What it amounted to was that Rio would take out of the marriage exactly what he brought into it."

"Which was nothing," I say.

"That was why I bought you the house in my name and then signed it over to you—"

"But you didn't tell me because…?" I ask.

"Because you'd have made me change it," he says.

"And Rio didn't tell me?" I ask.

He looks surprised and says he figured that by now Rio had, actually.

I tell him that Rio has never breathed a word of it.

Apparently my father, fearing I would somehow undo it, or hate him for the rest of his natural life, had made Rio promise not to. It sounds good, but I suspect that Rio had his own reasons—like he was content to let me think that half of everything I owned was his.

"And no matter what happened in our lives," I ask him, "no matter how many children we had or how long we loved each other, if we split up he'd still get nothing? Even if I died and he had to take care of the kids?"

My father says that no one is dying, but he sees it doesn't satisfy me. "Pretty much he gets nothing," he admits. "Unless you were incapacitated or something like that. To be honest, I never expected him to stay around long enough for it to matter."

"Nice confidence, Dad," I say, wondering if it was Rio he was doubting, or my own worth.

CHAPTER 27

I am waiting near the lobby when Bobbie and Diane come through the front doors, and I run into Bobbie's arms as if I have returned from a war. The Hundred Years War.

Bobbie and Diane flank me as we walk back to my room. We walk down the hall in silence, nodding cordially at anyone we pass, Diane and Bobbie no doubt wondering what is the matter with each of them.

"Probably a jumper," Diane whispers when a man on crutches limps by, his leg in a cast.

"Slicer," Bobbie say of the woman with gauze around her wrists.

A young man in his twenties who stands facing the wall whips around suddenly, exposing himself to us.

Diane starts to say something, but Bobbie interrupts her. "Forget the caption," she tells her sister. "I saw the picture."

"And you're in here," Diane says sadly, shaking her head at me.

"Yeah, I am," I say, "so a little respect for the shell-shocked if you please."

"Well, you look fine," Bobbie says, taking in my jeans and T-shirt as if what I'm wearing in here matters. I swear she would be busy telling people what to wear as they were getting into the lifeboats on the *Titanic*.

"It's still me," I say, and hold out my arm to reveal a plastic hospital band with my name on it. "The jewelry's a little tacky, but then, I'm not going to a cotillion at the Meadowbrook Country Club, now am I?"

"The what?" Diane asks.

"Nowhere," I say. I perch on the edge of my bed, leaving the desk chair and the easy chair for my guests. "I'm going no place, slowly."

"That beats getting no place fast," Bobbie says.

I ask if Bobbie has spoken to her girls, and if everyone is all right. Bobbie assures me that she's spoken to hers and mine and that everyone everywhere is fine. That I ought to pack my bags and come home.

"She can't do that," Diane says, and her gaze keeps returning to the window in the door.

"You on surveillance or something?" Bobbie asks. "What's with the window?"

"I hate that window," I say. "I hate that anyone passing by can look in here."

"It doesn't seem fair that you're in here," Bobbie says. "I mean, what about goodness and kindness and all? Shouldn't they take that into account? Isn't that like mitigating circumstances?"

Diane pulls the chair out from the desk and plops down in it. "She's not in prison, *Barbara!*" That's Diane's polite way of calling Bobbie *stupid*. She pronounces it in two syllables like Barbra Streisand, drawing out the first one overly long. "She's somewhere that they can help her."

"I don't need help," I say. "I need to turn back the clock. Go back to before Mike left you and my mind left me and Dana got her period."

"Dana got her period?" Diane asks. "No one told me Dana got her period."

"It isn't a crime, Officer," Bobbie says. "We don't have to report to you on every little thing."

The light bulb goes off over Diane's head. "She beat Kristin and Kimmie, huh?"

"It's not a race," Bobbie reminds her, the same way she's reminded her kids.

"Yeah, right. Save that for the Ks."

I look at my watch. Almost eight-thirty. Visiting hours will be over in a few minutes. "I think I'll give Mike a call," Bobbie says, reaching for my phone and ignoring the look Diane and I exchange. "I think he's coming home tonight, is all."

"Mike," she says into the phone, "listen to me and don't say a word. I've given it a lot of thought. I've decided that I was crazy when I fell in love with you. That's why I'm calling from South Winds. Because I'm crazy. I must be. Because after everything I still want you back."

"Bobbie!" Diane shouts and lunges for the phone, but Bobbie climbs up on the bed and continues.

"I will do anything you want…. Just please come home. Please love me again. I have no pride left. " She has fallen to her knees, and Diane seems frozen with horror.

"It doesn't matter…nothing matters but you…."

I am not frozen. I am furious. "Bobbie!"

She nods at me. "Teddi is yelling at me. She's right, of

course. Forget everything I said. I didn't mean it…really, I didn't. I mean, do you really think I'd let you screw me again? You already screwed me but good, didn't you?

"I hate you!" she screams into the phone before slamming it down.

There is dead silence in the room. Finally Diane says, "You scared the crap out of me, sister. I can't believe you told the SOB off. You were great!"

"Yeah," Bobbie says. "Imagine what I could have said if he'd picked up the phone!"

"You left that message on his answering machine?" I can't believe she'd do that. I mean what if Phyllis hears it?

"And risk him hearing it? You're the one in here, not me," Bobbie says. "Two rings and I pressed down the off button. But believe me, when I make up my mind what I want, he'll be the first to know…after me, that is."

"You weren't talking to him?" Diane asks. Obviously she is as disappointed as I am confused.

"Not for a second," Bobbie says. "You knew, didn't you, Teddi?" she asks, but I am in outer space, counting on my fingers, putting up one hand, putting up the other. The girls are staring at me as if I've taken a nosedive off the deep end. And the pool is empty. "Teddi?"

"Give me a sec," I tell them, biting a fingernail and studying the nubs in the carpet. "I'm thinking."

"I knew I smelled something burning," Bobbie says, trying to make a joke out of my short circuits. But I don't care. Pieces of the puzzle are coming together. If only I had the box top I'd know what the picture was supposed to look like in the end.

"Remember when the satellite went out at our house and Rio wanted to watch that Indie whatever race?" I ask. The sisters exchange a look, but Bobbie says she remembers.

Bobbie resists saying, "So what?" and instead says, "I had to crawl up on the freakin' roof to fix it."

"*You* did?" I say to be sure. She raises her eyebrows at me as if to ask if I think I did it. I drop it and ask instead if they are going home together. Bobbie tells me they are.

"Are you gonna watch a movie?" I press.

They don't have a plan beyond pizza.

"Could you do me an enormous favor?" I ask. "A favor for your confined, paranoid, psychotic friend?"

"You're not—" Bobbie starts, but my hand is up. I'm not sure whether I am having an epiphany or tripping out, but I am totally in the zone.

The Twilight Zone.

"Go home, now. Go in your basement and find your Ingrid Bergman tapes—"

"'Your mission, should you choose to accept it...'" Bobbie starts, trying to lighten the atmosphere, but I grab her arm and she realizes that I'm serious.

"And watch *Gaslight.*"

CHAPTER 28

When Dr. Benjamin comes into the room, the bed is strewn with bills and papers and notes. I am pressed up against the headboard with my feet tucked under me. I am sober, clear-eyed and seem to be in charge of what must look like either Command Central or a nesting party. I quickly introduce Bobbie, who is kneeling on the side of my bed, and Diane, who is beside her, rifling through my papers.

"Try to catch up," I tell the good doctor.

"You are joining a show already in progress," Diane says, and we all turn our backs on her and go on with our discussion.

But Dr. Benjamin isn't having any of it. "I don't think so," she says firmly, opening the door widely and asking Bobbie and Diane to give her a moment with "her patient." When they don't hop-to, she bullies them, threatening to restrict my visitors to immediate family.

I tell her she can't do that. She raises an eyebrow implying that she not only can, but will.

Diane grumbles something at her, but Bobbie, as she walks past her, nose in the air, is quite clear. "We *are* family," she says with great authority.

"Sly and the Family Stone?" Dr. Benjamin responds, giving her a bar or two of the song "We Are Family."

Bobbie looks at her with disgust and points to herself. "Sister Sledge."

"What if Sister Sledge married MC Hammer?" Diane asks me over her shoulder.

"She'd be Sister Sledge Hammer," Dr. Benjamin says. "Now, out!"

I look up from my work to see a doctor not satisfied with her patient's progress. "What?" I ask her when she can't seem to stop frowning.

"Your friend called and told me to drop everything and get over here, so I race here like a maniac, have to talk a state trooper out of a ticket on the Northern State Parkway, and then play Name That Tune with your friends. What is all this, Teddi?"

"Okay, you know how I kept asking you if I was paranoid?" I say, giving her just enough time to nod but not to tell me once again that I'm not. "You were right. At least I think you were. Otherwise I'm totally paranoid and there's no hope for me."

She tells me that isn't a good-enough hint, and I've got to actually spell out what the heck I am talking about.

"Well, call me John Nash, but I look at these—" I indicate the bills and notes on my bed "—and I see a message."

"You're in debt?"

I am digging in a stack of MasterCard statements, but I stop and look up at her. "Well, yeah. But look at what I'm in debt for—or to whom I'm indebted. CVS Pharmacy. Remember the toothpaste I swore I bought?"

She looks less convinced than confused, and before she gets the chance to tell me that the fact that I've charged something at CVS doesn't prove much, Bobbie and Diane come running back in, shrieking about the bank.

"We've got him! We've got him!" Bobbie is chanting.

"How about we start at the beginning, ladies," Dr. Benjamin says. "Slowly, calmly, rationally?"

Bobbie and Diane look at her with contempt and start saying things like "it's all here!"

"Humor me," she says with enough finality to calm the banshees down.

"Well," Diane says, warming to the telling of the tale, and gesturing toward her sister. "Teddi asked us to get her last bank statement, so Nancy Drew here and I went over to her house this morning and 'Nancy' told Rio that she thought she owed Teddi some money from the business. She said that she'd asked Teddi about it, but since Teddi can't remember squat—" Her face reddens while Bobbie jumps in to say that that was what they had told Rio, not what they thought—

"And the jerk gave us Teddi's last couple of bank statements like Teddi said he would. And he is so busted!" Diane shrieks like some kid whose arch enemy has been grounded for life.

Dr. Benjamin clears her throat and I look up at her. Suddenly I don't feel as euphoric as my friends.

"Why did you want the bank statements?" she asks me. "And what's with all the bills and paperwork?"

Once I say it, I feel there will be no going back. Merely suggesting it means the end of my marriage, the end of the life I've been living for twelve years. So I'm taking a minute to find the right way to phrase it, to give me a back door, an escape hatch. Bobbie has no time to wait. She tells her about the phone call to Mike starting the whole thing. And before I can explain, Diane interrupts her, urging her to get to the part about Charles Boyer.

"I think…" I say, and my voice comes out so softly Dr. Benjamin has to bend forward to hear me "…that it might be possible—and I'm only saying *possible*—that some of the stuff that I thought I was responsible for someone else might have actually done."

"Might?" Diane says, waving the MasterCard statement. "Might? Look. The location you make your deposits and withdrawals shows up on the statement. And unless you were driving to the Throgs Neck Bridge branch to make your withdrawals after you were at the Woodbury branch making your deposits, someone else was making them. In the Bronx. It's that or I need to issue you a speeding ticket for making the hour-and-a-half trek from Woodbury to the Bronx in roughly twenty minutes."

I ask if Diane is sure that the bank branch is in the Bronx. She assures me that it is not far from my father's store. She and Bobbie are so gleeful they don't seem to understand the full measure of what they are saying. They only want me not to be crazy. They don't care that I could have been married to a man who makes that husband in *Rosemary's Baby* look like a saint.

"You know, I don't think he could have made the withdrawals," I say, though of course I think he could. "I changed my PIN number and I never told him what the new one was.

So even assuming that Rio would ever do this to me, which is a large leap of faith, or lack of faith, I don't see how he could."

They are temporarily stymied, until Dr. Benjamin reminds us of my Palm Pilot—the one Rio fiddles with regularly. "We're talking *Gaslight* here, yes?" she asks, referring to the old Charles Boyer movie just to make sure. When I reluctantly nod, she asks if I didn't write the new PIN in there. "And I suppose that you didn't hide the thing. I mean, wasn't it right where Rio could find it?"

"But it doesn't make sense," Bobbie says. "If he wanted to loot the account, why put it in Teddi's wallet?"

"Why'd Charles Boyer fiddle with the lights…" I say in response "…when he could have sent her on a shopping trip to the mall?"

"They had malls then?" Bobbie asks. Diane whacks her on the arm.

"(a) that was rhetorical," Diane says, "and (b) it was so that Ingrid Bergman would think she was losing it. God knows, Teddi's always saying she's on the brink. He must have figured one little push…"

I really don't want to believe this.

"There could be another explanation," I tell them all. They look at me, waiting, and I wish I could think of anything besides an alien possession of my husband's body. "You realize that my father must pass that bank every day, too."

"And what would he gain by taking your money out and putting it in your wallet?" Diane says.

"Motive, means, opportunity," Dr. Benjamin points out.

"The toilet paper rolls coming and going? The food appearing and disappearing? Who else could have done it?"

"I forgot about the toilet paper," I say. "See? I have a memory problem. It could have been me."

"Putting a pool in the backyard," Dr. Benjamin says. "He knows your fears. I can't think of a better way to drive you right to the edge."

"Okay, but what about the nail place?" Bobbie asks. "They said that you called and left a message to cancel your nail appointment. How could he know when your appointment was for?"

"You know, I thought for a minute that *you'd* switched that appointment," I tell Bobbie. "You'd know when my regular appointment is, and if you weren't sure you could always…" I slap my forehead and say, slowly and deliberately, "Check the calendar on my fridge."

"Maybe," Bobbie concedes, "but how could he know when you wanted to change it to?"

"What about the to-do list in her Palm?" Diane suggests.

I concede that yes, it was doable, but how could Rio have sounded like me?

No one says a word. And then Diane says, almost apologetically, "Maybe there's a woman? A female accomplice."

I can't look at Dr. Benjamin, who, knowing about the nosedive my sex life has taken, must be thinking that this is a more-than-likely scenario. She asks Diane if she can find out who Rio is calling on his cell phone.

Diane seems to think this will be a piece of cake. "Give me his cell phone number," she tells me.

While we all watch, Diane identifies herself and asks for the last dozen numbers dialed from Rio's cell, scribbling only two phone numbers on the back of the bank statement on the table.

I point to the first one, indicating it is the main desk at South Winds. I've called it often enough in my life to check on my mother.

Diane calls the precinct and cajoles, wheedles and kisses butt until the officer on the other end provides the name of the recipient of ten of the last twelve calls Rio made.

We stare at the name below the number.

"Who is Marian Healy?" Bobbie asks. "Why is that name so familiar?"

For someone whose memory is in trouble, it doesn't take me a minute to remember Marian Healy. I don't think that the anger I feel has anything to do with jealousy. For that, I'd still have to care for Rio—and it has been a long time, when I think about it, since I have truly cared about the man himself rather than the institution of marriage. Well, being in one institution surely gives a woman a different perspective about being in another.

Maybe I never loved Rio. Maybe I wanted to love him so desperately that I convinced myself I did.

At any rate, I refresh Bobbie's memory of the woman in the yellow dress at the girls' Moving-Up Day Ceremony. "I guess she meant the biblical sense when she said she knew Rio."

"So he had an accomplice," Diane says.

I finger my neck while I sift through the bills on the bed. "I'll bet she's wearing a lovely diamond necklace, too."

"Are you finding anything else?" Bobbie asks. "Think about all the things you supposedly did or didn't do."

"Oh!" I say, looking through the papers for the tenth time, unable to find what I am looking for. "Tell Dr. Benjamin about the car."

Diane tells the doctor that Rio had rented a black Ford Expedition exactly like the one I drive.

Dr. Benjamin asks if I have any idea what he might have wanted another car for. She is tentatively getting on board.

I think about the man at the Dairy Barn asking me what I was doing with all the milk I kept buying. If Marian was driving the car…

"How did you find out about the car, anyway?" Dr. Benjamin asks.

If Diane was any prouder, she might explode at the table. "This is so cool. Best part of being a rookie. We're always supposed to be learning. So I went over to the precinct before we came here and had the sergeant show me how to run a few things through the computer. Then I called around. You know—'this is Officer Reynolds of the Nassau County Police. I'm checking out a possible 947 and…'"

"What's a 947?" Dr. Benjamin asks.

Diane appears to think a minute. "I forget, but the car rental company didn't know, either, did they?"

"But how did you know there was a rental car?" Dr. Benjamin asks.

"Right here on the bill," Diane says, pulling a paper out of her purse.

Across from me, Dr. Benjamin pulls the MasterCard statement away from Diane. "And you got this…how?" she asks her.

"Oh, I can't imagine how that happened," Diane answers, all wide-eyed innocence as she looks at Dr. Benjamin "Rio pulled out a bunch of papers this morning when he was getting the bank statement, and I guess when I put my purse down on the counter, they all stuck to the bottom. Teddi, you really ought to clean your counters more thoroughly."

Bobbie stares at her sister admiringly. "I see *Detective* in your future," she says, and Diane blushes.

"Bingo," I say leaning across the table and pointing out the E-ZPass charge to Dr. Benjamin and Diane.

"So?" Bobbie asks.

"So I'm pretty sure that the time you go through a toll is recorded by the machine that accepts the pass."

I look hopefully at Diane, who nods and picks up the ball. "So while we couldn't tell where Rio was when he got Teddi's call on Saturday night, because a phone bill doesn't say where a call is made from or received, we can at least tell when he was on the bridge."

"Or not on the bridge," I say quietly. "Or if he was ever on the bridge at all."

Diane's jaw drops. "You mean, if he never went upstate, but hung around…"

"Scaring her…" Bobbie jumps in.

"The sergeant says that I can find out everything he's ever charged to a credit card," Diane says, impressed with her own potential power. "It's amazing what you can find out about your ordinary Joe."

"But Rio isn't your ordinary Joe," I say, feeling all the steam run out of me—feeling more tired than after delivering my children, after staying up three days straight when Alyssa had the croup—but pressing forward, anyway. "He's my husband. The man I've lived with and slept next to for twelve years. For God's sake, I'm his children's mother. I refuse to believe that he could hurt them or me like this. Never."

"Right," Diane says. "Those calls to Marian Healy at 2:00 a.m. were probably business calls."

"And he rented the car because..." Bobbie is clearly stretching here. "He wanted to mate it with yours and get little Honda Civics."

Dr. Benjamin hushes my friends. "I guess I should go see about springing you, huh?" she says, sounding like one of us. "I'll just—"

"No," I say, laying my hand on her arm to stop her. "I need to know if what I'm thinking here, what I'm accusing Rio of, is true or not before I take one step outside this hospital."

"But you're not crazy," Bobbie says with a whine.

"Maybe not, but if I'm not, then I'm not all that safe, either, am I?"

CHAPTER 29

My father, with whom I've reached a delicate rapprochement, is visiting me when Diane and Bobbie come bounding into the solarium clutching one of those brown accordion files, calling out my name.

"Wait'll you see what we found," Bobbie sings like a first-grader at recess. "Wait'll you see what we found!"

That tiny piece of me that wants to go back, deny what is in front of my face, hopes vainly that in the brown accordion file is proof that Rio isn't really the scum of the earth. Since the girls left to investigate exactly what Rio has been up to, I've been trying to put two and two together. All I've come up with is more and more twos to add into the equation. There is so much to figure out and too little time to figure it out in. God only knows what Rio is doing out there, if Bobbie and Diane are right about him pushing me to the edge.

And let's face it. They're right.

My father is ready to go after him with a shotgun, but I convince him that would be pointless—we have to be calm.

I swallow my wishes and gesture for Diane and Bobbie to show me what they've found. Diane smacks the Redweld file on the table. "Plenty," she says, presenting me with a copy of a bill from the Bloomies in Manhattan, signed by Mario Gallo for bra and panty sets in a size small. With a bit of embarrassment she guesses they weren't for me and hurries on to the three receipts from CVS Pharmacy for a total of a dozen tubes of toothpaste among other things, all signed by me.

"There are the toothbrush holders and soap dishes," I say, reading the receipts line by line. "I did buy them!"

"This is the tip of the iceberg, honey, and the Rio-tanic is going down." Bobbie rifles through the papers and puts the cell phone bills on top. There are a million calls to that same number in the Bronx.

"More Marian Healy," I say. No wonder he didn't need to have sex with me. The poor man must have been exhausted from all the phone sex he was having with Miss Healy.

"Marian Healy?" Marty asks. "From Rothman's?"

"The deli?" I ask.

"Mr. Bayer, what does this Marian Healy look like?" Diane asks my dad, and before Bobbie and I can tell her, my father looks guiltily at me.

"To tell you the truth, she reminds me a little of Teddi," he says. "Not as pretty, not as good a figure, not that I notice such things…"

"Could she pass for Teddi?" Diane says.

"Funny, she's even got a necklace like Teddi's. Wore it once at the deli. Of course, she's maybe ten years younger, but—"

"My necklace! And he brought her to Dana's graduation! Can you believe he'd—"

Bobbie looks at me knowingly. Of course she can believe it.

I study the photocopies while my father goes berserk. *Bad back, my ass*, he yells. *Sure! Guilt is heavy*. He is pacing fast enough for a stress test. *Gotta go to the physical therapist—ha!*

This is, he tells Diane, a matter for the police, and he demands to know what is being done about it. When Diane says "nothing" and starts to explain, he is in no mood to listen and he storms from the room, yelling about how he will "just see about that."

After my father is gone, she admits to me that there is no law against trying to drive your wife crazy. What did Rio do, after all? Rent a car? Lie to his wife? Give his mistress his wife's necklace? How many men would be in jail for that particular crime?

He took his own money out of the bank and put it in my wallet. Hardly indictable. He poured out milk and replaced it. Or maybe he merely hid it and brought it back.

While Diane shows me still more papers, Dr. Benjamin comes in and joins us.

"Hello!" she says, her eyes twinkling. "Don't you look like the cat who swallowed the canary?"

"Hardly," I tell her. "But at least he didn't swallow me."

"Speaking of the cat, or is that *cad*, have you seen Rio?" Bobbie asks.

"I've been feigning sleep since I started putting things together. He comes, he goes, he leaves flowers or candy or a note."

"Well, you can't hide in here forever," Dr. Benjamin says. "I've signed your release papers and you can go as soon as you want. You just have to decide—"

Dr. Benjamin stops, distracted by the yelling in the hallway. I recognize not merely the voice, but the tone. A little voice deep inside me says *placate. Diffuse.* But I've cowered to that tone for too many years, never really aware of how hard I was trying to be a good wife, a good mother, and losing myself in the process. That life is over.

"Where is she?" Rio is demanding. "I'm taking her outta here and taking her over to Bellevue. Didn't Dr. Peller call you guys? He's her new doctor. Benjamin is out."

He is ranting closer, and I nod at Diane, who goes to the doorway and asks, "You looking for Teddi Gallo?"

"If it isn't the third witch…er, watch," Rio says. "You know where—" He comes into the room and lets out a sigh when he sees me sitting in the big rattan chair, dressed and ready to go.

"Rio," I say politely, as if I am at some tea party and it is a pleasure to meet him. I clasp my hands together to stop the shaking. "Do come in. We were just talking about you."

For a moment he looks wary, but it passes. Of course it does. He knows how to play this game better than all of us. But this time he isn't going to win.

"Good thing I found you. You feeling okay? You look great. Must be all the rest you got. I told you this'd be a good idea, didn't I?" He glances around the room. "Doesn't she look good?"

"I'm well," I say. "Mentally sound. Stable."

"Of course you are," Rio says. "And don't you let anyone tell you otherwise. You were a little stressed out is all. Like your mom, you know, but a little treatment, some of that whaddaya call it, that shock therapy, and you'll be good as new."

"I am a lot like my mother," I admit. "Or I was. But somehow I don't think I'm going to need any shock therapy. In fact, you might be the one due for a little shock."

"Me?" he says, following it with a nervous little laugh. "Okay, Teddi, honey. Whatever you say." He does that macho swagger thing, pandering to the crowd around us, showing that he is simply humoring me. But I can see that he is nervous. In my whole life I have never felt so powerful, so in control. "You got a purse or anything? I got the Expedition parked out front and we better get going before some cop decides to tow it."

"The Expedition? Would that be mine, or the one you rented?" I ask.

"I'm afraid, Mr. Gallo, that Teddi's not quite ready to go anywhere," Dr. Benjamin says. "At least not with you."

"Why not have a seat?" Diane asks Rio, pulling out a chair. "I think there may be a few things that your wife wants to ask you."

"What's this all about?" Rio asks. He licks his lips and stares at the seat but doesn't take it.

"Diane's been earning her detective's badge," I say, stretching out the moment, reveling in it, knowing I am holding the bomb that will be dropped right in Rio's good trousers—exactly where he deserves it. Giving a credit card to his girlfriend and telling me I should watch my spending! "And she's been very busy and very successful—investigating you."

I let that worry him for a while, wondering if Rio is

into other things I have no idea about. Like business with the Nose.

"She even saw some tapes from a bank in the Bronx." Okay, so I am making that part up. All banks have security cameras, don't they?

He has no response at first. Of course he doesn't. But it doesn't take him long to make a joke of it. "Films, huh? Was I dressed, at least?"

"Fully dressed, and taking out seven hundred dollars each time. The same seven hundred dollars you accused me of withdrawing…"

"No way," Rio says, as if he is sure he hasn't done it. I think for a second that maybe I am wrong, that Diane and Bobbie have made mistakes, until Diane speaks up.

"We know all about your accomplice," she says. "Ms. Healy?"

Rio pales. So it is true. All of it.

"Okay," I say. "I get it. I see how you did it. I see how easy it was and how it worked. But I didn't see why until my father told me about the agreement you signed with him. If you left me, you'd walk away with nothing, right?"

Rio doesn't say anything at all. He grimaces, looks at Dr. Benjamin as if she is at the bottom of everything, and seems to be considering what to say.

"But what I don't get is why you didn't simply kill me. We had insurance on my life. You fixed my car all the time. Why didn't you do something to my brakes? Get it over with if you hated me so much?

"The kids were away, so they wouldn't have been in the

car with me…why didn't you just kill me?" I ask. I don't realize that I am crying until I feel the wetness on my cheeks.
I backhand them away and stare at Rio, waiting for him to
answer.

"Who said I hate you? See, that's what she always does,"
he tells Dr. Benjamin and Diane, still playing to the crowd.
"She makes something out of nothing. If I hated you, Teddi,
would I be here?"

"If you loved me, would I be? You tried to make me crazy,"
I say. "I have all sorts of proof. If that's not hate—"

"That's ridiculous and you know it. You've had two toes
over the edge from birth, Teddi, and you fell over and I caught
you. How the hell does that make me the bad guy?"

I try to draw an even breath. I am not going to come apart
here, prove him right. I can fall apart later, alone, cry and
shout and throw whatever I want. Here, now, I want to be
completely in control. I swallow, lift my head and pray my
voice will come out steady.

"I'll ask you again, why didn't you just kill me if you hate
me so much?"

"And I'll tell you again. I don't hate you. *Ti amo con tutto
il cuore*," he says in the private voice he uses in our bedroom
to say he loves me with all his heart. "*Tirami su.*"

Tirami su, I think. *Hold me close*.

And then I don't have to work at it anymore. Those two
little words we always laughed over tear it all. "Oh, please!"
I say, only now I am laughing alone.

"You don't think I do? You don't think I coulda walked
loads of times, that I coulda found someone who—"

"*Could have?* You did. And you gave her my necklace and lingerie from Bloomingdale's and then you accused me of losing one and spending too much on the other. And on top of that, you gave her—" how was I suppose to put it? "—the physical affection that was supposed to be mine."

There is some satisfaction as the blood drains from Rio's face. "Come on, Teddi. You know how things were between us. I was so afraid to push you, to make demands. Marian was only a piece of ass, you know? A *goomah* without an ounce of your goodness. It wasn't like it was with you. It wasn't even good for me. Men need—"

Beside me, Bobbie groans loudly. The truth is that I don't really care about Marian. How long ago did I let go of Rio in my heart and hold on by inertia? He is a twelve-year cigarette and it is time to kick the habit before it kills me. "Who cares? It wasn't like our sex life was satisfying, anyway," I say, letting him cringe in front of Dr. Benjamin and a bunch of strangers. "But driving me crazy, Mario?"

I keep calling him Mario to remind myself that this isn't the man I loved, gave my heart and soul and body to, had children with. God, what if my friends didn't believe in me when I'd stopped believing in myself? What if I'd had to stay at South Winds, believing that I really did lose my mind? What if my children had to grow up with the fear that they, too, would need to be put away in the end, the way I'd been so sure about myself? "Why the hell didn't you kill me?"

"She's getting all upset, Doc," Rio says, pointing at me while, if the looks on their faces are any indication, everyone around us seems to think I am doing pretty well. "Shouldn't you maybe give her something to calm her down?"

Dr. Benjamin answers. "She's angry Mr. Gallo. A perfectly natural response. In fact, she's calmer than I am."

"She's a freaking wack job, just like her mother," Rio says. "Look at June..."

CHAPTER 30

"**If** you think for a second I'm going to let you open my valise and steal my Godiva chocolates like you did the last time…" I hear my mother shouting from down the hall "…you're loonier than I am. Call my doctor and tell him I'm baa-aack."

"And speak of the devil," Rio says, gesturing with his head toward the hall. "This is my life. If even one of you knew what my life was like—I just needed somebody who—"

He is still hung up on his infidelity, as if that is what matters to me.

"And it was only once, Teddi. She was a whore who didn't charge me nothing. I mean, yeah, I called her a lot and we talked about it a lot, but I was trying to be faithful to you. I was with her twice, I swear it." Only he isn't looking at me anymore, he is looking at the doorway, where my father stands fuming and my mother fiddles with her valise.

"Marty!" Rio shouts. His voice cracks before he can get control of it. "Thank God you're here. Teddi's got this crazy idea into her head, and the doc here—"

"Rio, Rio, Rio," my mother says, shaking her head. "Whatever happened to 'hello June, how are you'? I got that much from the nurse in Admitting. She always tries to butter me up when I'm here. Wanted to go through my suitcase and take my Godiva chocolates, no doubt. Well, I told her we'll have none of that this time."

My father looks wide-eyed at everyone, as if to say, *See? I'm not the only one that lets her get away with it.*

"I'm going to put my things in my room," my mother says, putting up a finger to keep everyone quiet. "Don't say anything until I come back. I don't want to miss a word."

For a moment after she leaves, no one says anything, as if we are going to respect her wishes and wait for her while she rolls her Louis Vuitton drag-a-long down the hall. But then we all begin to speak at once, my father calling Rio a goddamn son of a bitch, swearing he'll get him even if the police can't do squat, Rio saying that he has to get me to Bellevue because a doctor who can really help me is waiting, Dr. Benjamin saying that Rio has played a very dangerous game and is lucky that he's been found out before it is too late, and me repeating the same question over and over.

"Why didn't you…?" I stop midway when I see my mother coming back into the room. She is wearing yet another ecru knit outfit. In her left hand she has her Gucci mock-croc handbag. In her right, she carries what looks like one of Rio's smaller rifles. "What the hell is that?"

"I believe Rio calls it his Saiga-12," she says, raising her eyebrows at Rio. "Isn't that right? This was the one you were showing off to that police officer at the house, isn't it?"

"June, for Christ's sake!" my father says, stepping toward her to find the gun pointed at his midsection. "Where did you get that?"

"While you were running around Teddi's throwing all Rio's stuff out onto the lawn, I was checking out his shed," she says simply.

"Well, that's great," Rio says. "You ever hear of private property? You better give it to me, June. It could be loaded."

"Oh, it is," my mother says with a Cheshire cat grin. "You're really anal-retentive about your ammunition, aren't you? All those little boxes, labeled so carefully…"

"Loaded! Oh, my God. Put it down, June," my dad says, his hands doing that calming thing that people inexplicably do. "Gently. Don't drop it."

"You know," Mom says, casually pointing the stubby rifle this way and that, first at Rio, then at Marty, even for a minute at Dr. Benjamin and Bobbie. "I was a lousy mother." She waits a minute for someone to disagree with her. Even with a gun in her hand, no one denies it.

"Don't all yell at once," she says sarcastically. "Anyway, it was a worthless life. I did nothing right after Markie. I did nothing at all. Nothing seemed to matter. I failed you, Marty, as a wife."

"No," he says softly. "That I can't agree with. Even with a gun to my head."

"Then how do you explain Angelina?" she corrects him.

"That was my failing, not yours."

I have never found my father noble, but with those words, there is something new there. Something gentle and admirable.

"What I did to David!" she says, shaking her head. "Driving him away, so I could have you to myself."

"David's back," Marty says. "He's home now, for good."

The rifle is getting heavy, and my mother puts down her handbag so that she can hold it with both hands. "He's already packed, Marty. He's already got his reservations. They haven't changed any more than we have. He still wants something we can't give him, the same as Teddi does. Only she's more forgiving."

"What do they want?" my father asks, but I already know the answer.

"They want to grow up in a normal house with a normal mother and father," June says with a quick shrug that acknowledges that is never to be. "They want to rewrite history. I think they get that from me."

She swings around with the rifle, taking aim at Rio, who has moved several feet closer to the door.

"Where do you think you're going?" she asks him.

"Look, June," Rio says. "Don't you want to help Teddi? Don't you want me to take her out of here, and then you—"

"How the hell do they expect me to rewrite history?" my father asks, and slumps into a chair, but my mother ignores him.

"You never answered her question," my mother tells Rio.

"What question is that?" Rio asks, as if he doesn't know.

So I ask again why he didn't kill me. "Did that agreement say you got nothing if I died? Was that it? So even though you hated me…"

"I don't friggin' hate you," Rio shouts, throwing up his hands. "You think I want to see the mother of my children dead? You think I could hurt them like that…?"

"But it was okay to hurt me, to make me think I was losing my mind?"

"You gonna tell me you're not losing your mind? That you haven't been losing it since day one? You're always expecting it. How many times do you ask me if I think you're normal 'cause you feel this or that? Alls I did was make sure that it happened while the kids were away. Did you want to lose it in front of them?"

"*All*," I say, interrupting him. "Not *alls*. *All*."

"All," he says sheepishly, and I know he is seething with embarrassment and I am so small and petty I enjoy every second of his discomfort.

"Not that this is about grammar," I concede.

"Right," he agrees readily. "The important thing is that you'd get better. And when you were fine again, I'd be there for you."

"You're the one who's out of your mind," I say, staring at him. Can he really think he's done me some sort of favor? "And Marian? She was to relieve me of the strain of having sex with you? You're too good to me, Rio, really you are."

"It sounds bad, but that's not the way it was. Try to put yourself in my shoes for a minute instead of always looking at it from your side."

Diane is trying to sneak up on June, who keeps shooting looks at her that back her up. Bobbie, totally ignoring the fact that my mother is standing with a rifle pointed at all of us, is huffing and puffing and making indignant noises as loudly as she can. Dr. Benjamin looks at me with utter confidence. *You're fine*, the look says. *Better than fine*.

I nod at Rio to continue.

"It's your fault, you know. If you just agreed to come here in the first place, a month ago, you'd be getting out of here by now. But no, you had to be strong. I waited and waited, but you didn't get it. I had to have some space, don't you understand that? Do you have any idea what it's like for me? I leave you and your father expects me at the store an hour later. I leave work and you expect me home an hour after that? Where's my time off for good behavior? When do I get to do what I want to do?"

My mother bangs the rifle butt against the floor. "This isn't about you," she says. "It's about me."

I can't help smacking my forehead. Here Rio is, admitting that he tried to drive me crazy, and it's still all about my mother. I glance over at Dr. Benjamin, who, despite the seriousness of the situation, can't help smiling, too.

"Let's move on to how I failed Teddi," Mom says. "That was the worst of it, I think. I showed her how to blow a marriage, and I showed her that she was worthless because she's a woman.

"I really blew it," she says, her gaze wandering to the window, where we can all see two police cars, their sirens blaring and their lights flashing, pulling up in the circular drive in front of the hospital. "I think I'll have to skip the rest of the speech," she says, and for the first time I've ever seen her do it, she bites at the side of her lip.

"June," my dad says softly. "Put down the gun. Give it to me, or to Diane there. She'll know what to do with it."

"I didn't do one thing right," she says sadly. "I dragged

everyone I loved to hell and back, and for what? To live to be embarrassed when the neighbors finally found out that my husband was fooling around with my maid, to see my daughter being driven crazy by her husband, to watch my son take off from our lives again ..."

"Who?" Marty asks. "Roz? Are you saying that Roz Adelstein found out about Angelina? Is that what this was all about?"

My mother looks at him as if he is stupider than dirt for not having figured that out.

"Listen to me," Marty says. "Who cares who knows what? I love you, June. Don't ask me why, but I do, and I'll try harder."

"What about you?" June asks Rio.

"Me?" Rio asks, and I can see it is the wrong answer.

She glances at the window. "I don't have time for this, Rio," she says, listening for the police in the hall and bracing her elbow on her hip. Diane lunges forward, but before she can get to her, my mother pulls the trigger.

I am screaming. I try to run to Rio, but someone is holding me back. I see Rio fall, and try again to get to him but the arms hold me firmly. "You'll be in the way," Bobbie tells me, turning so that I have to look over her shoulder to see Dr. Benjamin and Diane crouching beside Rio.

"Shit!" he is shouting, smacking one of his imported leather shoes against the linoleum floor. "She shot me! Oh, shit, it hurts. Did you see that? She shot me!"

Actually, he has a lot of energy for a man who's been shot.

"Am I gonna die?" he asks Dr. Benjamin, grabbing onto

her lapels while she rips open his good trousers, the ones I had cleaned for him all those weeks ago.

"Probably in fifty years or so," Dr. Benjamin tells him, apparently very unimpressed with what she calls a flesh wound to Rio's thigh. "A couple of inches to the right and you'd be a soprano, but you'll live."

"I should have gone to riflery more often," Mom says, handing the gun to Diane and nodding at the nurses standing in the doorway, their faces frozen in horror. "But they gave you a choice at Camp Runamok, and I always chose golf. I'd have gotten him where I was aiming with a five iron, I think."

And then, head high, elegant as ever, she announces that she will be in her room, should anyone need her.

A nurse takes over for Dr. Benjamin, applying pressure on Rio's leg, while she rises to meet the police.

A minute later, two EMS workers come in and carry Rio out. "I'll come back and see you as soon as I can," he calls to me from the stretcher. "We'll work it out. *Ti amo.*"

Bobbie, still holding on to me, makes a guttural sound and says something like "work it out, my ass." Then she asks me, "You all right?"

I survey the room. The police allow my father (the adulterer) to take my mother (the assailant) to her room (in the looney bin) for now. They are talking to Dr. Benjamin (the psychiatrist who's medicating me) and Diane (the rookie who is eating all this up), who are nodding and throwing a glance my way every now and then. Dr. Benjamin must have told them about the paintball accident at the house because I can see a spark of recognition flare in one of the cop's faces.

A nurse is cleaning up the blood (of my two-timing, conniving, black-hearted husband) on the linoleum.

"Are you crazy? Of course I'm not fine!" I tell Bobbie. I figure it's going to take some time to put all the pieces back together. "But I will be."

CHAPTER 31

My father wanted me to go home with him. Bobbie offered to stay with me at the house. Dr. Benjamin suggested I not rush home, but take another day or two at South Winds before the kids come home, to "get my bearings."

But I have come home alone. Home to the kitchen full of red paint and the yard full of dirt and one enormous hole, not unlike the one in my life. I've wandered around the house for two days, trying to separate what really happened from what I thought was the truth. There are a million reminders of the tricks Rio played on me—I can't reach into the fridge for milk without thinking it's a miracle there's any in there.

I call Rio's mother and tell her that there has been an accident and that Rio is in the hospital. I offer no details but suggest that it would be best if Rio goes home to her house to recuperate. Rio can tell his mother whatever he pleases, as far as I am concerned.

All I am worried about is the children.

Dr. Benjamin, now that she has released me as a patient, insists on my calling her Ronnie, stops by with a box of rugelach. I invite her in and get a thrill that we are on my turf for a change.

"Did I tell you that Bobbie finally figured out why the house was such a mess even though Rio had a girl in to clean?" I ask her as I usher her into my kitchen—better known as the scene of the crime.

"At least tell me she wasn't cleaning in your necklace," she says, figuring out for herself that Rio's "maid" was Marian. My father, with Diane in tow, has already gotten the diamond necklace back.

"Rio the Hood and—" I start.

"Maid Marian," she finishes with a laugh while I place little pastries on a plate and turn on the coffeepot.

"So," I say, gesturing at the paint-splattered walls. "I'm thinking of Barely Salmon in here. It'll be brighter than it was."

She takes a bite of the fresh rugelach and nods appreciatively. I don't know which she likes, the pale walls or the cookies. I don't care. Just being in my own kitchen, having a normal conversation here, shooting the breeze, is heaven. "Barely Salmon. Sounds like that lox-and-cream-cheese mix they sell in the deli."

We sit down at the table and I tell her about possibly selling the house, and changing some things I can't live with. I talk in detail about every room, and what it will take to make the house ready for the market.

"I can do all that," I say. "But I'm worried about the kids. I mean, is that one thing too many for them? Coming home to only me and then having to move and make new friends and—"

She asks what I'm going to tell them.

"You mean after I tell them that their grandmother shot their father while I was in the mental hospital?"

"Yeah, after that," she says with a grin.

"That their grandmother could go to jail if their father decides to press charges?"

She takes a good look around the room. Rio was clever to have loaded the rifle with red paint. Even knowing the truth, it still looks like a murder happened here. "When do they come home?"

"The end of next week. I've got the painters coming in tomorrow to do the kitchen," I say.

"Good," she says. It's different now that she has resigned as my doctor, now that she is my friend. She doesn't push me, she doesn't tell me that I am avoiding the real issues with my decorating plans. She doesn't tell me how symbolic it is that I am painting over the problem. If only I can stop trying to show her I am now fine.

"Did I tell you that I'm having the pool filled in?" I ask. "If we stay or not, I'm not comfortable with a pool in my backyard, and I'm not apologizing for my feelings."

"Good for you!"

"Well, I really am sorry, and I wish I didn't have to do it, but I'm going to *try* not to apologize, anyway."

"Teddi, you've got nothing to apologize for," she says. "And that's the last professional opinion I intend to give you."

She pops another rugelach into her mouth with a shrug that says she simply can't resist. Then she looks out into my hallway, gets up and strolls through it until she is standing in my living room and gazing toward the dining room.

"This place is really fabulous. Who did your decorating?" she asks.

When I tell her I did it all myself, she asks if I'd consider doing her office over for her. She starts to tell me that it's getting a little shabby and we both laugh at her forgetting that I've seen it firsthand.

"I would love to do it," I say from the heart. "The first thing that goes is that dreadful leather chair."

She asks if this is what I plan to do with my life and I tell her about the money I've made from my business with Bobbie, and that I thought I'd use it to start a decorating business of my own. I've also asked my father if I can work at Bayer three days a week offering decorating services free to his customers, like they do in Bloomingdale's, and he's agreed. "With Alyssa in full-day kindergarten I'll be able to work until about two and still get home for the kids. And Bobbie says she'll cover for me if I'm late."

She tells me that she thinks that's terrific, and acts as though my life is settled. As if everything is over.

"But it really kills me that there isn't anything to nail that husband of yours on," she says as she balls her fist and grimaces.

"You ought to hear Bobbie and Diane. Last night they came over and we sat around trying to figure out what we could do to get even without getting Diane thrown off the force, of course."

"Did you come up with anything?" she asks. "Anything I can help with? Do? Don't think I haven't considered having him committed, but—"

"Well, when we ruled out illegal things like poison and blowing up his car, no. And you are helping. You're seeing me through this and letting me know that it's all right to be angry. That's not something I've ever been allowed before."

Ronnie nods, but her look says that isn't enough for her.

"So," she says after a while, drawing out the word and making it clear that it is time.

"So," I agree. "What am I telling the kids? Well, my big fear is what Rio will tell them."

"Is he still in the hospital?"

"No. He's at his mother's. He calls me three times a day to tell me he loves me and wants to come home."

"And will you let him?" Her eye begins to twitch, something I never noticed before.

"Hey—remember, I'm not really crazy" is all I say.

CHAPTER 32

I am not a vindictive woman. I repeat this to myself several times as I sit across from the attorney Diane and Bobbie have insisted I consult.

"Because Citibank is FDIC insured, the forgery is considered a felony," she explains to me as she examines the loan application I found in Rio's kitchen junk drawer—the one with my name on the signature line.

I tell her that I've called the bank and canceled the loan. She shrugs noncommittally, raising an eyebrow as if to say that it doesn't matter in the scheme of things. Only I'm not a schemer, and I don't know what she's getting at.

"That doesn't change the facts. You can still bring this to the police, have your husband arrested and—"

"—my children would then have a felon for a father," I remind her. And then I remind myself again that I am not a vindictive person. As tempting as it is, it's not a place I can go.

"Does he know you have this?" she asks me, tapping the loan application with a well-manicured fingernail. My own nails are gnawed to the quick, but I make no effort to hide them. Ironically I see them as a badge of courage, or a medal of honor. I may be a little the worse for wear, but I made it through—I survived.

"Mrs. Gallo?" she asks when I don't answer.

"Bayer," I correct. "Teddi Bayer. It may not be a great name, but it's mine. I want it back."

She assures me that will be no problem, she will take care of it along with the divorce.

"But there's still the matter of Mr. Gallo. A man who could pull something like this isn't going to just tuck his tail between his legs and go away."

"Well…" I say slowly, as a plan begins to take form "…I might be able to make him do just that." Maybe, it seems, I am a schemer after all.

"How so?" The attorney asks, and follows my gaze to the papers she's holding. She smiles and asks again whether Rio knows I've found the loan application.

I shake my head. I knew when I found it in the junk drawer that the loan application wasn't junk. He'd submitted it and the bank had approved it. I suppose he thought he could tell me I didn't remember signing, but I am past falling for any of that stuff now.

I called Diane right away and she assured me Rio had committed a crime and then she'd set up the appointment with the best divorce lawyer on Long Island. Still, I didn't know what it all meant until this moment.

"If I were to turn that application over to the authorities, that would be the end of the line for Mr. Gallo, right?" I ask. The power I feel is almost physical—it seems to surge through my body. It scares me, but only a little.

"But as you've pointed out—" the attorney begins.

"And the statute of limitations?" I ask.

She starts to tell me that I don't have to worry about that, that it's seven years and it's only been a few weeks, and then she stops. "I see where you're going with this," she says. "Does Mr. Gallo have an attorney?"

"I guess he'd better," I say.

She asks what exactly it is I want from him. I take a deep breath and find it easier than I expected to pinpoint. "I want him out of our lives, but I want the children as unscathed as possible. And the way I see this happening, the only way, would be for him to leave me for another woman." I think of Kimmie and Kristen, who never thought that Mike didn't love them when he left, never blamed themselves. The Ks never felt abandoned because they knew that Mike was leaving Bobbie, not them. "I want him to tell the kids that he loves them but that he's fallen in love with someone else. He couldn't help himself. He's sorry, they'll always come first with him, even if he and Marian have children of their own, but he has to follow his heart and find happiness with her."

"Marian?" she asks, and until she does I don't even realize what I've said. And it's so perfect. So fitting. I explain how Marian helped him in his plot to drive me crazy.

"They deserve each other."

"Is it blackmail?" I ask, suddenly worried that my children could have two felons for parents.

"Are you asking him for money to keep quiet?" she asks me.

"I'm asking him to go away and not hurt my children in the process," I say.

"And child support?" she asks.

I can't help laughing. The chances of Rio earning legitimate money anywhere but Bayer are even smaller than the chances of my father letting him stay on there. I repeat that I just want him to go away.

"Not blackmail," she concedes.

"Can I really make him marry her?" I must admit that I am a little giddy with power.

"Is that what you really want?"

I suppose it isn't. But since I can't have what I really want—to change the past, to make Rio the husband I pretended he was—I admit that I do want some measure of revenge. I can just hear Ronnie Benjamin asking me if knowing Rio is miserable will make me happy.

I think long and hard before I answer.

"No, but, to quote my soon-to-be-ex-husband, it makes a helluva down payment." I smile like I haven't smiled in what feels like years.

"Have someone tell him to get himself an attorney pronto," she tells me. "I'll take it from there."

I give her all my particulars and head for the parking lot, where I find Bobbie shouting into her cellphone as she paces anxiously. She raises an eyebrow at me in question and I nod. "Whoo hoo," she shouts into the phone. "Teddi rules!" She closes the phone and we are both giggling as we head toward my car.

"Retail therapy, anyone?" she asks once she's settled in the shotgun seat. "Next stop, Designer Shoe Warehouse?"

Tomorrow I'll have to figure out how much to tell my parents. I'll have to figure out how to tell the kids that their father has "left me." I'll have to finish removing any trace of Rio from my house and my life. I'll have to insist that there are letters to each of the kids from Rio which explain and apologize for no longer loving their mother. I'll have to make him understand that he is to fade out of their lives. And I'll have to get myself set up at Bayer Furniture.

Tomorrow I'll have to call Ronnie Benjamin and tell her where things stand.

But today some retail therapy sounds perfect. I shift my 1961 candy apple red vintage Corvette convertible into Drive while Bobbie slides a CD into the player Rio had installed and cranks up the volume so that the entire parking lot can hear Gloria Gaynor's *I Will Survive!*

Cliché? Maybe, but for the first time in a long time—maybe my whole life—I finally believe I will.

Detective Maggie Skerritt is on the case again!

Maggie Skerritt is investigating a string of murders while trying to establish her new business with fiancé Bill Malcolm. Can she manage to solve the case while moving on with her life?

Spring*Break*

by *USA TODAY* bestselling author

CHARLOTTE DOUGLAS

HARLEQUIN®
N&xt™

Available March 2006
TheNextNovel.com

HN33

You always want what you don't have

Dinah and Dottie are two sisters who grew up in an imperfect world. Once old enough to make decisions for themselves, they went their separate ways—permanently. Until now. Will their reunion seventeen years later during a series of crises finally help them create a perfect life?

My Perfectly Imperfect Life

Jennifer Archer

HN34

Available March 2006
TheNextNovel.com

REQUEST YOUR FREE BOOKS!

2 FREE NOVELS TO INTRODUCE YOU TO OUR BRAND-NEW LINE!

There's the life you planned. And there's what comes next.

NEXT05

What happens when new friends get together and dig into the past?

Ex's and Oh's
Sandra Steffen

A story about secrets, surprises and relationships.

Where can a woman who has
spent her life obliging others truly
take time to rediscover herself?
In the Coconut Zone...

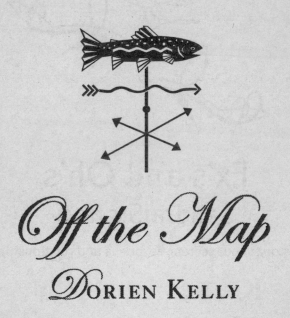

Off the Map

DORIEN KELLY

HN31

Available February 2006
TheNextNovel.com

HARLEQUIN®
Next™

Since when did life ever tell you where you were going?

Sometimes you just have to dip your oar
into the water and start to paddle.

T H E
SUNSHINE
COAST
N E W S

KATE AUSTIN

If her husband turned up alive—she'd kill him!

The day Fiona Rowland lifted her head above the churning chaos of kids, carpools and errands, annoyance turned to fury and then to worry when she realized Stanley was missing. Can life spiraling out of control end up turning your world upside right?

where's Stanley?

Donna Fasano